THE
INVITE

SHERYL BROWNE

bookouture

Published by Bookouture in 2022

An imprint of Storyfire Ltd.
Carmelite House
50 Victoria Embankment
London EC4Y 0DZ

www.bookouture.com

ISBN: 978-1-80314-175-6
eBook ISBN: 978-1-80314-176-3

THE
INVITE

BOOKS BY SHERYL BROWNE

For Lyn, my beautiful sister, whose hand is always there when I need it. XX

You can't hide from yourself.

PROLOGUE

'Is Grandpa coming on holiday with us?' Ruby looked trustingly at him as he straightened the cute two-pompom beanie he'd bought her over her curls. Her pretty green eyes, a myriad of forest greens, were so like her mother's it was heartbreaking.

'No, cupcake.' He checked her coat buttons and made sure her matching scarf was snug around her neck. 'Grandpa's having a little lie-down. We don't want to disturb him, do we?'

'Is his chariot close by?' Ruby asked, a worried little furrow forming in her brow. Realising she was concerned that the old man might not be able to reach his wheelchair, he swallowed back an emotional lump in his throat. She was a beautiful child, inside and out, caring and intuitive. He'd told Kaitlin he would die before he would let any harm come to her. He'd meant it.

'It is.' He gave her a reassuring smile and collected up the Barbie doll she was insisting on bringing with her in case it got lonely.

'He can't walk without it,' Ruby reminded him, still fretting about her grandpa.

'I know, sweetheart.' Quickly checking the bedroom she and Kaitlin had been staying in for anything obvious the little girl might need, he handed the doll to her, then swept her into his arms. 'I made sure it was nearby, don't worry.'

'And his phone?' she asked as he carried her along the landing.

He looked at her to find her eyes locked on his. She was more like her mother than ever, studying him intently, quietly assessing him. Kaitlin had done that a lot lately.

'And his phone.' He squeezed her closer as he carried her down the stairs. She was quite capable of making her own way down, but he didn't want to risk her falling before they left. 'It's right next to him, I checked.'

Seemingly satisfied, Ruby nodded, though her eyes flicked to the partially open lounge door. He understood. She had a tight bond with her grandparents. Naturally she would want to say goodbye to her grandpa, but time was of the essence.

'He'll be fine.' He gave her another reassuring smile. 'I've just spoken to Nana on her phone. She'll be here soon.'

'In five minutes?'

'Less than.' Setting her down on her feet, he took hold of her hand and opened the front door, checking to see if there was a car actually about to pull up on the drive.

'Are we going to get Mummy now?' Inquisitive as ever, Ruby had yet another question.

'We are,' he promised, taking a breath and heading on out. 'She's at home packing your clothes right now.'

'And Cocklepoo?' Ruby asked as they walked the short distance to where he'd parked his own car around the corner.

'Absolutely.' It was her favourite toy, he recalled. A cock-apoo cuddle toy she wouldn't go to bed without. He gave that pause for thought, then dismissed it. He would cross that bridge when he got there. Right now, his priority was getting this little girl, who he loved as if she were his own flesh and blood, somewhere she would be safe. He'd sworn he would protect her and her mother, and that was exactly what he intended to do.

Kaitlin wasn't the person he'd thought she was when he'd first met her, but he still loved her. He could forgive her for turning away from him, her neglect of her daughter. She'd been led astray, he could see that. Even if she didn't know it yet, in time she would realise that he was simply trying to do what was best for her and Ruby.

ONE

KAITLIN

Watching her five-year-old daughter's eyelids grow heavy, Kaitlin lowered her voice to a whisper, then paused her bedtime story at a suitable juncture and eased herself off the bed. She was bending to kiss her cheek when Ruby's eyes sprang open. 'I'm not sleepy yet, Mummy,' she announced.

Kaitlin hid a knowing smile. 'It's late, sweetheart,' she reminded her. 'Time you were in dreamland.'

'Oh Mummy, just one more page. I'm really not sleepy at all.' Ruby's big green eyes were now wide and beguiling, the gorgeous copper curls framing her face making her look like a little angel – almost.

'No more pages.' Kaitlin rounded her eyes in turn and did her best to look stern.

'But I want to know which fantastic character Ellen the Elephant meets next.' Ruby's forehead creased into a frown.

Kaitlin had a feeling Ruby knew quite well what *fantastical* character Ellen met next, since Greg had read her the story twice already this week. 'You'll just have to find out tomorrow, won't you? Sleep, madam,' she insisted. Aside from the fact that she couldn't let Ruby win the bedtime battle, she would be tired tomorrow. Kaitlin's mum was babysitting while she and Greg were at the party Greg had arranged for Kaitlin's birthday, a beautiful, lavish affair, and the last thing she wanted to do was saddle her with a fractious little girl.

'But Greg always lets me have one more page.' Poppy's bottom lip protruded petulantly.

'Okay, fine.' Kaitlin sat back down on the bed. 'I'll have to tell Nana you'll be too tired to stay up an extra half an hour tomorrow night,' she said with a sorrowful sigh, 'but ...'

'Oops.' Ruby's eyes grew wider, if that were possible. 'I forgot I was going to Nana's,' she said, tugging the duvet up to her chin and snuggling hurriedly down.

Kaitlin had guessed that bit of subtle blackmail might work. Next to playing Super Mario with Greg, or whatever video game she often found the two glued to, Ruby loved being at her nana and grandpa's, spoiled by Nana, whom Kaitlin had no doubt would let her stay up no matter what time she stipulated she should go to bed, and being given wheelies along the hall in Grandpa's wheelchair. 'Eyes closed,' she instructed, reaching for the night light.

'They *are* closed,' Ruby replied, peering at her through one half-closed eye.

Kaitlin couldn't help but laugh. 'Night, night, sweetheart,' she said, giving her a goodnight kiss.

As she headed for the landing, she marvelled at how content and outgoing her little girl was lately. She felt a familiar dip in her chest as she recalled how, after a particularly nasty argument with her ex-husband, she'd hurried into the nursery to find Ruby standing at the bars of her cot with tears streaming down her bewildered little face. That was what had made Kaitlin decide to gather her up and leave there and then. In suffering Sean's abusive behaviour, she was damaging her daughter. Fortunately, her best friend, Zoe, had come in a flash to collect her, and given them a safe haven to go to.

Ruby had soon forgotten about the incident, but Kaitlin had worried that she'd seemed subdued for a while, that she might even be missing her father, who'd miraculously shown an interest in his daughter recently. Kaitlin suspected that was because Greg had come into their lives. Sean hadn't wanted to be with her, but it would rankle if he thought she might find happiness with someone else. He'd never paid any attention to Ruby before. He hadn't even turned up for her first birthday party, preferring to spend the evening in the company of a woman – one of many. Recalling how devastated she'd felt for her little girl, Kaitlin swallowed back an emotional lump in her throat. Ruby was doing just fine now without him. She never mentioned him; possibly didn't even remember him. She'd thrived in Greg's company. He made a special effort to listen to her and play with her on her level, something Sean had never done. Kaitlin trusted him completely.

She couldn't wait to see Zoe, who'd taken some leave from her job in Portugal to come home especially for her birthday. They'd shared everything since meeting at sixth-form college, but they hadn't been in touch much lately, Zoe being busy with her new job and the new man in her life, Kaitlin similarly so. They had so much to catch up on. She would have to be careful not to sideline Greg – not that she imagined he wouldn't understand why she would be excited to see her friend. She couldn't wait to wear her new dress either.

Slipping into her bedroom, she went over to where it hung on her wardrobe door, a gorgeous off-the-shoulder empire dress in flame red, a colour she would never have worn in Sean's company. She'd fallen in love with it immediately. She hadn't been sure about the colour, though. 'Why?' Greg had asked her, his eyebrows arched in surprise as she'd run her hand over it, loving the feel of the sheer satin fabric under her fingertips. His face had darkened when she'd explained that Sean's pet name for her had been 'rusty head'; that she thought the dress would draw too much attention to her hair.

He caught her hand and pressed his lips softly to the back of it. 'It will complement it,' he'd said, his brow furrowed in consternation. 'You're a beautiful woman, Kaitlin. Every hair on your head, every freckle on your face is beautiful. The man clearly didn't want you to believe that you are.'

It was the first time she'd shared such an intimate detail, sure that no one could understand how soul-crushing such sarcastic comments could be. Greg got it, totally. She'd almost burst into tears, right there in the boutique. Yet she still hadn't been sure. It was expensive. She'd had to count every penny for a while after finding the courage to leave her marriage. Could she really justify being so extravagant on a purchase for herself, one she possibly wouldn't wear again? Greg had secretly gone back for it. 'I like it,' he'd said, when she'd stared at it in bewildered surprise. 'Wear it for me.'

She would. She gathered up her hair, glancing at herself in the mirror as she wondered whether to style it in an updo. And she would wear it with pride.

Heading down the stairs, she stopped part way down as she heard his key in the lock. Stepping in, he glanced up at her. He looked absolutely drained. His face was ashen, and even from where she was standing, she could see his eyes were tortured by whatever he'd had to deal with today. He tried to play it down, but his work as a forensic fire investigator didn't come without risks. One time, when he'd had a late-night call-out to an explosion caused by gas, she'd been so worried, she couldn't eat, couldn't sleep.

He'd clearly had a traumatic incident to deal with today, yet still he'd made the sweetest gesture.

'For your birthday,' he said, looking from her to the beautiful bouquet of roses and lilies he held in his hand. 'They looked nice when I bought them, but they're wilting a bit now, after sitting around in the office. Sorry.' He shrugged apologetically.

Unable to believe that she was with such an incredibly caring man, Kaitlin ran the rest of the way down. 'They're beautiful,' she whispered, taking them from him and stretching to brush his cheek with a kiss. 'Thank you.'

'Thank *you*,' Greg responded. 'For being so wonderful.' Cupping her face in his hands, he scanned her eyes for a moment, a soft glint in his own, then leaned to kiss her lips.

'Did you have an awful day?' she asked, easing away from him to allow him to take off his jacket.

He nodded and ran a hand over his neck. 'Pretty gruesome. I've spent the best part of it excavating fire debris and collecting evidence. We still have to test a couple of theories until we have a solid credible cause, but it's looking as if the fire was started deliberately. There was loss of life on this one,' he drew in a breath, his expression grim, 'so obviously it's important to be thorough.'

'Oh no.' Kaitlin's stomach turned over. 'An arsonist?' she asked.

He shrugged. 'Not your regular random arsonist. It's possibly drugs-related, according to the police. Some kind of revenge attack for drugs gone missing. I'll most likely have to provide evidence in court, hence the extra time spent collating everything. Drink?' he asked her, heading for the kitchen.

'Not for me. There's a bottle of red on the side, though,' Kaitlin said, following him.

'Cheers.' Greg smiled back at her. 'I could use a glass.'

She'd guessed he might. He would undoubtedly have been trying to contain his emotions as well as preserve the scene. Still, she felt she had to talk to him. Tomorrow was her birthday party. If she couldn't share the news publicly that they were thinking of getting married – which she couldn't if she went along with Greg's plans for an exotic wedding – she wanted at least to tell Zoe. Zoe had always been there for her. Kaitlin might never have found the courage to leave her marriage without her support. It was Zoe who'd convinced her she was worth so much more than being treated the way she was; that none of the awfulness that had gone on in the marriage was her fault. She'd helped look after Ruby while Kaitlin had continued her studies to become an occupational therapist, studies she'd had to keep secret while she'd been married for fear of her husband either ridiculing her or making it impossible for her to carry on. Zoe had helped her rebuild her self-esteem and, eventually, a new life for herself. She couldn't exclude her from this, and that was exactly what she would be doing if she went off and got married without her.

Going into the utility, she rested the flowers in the sink and then went back to check on the casserole that was simmering in the oven, hoping that Greg had an appetite for it.

'Smells good,' he said, to her relief.

'Beef bourguignon. A packet mix,' she admitted, knowing she didn't have to impress him. She doubted she could. He was a far better cook than she was.

'Perfect.' Pouring his wine, he took a gulp, then placed the glass on the work surface and walked across to circle his arms around her. 'Okay?' he asked, kissing the nape of her neck.

Kaitlin nodded and leaned into him.

'Ruby's in bed, I take it?' He kissed her again, sending a tingle of sexual excitement down the length of her spine.

'Fast asleep, hopefully.' She wriggled to face him before she lost her courage in fear of spoiling the moment. If she was going to speak to him, it was now or never. She wouldn't have a chance before work tomorrow, particularly as he would probably have an early start given the seriousness of the incident today. 'I need to talk to you, Greg,' she started hesitantly. 'I know it's been a difficult day for you, but ...' She faltered, trying to choose her words. It was a wonderfully romantic idea, but unrealistic. He would see that. She was sure he would.

He picked up on her anxiety. 'You're not sure about the wedding arrangements?' He searched her eyes, nothing but concern in his, and Kaitlin felt a huge surge of relief. 'It's okay, Kait, I get it.' He smiled reassuringly. 'I've been a bit thoughtless, haven't I?' He shrugged sheepishly. 'I was trying to be romantic, but it's not what you want, is it, to get married miles away without your parents and Ruby there?'

Kaitlin stared at him in wonderment. She'd imagined he would be put out, hurt that she wasn't thrilled at the thought of being whisked off to some romantic location. But he wasn't Sean, she reminded herself. He was the polar opposite of the man she'd been married to: caring, kind and most importantly of all, prepared to admit he was wrong. 'I think it's a lovely idea, Greg, truly I do.' She smiled, and placed her hand on his cheek. 'But yes, I would want my mum and dad there, and Ruby, of course.'

He nodded. 'Of course you do. I only want what you want, Kait. I would hate for you to feel I was monopolising you.'

Kaitlin felt something inside her melt. God, she did love this man. She could take him upstairs and eat him. 'There are friends I would like there too,' she ventured. 'We could still keep it small,' she added quickly, aware that he didn't yet have many friends locally, 'but I really want Zoe to come.'

Greg looked puzzled. 'Zoe?'

'My best friend,' she reminded him. 'Remember I told you about her? She helped me through one of the worst periods of my life. I can't imagine getting married without her there with me.'

'Oh, right.' His brow creased into a frown. 'Sorry, I should have remembered. I haven't met her, have I?'

'Not yet, no. She's coming to the party tomorrow, so you'll meet her then. I wanted to tell her that we were thinking of getting married. I didn't want her to think I'd gone ahead and made arrangements without even mentioning it to her. I love her to bits. I know she would be terribly disappointed.'

Greg nodded again, thoughtfully. 'I suppose she would. I'm sorry. I honestly wasn't thinking.' He raked his hand through his hair in that way he did whenever he was troubled. 'I'll cancel the holiday. I should be able to get the deposit back. Maybe we should look at booking the—'

Kaitlin caught hold of his hand. 'Or maybe we could change the booking?' she suggested. 'Look at flying people out, possibly? I know it would mean extra expense, but I have some funds in my bank account from the sale of the house. And Mum and Dad's wedding anniversary is coming up. It would be perfect if we could fit it around that.'

She found herself growing quite excited at the idea of getting married somewhere warm and exotic now she knew that those dearest to her could be there with her. And with Greg too. Her family would be his family once they were married. Her friends would be his friends. 'What do you think?' she asked him. 'Zoe would probably insist on paying her own air fare, and that would cut the costs a bit. Where is it, by the way?' She looked at him expectantly.

Greg seemed deep in thought. 'Portugal,' he said distractedly.

'Portugal?' Kaitlin eyed him in surprise. 'But that's amazing. That's where Zoe's been working.'

Now Greg looked surprised. 'Really?'

'At a hotel there. Small world. It could almost be fate, couldn't it?' Kaitlin was growing more enthusiastic by the second. Perhaps it *was* fate. Zoe and Greg would have lots to talk about. They were bound to get on. 'I bet she knows the hotel you've booked, and she'll be able to give us lots of tips on where to eat and what to see.'

'Sounds like the right sort of friend to have.' Greg smiled indulgently.

'She is. I can't imagine not having her in my life. I think she actually *saved* my life. Or at least gave me a reason to want to keep living. She was there for me, you know. My shoulder whenever I needed one.'

Kaitlin closed her eyes, nightmare scenarios of her past coming back, where her ex would accuse her of sulking if she didn't talk to him – which half the time she had no idea how to – and they would argue. Or of talking too much when she tried to voice an opinion, and they would argue. And then he wouldn't speak, deliberately ignoring her before he stormed out, and she would feel sick to the pit of her stomach waiting for him to come back, his resentment of her for whatever reason – simply being, she'd often thought – having festered inside him.

Shaking off a shudder at the memory, she looked back at Greg to find him watching her, perturbed. 'I'm sure you'll like her,' she hurried on rather than dwell on the past. She was free from him now. She was safe. 'She's the life and soul of the party.'

Greg's face relaxed into a smile, but still he looked concerned. 'I'm sure I will,' he agreed, taking her hand and gazing contemplatively down at it. 'She's obviously a good friend to you. I can't wait to meet her.'

Kaitlin smiled, pleased that the two people she loved most in the world, along with her precious daughter and her parents, were at last coming together.

'And just in case she thinks I'm a cheapskate ...' Kaitlin's heart skipped a beat as he moved away from her, reaching into his trouser pocket and then dropping to one knee. 'I didn't do this properly before, but ...' He presented her with a tiny black velvet box. 'Kaitlin Chalmers, will you do me the honour of marrying me?'

Eyeing him in amazement, she took the box and prised it open.

'Do you like it?' he asked her nervously as she gazed at the contents, an engagement ring with a beautiful intricate twist design and a dazzling solitaire diamond. It must have cost a small fortune.

'I love it.' She looked back at him, feeling suddenly overwhelmed. 'But ...'

Greg raised his eyebrows. 'But?' he urged her.

'Nothing, it's nothing. Just ...'

'I'll take it back,' he said, a frown crossing his face as he reached for the box. 'You obviously don't like it.'

'I *do*.' Her heart flipping, Kaitlin placed a hand over his. 'I love it, Greg. Truly I do. I just thought we might choose the ring together. But it doesn't matter,' she added quickly as his frown deepened, making him look almost angry, which surprised her. She'd never seen even a flicker of annoyance in him. But hadn't he got a right to feel peeved? After going to so much trouble to choose a ring, pay for it and propose properly, of course he might feel disappointed, embarrassed even, at her appearing to be unimpressed.

'I'm a bit overwhelmed, that's all. Everything's happening so quickly. I do love it, though.' She held his gaze as he studied her uncertainly. 'I love you too,' she assured him. 'It's a wonderfully romantic gesture and I do appreciate it.'

Greg nodded, but still he looked troubled. 'You don't want another design, then? A bigger diamond, or—'

'*No*.' She laughed at the preposterousness of that notion. The size of the stone didn't matter. A ring given with love was enough for her. It would always be enough. 'It's perfect.'

'And you reckon your friend will like it?' he asked, still looking a little moody as he scanned her face.

Kaitlin smiled. He put her in mind of a child needing reassurance. 'I'm sure she will.' She actually suspected that Zoe would be astounded at the speed at which things were moving. Greg had made all the arrangements so fast, Kaitlin's head had spun. He'd said he was thoughtless. He wasn't. How could choosing such a beautiful ring for her ever be that? He was simply impetuous, but thoughtfully, romantically impetuous, and she could only love him more for it.

TWO

ZOE

Feeling the unseasonable cold of the British climate right through to her bones, Zoe eyed the bulbous grey skies as the taxi pulled up a short way away from her apartment building on the Water's Reach dock. She hadn't envisaged coming back so miserably. While she'd been out in Portugal, she'd considered selling the apartment. It was shared ownership and probably didn't have much equity in it, but she'd imagined that she and Daniel might move into his villa together. God, she'd been such a fool.

'You can tell you're in the UK as soon as you touch down, can't you?' the taxi driver commented as she gathered up her bag. 'Bet you wish you'd stayed on the plane now.'

'Mmm.' Her chest feeling too full to speak, she wrapped her flimsy linen jacket more tightly around her and climbed out. She pulled out a ten-pound note and handed it to him. 'Keep the change,' she managed with a weak smile.

Standing alone on the waterfront with her hastily packed suitcase, she felt her heart plummet to new depths. She and Daniel were supposed to have been coming back for this trip together. She'd been planning it for ages to coincide with

Kaitlin's birthday, secretly wanting to show him off. She'd had to beg the time off from the Poolside Café, where there'd already been one member of staff booked off for holiday this week. She'd been worried that insisting on taking the time might sour relationships with her colleagues. She didn't have to worry any more. Thanks to Daniel, she could take all the time she liked.

He'd lost her her job. Lied to her, broken her heart and her faith in herself. She squeezed her eyes shut to stop the tears falling. Still she couldn't block out the image of his wife's face, her eyes wild with hatred as she'd burst Zoe's bubble about any hopes she'd had of a life with Daniel. 'I suppose you thought you'd found your white knight, didn't you? Did you imagine he was going to sweep you off your feet and keep you in the luxurious style to which you would like to become accustomed? If you weren't such a calculating little slut, I might almost feel sorry for you.' She'd looked Zoe over with a mixture of sympathy and ice-cold contempt. The villa she'd found them in, she'd gone on to inform her, wasn't Daniel's, as he'd no doubt told her it was. It was a show home in one of the holiday villages he sold property for. He'd clearly been trying to impress her. Problem was, he didn't have anything to impress her with.

Zoe didn't care about the villa. If he were penniless, she would have loved him, the person she'd thought he was, the man she'd thought had loved her. She had wanted more from life, a better, richer, more fulfilled existence. After being brought up in care, she felt she deserved it, but materialistic things mattered little against what she truly craved: to be loved, to be able to love back and feel safe emotionally. To be able to trust that someone cared for her enough not to hurt her.

She swallowed hard, hearing the urgency in his voice as he'd tried to persuade her he wouldn't. He'd actually said it: 'I won't hurt you. If it's too much, just whisper the word and we'll stop, I promise.' His piercing blue eyes had held hers, such palpable lust in them, Zoe had felt her own desire spike. Her heart thrumming a nervous drumbeat in her chest, she'd lowered her gaze, her eyes coming to rest on his lips, which were just full enough to be sensual, and her will to resist had evaporated. She'd never done anything like that before, but she'd felt safe with Daniel, telling herself he would never overstep the mark. She'd trusted him completely. It was a sex game, that was all, she'd reassured herself. A fantasy acted out between consenting adults. She hadn't wanted him imagining she was so inexperienced and unadventurous she wouldn't explore new avenues with him.

She still couldn't believe he'd left her there, frightened and alone, trussed to the bed in that damn villa like a cheap tart in a porn movie.

With no way to escape, she'd been there for hours, until her manager had reported her missing and the Portuguese police had finally freed her. One of the men had made lewd eyes at her. Zoe's skin crawled afresh as she recalled the suggestive comments he'd made. He'd clearly thought she was into S&M. She obviously did have some sort of masochistic streak. Why else would she have allowed a man to hurt her so badly? A man who, having run away to save his own worthless skin, now seemed to have decided he wouldn't leave her alone after all. He'd inundated her with texts and calls since she'd scurried from her Portuguese apartment with her things thrown in her suitcase and her life in tatters. Hearing her phone buzz in her pocket for the third time since she'd arrived at the airport, she guessed it was him. She'd put an ocean between them and still he wouldn't stop. Because *he* was frightened now, she knew, after his meek little bit on the side had grown fangs and threatened to expose the full extent of his cruel deceit to his wife, the woman who, her colleagues had confirmed, was funding the bastard's luxurious lifestyle.

Her manager had been utterly incredulous at her naivety,

shaking her head in despair after delivering the news that the powers-that-be at the exclusive Algarve hotel where she worked had decided they couldn't tolerate such deplorable behaviour. 'Was he worth it?' she'd asked her.

Zoe had never been more humiliated and hurt in her life. The worst hurt of all was that, while grappling for an excuse for his adulterous behaviour, he'd told his wife she was a prostitute. She would never understand why he'd done that. She'd obviously meant nothing to him. Impotent anger churning inside her, she tugged her phone from her pocket, braced herself and read his text. *Zoe, don't do this to us. Please talk to me. I love you.*

She felt her blood boil. Don't do this to *him* was what he meant. Don't ruin *his* life, as he had hers. She should rise above it. In time, maybe she could, but right now she was incandescent with rage. She wanted him to squirm as she'd squirmed, struggling to pull herself free until the bindings had bitten mercilessly into her wrists.

Fuck off, Daniel, she replied, before picking up her suitcase and marching on towards her apartment. She supposed she should count what small blessings she had. At least she still had a home to come back to.

I can't live without you, he texted as she keyed her security code into the gate and struggled through it with her luggage.

Unbelievable! She plonked the case down. He would say anything, wouldn't he, in an effort to stop her from sharing things with his wife that would make sure his marriage was over. *Without your wife's income, you mean. Tough*, she sent back. She swiped away the tears that mingled with the rain on her face and headed onwards. Reaching her apartment, she unlocked her front door and threw her suitcase in before her. She'd barely followed it when her phone rang.

Why was he doing this? Tears sprang again to her eyes. Why couldn't he just leave her be? 'I don't want to *speak* to you!' she seethed, jabbing the answer call button. 'Just piss off, will you?'

'Charming,' Kaitlin replied, somewhere between alarmed and bemused.

'Oh hell. Sorry, Kait. I didn't mean you, obviously.' Gloomily Zoe closed her door behind her and took in her suddenly small world. It looked as grey and uninviting as the weather. She would have to decorate, she decided. The walls were still the builders' original magnolia; she would have to paint them bright yellow or something, cheer the place up a bit, and then pull herself up by her bootstraps. She'd done it before. Coming out of care, she'd been determined not to let her past define her, though that had been bloody difficult when her mother had decided she couldn't afford to feed her daughter as well as her drug habit and abandoned her at five years old. That was what her new start in Portugal had been all about. After finding her previous boyfriend had cheated on her, she'd decided to leave her past behind her and make a new life for herself. Hadn't worked out so well, though, had it?

'I should hope not,' Kaitlin said, her tone concerned. She'd obviously cottoned on to the fact that something was wrong.

Zoe was glad to hear her voice. Her one consolation in coming home was that her best friend was here and would lend her a shoulder.

'Trouble in paradise?' Kaitlin asked intuitively.

'Definitely.' Zoe blinked back her tears. 'I've come back on my own.'

'Oh,' Kaitlin said, clearly getting the drift.

Zoe filled her in anyway. 'Daniel and I are over. He's a complete bastard.'

Kaitlin didn't say anything for a second. Didn't bombard her with questions, which Zoe didn't think she could have borne yet. 'Are you okay?' she asked gently instead.

Zoe swallowed and nodded and squeezed out the words. 'I

will be,' she assured her, though she didn't feel very assured herself, not with the stark choice she now had to make. 'He's married,' she blurted. 'Daniel, he's married with two children.'

'Oh no,' Kaitlin groaned sympathetically. 'And you had no idea?'

'None.' Zoe sniffed and wiped a hand under her nose. 'You haven't heard the best of it yet,' she said, taking a breath. 'His wife caught us having sex. If that wasn't bad enough, it was risqué sex. I was tied up, humiliatingly. I'm wondering how much of a kick he got out of leaving me there.'

Again Kaitlin paused. 'Do you need to talk?' she asked eventually. Zoe was about to leap at the chance when Kaitlin added, 'I have to pick Ruby up from school, and then we were going to take her to McDonald's before dropping her off at Mum's, but I'm sure Greg won't mind taking her on her own.'

'Oh.' Zoe felt that like a slap. Kaitlin had a life. Of course she did. Zoe hadn't realised that this Greg was such a big part of it, though. She felt a pang of guilt that she'd been so busy living her own supposedly exotic life with Daniel that she hadn't kept in touch with Kaitlin quite as much as she should have. 'No, it's fine. You go,' she said, making an attempt at cheerfulness. 'I have my unpacking to do and I have to grab some groceries. I'll catch up with you later.'

'You're sure?' Kaitlin didn't sound convinced.

'I'm sure. I'd be lying if I said I wasn't feeling a bit down, but it's nothing a glass or two of wine won't fix.' She wouldn't have any wine. She was tempted, very, but she'd made her decision and would steer clear of alcohol. 'I know you have loads to do for the party, and I need to clean this place up. I left it in a mess, and you know I'm borderline obsessive about having things neat and tidy. We'll talk later, promise.'

'Okay.' Kaitlin still sounded doubtful. 'You're absolutely sure you'll be all right, though?'

'I just said so.' Zoe smiled, relieved that she had someone

who cared in her life. Someone she could confide in who wouldn't judge her.

'And you are definitely still coming to my party?'

'I'll be there. I'm going to grab something glam to wear while I'm out,' she said determinedly. She'd been tempted not to go, given her new single status and the way she was feeling, but she could hardly cry off. She and Kaitlin had been together through thick and thin. Her friend would probably need her advice about the new man in her life. Zoe hoped Kaitlin wasn't planning on doing anything drastic, as she'd done with Ruby's father. She'd barely known Sean for two minutes before she was waltzing down the aisle with him, making the biggest mistake of her life.

'Brilliant,' Kaitlin said enthusiastically. 'I'll see you there. You know where it is – the Manor House, on the main road into Worcester. Don't worry about bringing wine or anything. Greg's laid everything on.'

That was nice of him. He was evidently very attentive.

'Or you could come here and go with us,' Kaitlin offered. 'Greg's booked a taxi, but there's room for one more.'

Definitely nice of him. It sounded as if he was getting his feet under the table. Kaitlin couldn't seem to utter a sentence without mentioning ... Hang on a second, *was* he getting his feet under the table? 'He's there a lot, isn't he?' Zoe asked warily.

Kaitlin fell silent. Then, 'He lives here, Zoe,' she said hesitantly. 'I told you we were moving in together.'

What? When? Zoe racked her brains. She couldn't remember Kaitlin mentioning anything about Greg moving in with her. If she had, she would most certainly have tried to dissuade her. It was too soon. How long had she been going out with him? Six months tops. Surely she should be taking it more slowly, after all she'd gone through? After all little Ruby had gone through? 'Right,' she said, and paused, aware of the need to choose her words carefully. 'So he's been living there for a while then?'

'A couple of months,' Kaitlin confirmed guardedly. 'I take it from your tone that you disapprove?'

'No.' Zoe spoke quickly. 'It's just ... Hasn't this all happened a bit fast? I mean, you can't really know him that well yet, can you?'

'I do,' Kaitlin assured her, now sounding defensive. 'He's okay, Zoe, I promise. I know you'll like him.'

'I'm sure I will,' she responded, less enthusiastically than perhaps she should have. Whether she liked him or not, though, was immaterial. Her concern here was that Kaitlin had had her self-esteem reduced to nil by a man, a feeling Zoe herself now knew only too well. She'd watched her friend reach rock bottom, feeling that somehow she was to blame for the fact that the person she'd fallen in love with had anger issues, commitment issues and basically didn't want the responsibility of fatherhood. Kaitlin had had to claw her way back up, rebuild her life, which she'd done with nothing but sheer determination. Was she really ready to rush headlong into another relationship, putting all that she'd worked so hard to achieve – her independence, her self-worth – at risk again? Zoe might be wrong – this new man might be perfection personified – but if there was one thing she knew, it was that nobody was perfect.

THREE

In the foyer at the Manor House, Zoe checked her new pixie haircut in the huge antique mirror. The lowlights were more copper than the caramel she'd asked for – similar to Kaitlin's colour, in fact. It was also a little shorter than she'd anticipated, but she'd had to agree with the hairdresser that it suited her face. She might not have a lot else going for her, but she did have a good bone structure. She tugged at the hem of her new blue satin ruched minidress and wondered if she wasn't showing off too much leg. Daniel would have approved. But then he'd got her down as a cheap tart, hadn't he?

Shut it out. She tried desperately to block out the image of him scrambling away from her after indulging his fantasy, searching frantically for his clothes as his wife eyed him murderously from the bedroom door. 'It was a mistake.' She heard his panic-filled voice. 'A one-off, I swear. Please, I can explain.' Scrambling into his trousers, he'd half stumbled, half hopped towards her.

'A prostitute, then?' the woman surmised. 'Why am I not surprised?'

'No!' Daniel exclaimed. Then, 'Yes,' he'd said throatily. 'I'm sorry. I ...'

Zoe felt it again, a low blow to her stomach, as if he'd just punched her.

He was obviously right. She'd been bought and paid for with a few fancy meals and fine wines. She might as well go into the party tonight and flaunt herself. You never knew, she might even get lucky and meet a man who wasn't a complete bastard under the superficial charm.

Unlikely. She clearly didn't attract that kind of man. She didn't want a man anyway. She was perfectly capable of managing without one. She was a survivor. Swallowing back the tight lump in her throat, she held her head up, and headed for the hall.

She paused outside the double doors. The music was thrumming loudly inside, Chris de Burgh's 'Lady in Red'. Gorgeously romantic. She fixed a smile in place for her friend's sake, took a breath and pushed on through with a flourish. Then she stopped, realising that it was Kaitlin who was the lady in red, and that she was dancing intimately with someone, presumably her dream man. She strained to get a better look, but her view was blocked by two women bobbing in front of her on the way to the dance floor.

As she twirled in Zoe's direction, Kaitlin's face lit up in delight. 'Zoe!' she exclaimed, abandoning her partner and dashing across to squeeze her into a hug. 'You look fabulous!' she said, standing back to look her over. 'So *tanned*. And that hair. Wow! I love that colour on you. Oh, and I adore the bag and matching earrings.'

'My cheer-myself-up gift to me.' Zoe glanced down at the pretty crystal-embellished bag she'd spent more on than she ought to. 'You look amazing too,' she said, taking in her friend's radiant complexion and the off-the-shoulder pillar-box-red evening gown she was wearing, which looked utterly stunning with her wild copper hair. Gone was the meek, self-effacing Kaitlin. In her place was a new, confident woman, one Zoe hadn't seen in a long time. 'Whatever you're doing, it's obviously working,' she said, with subtle innuendo.

Kaitlin's cheeks flushed such a deep shade of crimson they almost matched her dress. Laughing, she glanced self-consciously down and back, then grabbed hold of Zoe's hand. 'Come and meet him.'

Zoe allowed herself to be led, her eyes sweeping the room as she went. They were halfway across the hall when Kaitlin said, 'I have some news to share with you, but you have to keep it under your hat. I wanted you to be the first to know. Obviously I would want you to be—'

'Kait, wait.' Zoe stopped, tugging Kaitlin to a halt alongside her. 'Know what?' she asked, immediately wary as she picked up on the excitement in her friend's voice.

Kaitlin glanced at her, guiltily, Zoe noticed.

Her apprehension growing, she narrowed her eyes. 'You're not thinking of getting engaged, are you?'

'Well, um...' Kaitlin couldn't quite meet her gaze.

'Please don't tell me you're *already* engaged.' Zoe stared at her, bewilderment running through her. She hadn't told her. Such an important, life-changing decision – a monumentally *bad* decision, since she'd only know this man for five minutes. 'And you didn't think to mention it to me before now, your *best friend*?'

Out of nowhere, Zoe felt tears rising. Suddenly she felt as if she was losing everyone in her life all over again, and she just couldn't bear that.

Kaitlin looked confused for a second, and then, 'Oh my God,' she murmured. 'I'm so sorry, Zoe. I didn't mean not to tell you. Everything's happened so quickly. He only ...'

She trailed off, glancing towards the band, who decided that now was a good time to strike up with a rock-and-roll number. 'Come on,' she shouted above the music. 'We need to talk.'

Nudging people out of the way, apologising as they went, she tugged Zoe back to the foyer. Once there, she caught hold of both of her hands. 'Zoe, I am *so* sorry I didn't tell you before,' she said, her eyes full of remorse. 'I didn't get a chance, honestly. He only proposed to me properly last night. And with the wedding plans all being so—'

'Whoa.' Zoe snatched her hands away. 'Could you back up a little, please, Kait? *Wedding* plans?'

Kaitlin's eyes flickered down. 'Yes,' she said, looking back at her. 'I was going to mention it on the phone, but when you told me about you and Daniel ...'

'I see.' Now Zoe was hurt, indescribably. 'These would be wedding plans you've presumably been making for some time – by the nature of the fact that weddings take a while to organise?'

'No! It's not like that, Zoe, I promise. I wouldn't dream of not sharing something as important as this with you. You're my best friend.'

Her throat tightening, Zoe looked away.

'Greg organised it,' Kaitlin blurted, a desperate edge to her voice.

'What?' Zoe's gaze snapped back to hers. 'Not everything, surely?'

'Yes.' Kaitlin looked extremely awkward.

'So he just sprang wedding arrangements on you and you went along with it?'

'Yes. I mean ... No, not initially.' Kaitlin shook her head, flustered. 'We discussed it, but ... I hadn't even agreed until last night. Please don't be angry with me, Zoe. I honestly didn't mean to—'

'I'm not,' Zoe replied shortly. 'I'm shocked. I'm also scared for you, Kait. Surely you can see why I would be?'

'I know, and I can,' Kaitlin conceded, looking anguished. 'But there's no need to be. You'll see once you meet him.'

Zoe didn't think she would see anything, other than what was happening here. Kaitlin was being manipulated, and she obviously didn't realise. 'These wedding arrangements,' she said, unable to stop the cynicism from creeping into her voice, 'where exactly is he planning on you getting married?'

'Portugal,' Kaitlin replied, her gaze dropping back to the floor.

'Portugal?' Zoe blinked. This was growing weirder by the second. Kait *must* see that. 'Did he know I was out there?' She struggled to give him the benefit of the doubt. *Really* struggled. It might be that he'd genuinely tried to arrange a lovely surprise. In which case, shouldn't he have been in touch with *her*, Kaitlin's best friend and surely someone he must know she would want at the wedding?

Kaitlin drew in a breath. She looked close to tears. Zoe just wanted to hug her and reassure her. But how could she? 'No,' she said eventually. 'I did mention you were there, but I don't think he'd remembered.'

No, Zoe would bet he hadn't.

Silence hung heavily between them for a second. Then, 'You'd better go back in,' Zoe suggested, her voice tight.

Kaitlin blinked at her, startled. 'Aren't you coming?'

Zoe hesitated. She didn't want to upset Kaitlin, but even at the risk of their friendship, she would have to. She had to talk to her, caution her to take things more slowly. Kaitlin was bringing this man into little Ruby's life too, permanently. It was a major decision, one that she wouldn't be able to easily extract herself from. Zoe prayed she knew what she was doing.

Breathing deeply, she made her decision. She would talk to Kaitlin later, preferably away from here. 'I'll follow you in in a minute,' she said, nodding towards the loos, where she suspected she might need to paint on her smile.

Clearly gathering that she needed a moment, Kaitlin didn't offer to go with her, nodding forlornly instead. Then, 'Zoe, *wait*,' she called tremulously as she walked away. 'I'm pregnant.'

Zoe froze. Stunned, she turned slowly to face her friend, her gaze drifting down past her waistline. The empire cut of the dress gave nothing away. Her gaze travelled back to her face. Kaitlin's eyes, which were full of nervous apprehension, confirmed in a heartbeat that she was telling the truth.

'I should have told you that too. You seemed so negative about us living together, though, I ...' Kaitlin looked away and back again. 'It's me who wants us to get married. Greg's not pushing me into anything I don't want to do. You're judging him, Zoe, and you shouldn't be.'

Noting her friend's expression, a combination of disappointment and defiance, Zoe felt awful. Was it possible that she was jealous because of what had happened between her and Daniel? She'd trusted Daniel because she'd wanted to, because her own self-esteem had felt battered when she'd gone out to Portugal. She'd been wrong to. Was she wrong about this man, who it seemed wanted to marry Kaitlin for all the right reasons? She felt threatened by him, she realised with a jolt. Was that because she feared he would take Kaitlin away from her? Kait was her best friend. Zoe needed her now more than ever. In order to keep her, though, she needed to rise above this. She couldn't believe they had been verging on arguing for the first time ever.

'Greg's not one of the bad guys, Zoe.' Kaitlin smiled sadly. 'I understand your concern, but please give him a chance. I just know you'll like ...' She stopped, her eyes swivelling to the hall doors as they opened.

'Greg,' she said, almost wilting with relief.

'Is there a problem?' he asked, looking between them.

Zoe's breath caught in her chest as his gaze settled on her. Dressed impeccably in a black dinner jacket and tie, he was so good-looking it was obscene. That in itself sent another wave of trepidation through her. But it was his eyes that really caught her attention. Piercingly blue, incongruous with his stylishly messy dark hair, they were so intense they were electrifying. Apprehensively she looked him over and felt a glimmer of recognition. And then it was gone. Did she know him? Or was it simply that his colouring and build put her in mind of Daniel?

FOUR

'Can I get you two ladies a drink?' Greg asked once they'd gone back inside. He'd pointed out that people were wondering where Kaitlin was. By people, Zoe assumed he meant himself.

'I'll get them,' Kaitlin offered, her bright smile back in place. 'I need to have a word with the band about breaking for the buffet anyway. You two have a chat, why don't you?'

'Right.' Zoe smiled, and tried not to actually fall against him as Kaitlin all but pushed them together. She was so close she could smell the spicy, woody smell of his aftershave. See the curiosity in his electric-blue eyes as he scrutinised her. 'I'm Zoe,' she said, extending her hand. 'Nice to meet you.'

'Gregory Walker,' he said, smiling charmingly as he reached to shake it. 'Most people call me Greg. Nice to meet you too, Zoe. I have a feeling my fiancée is manipulating us into getting to know each other a little better.'

Interesting that he should use the word 'manipulating'. The word 'fiancée' jarred too. It was almost as if he were staking his claim. 'Greg,' she said. 'Do you have a middle name?'

He squinted at her. 'Mark. Why?'

'I just wondered. I knew a Gregory Walker, years ago. You're obviously not him.'

'No.' He looked puzzled, briefly. 'I think I would have remembered if we'd met before. So, Zoe, I've heard a lot about you,' he said, moving on. 'You and Kaitlin are obviously close friends.'

'Since we were sweet sixteen. We went to sixth-form college together.' She felt as though she were the one staking a claim. Was she? She'd felt pushed out realising that Kaitlin hadn't shared her news with her, about the pregnancy, their plans to get married. She still wasn't convinced that she'd mentioned that Greg had moved in with her either. 'Are you from around here?' she asked him. 'I don't really know that much about ...'

She paused as Kaitlin reappeared with the drinks. 'One red wine,' she offered Greg a glass, 'and white for you, Zoe, Pinot Grigio. Hope that's okay?'

'Great, thanks.' Zoe accepted it, though she wouldn't drink it. She would grab a soft drink later, rather than send Kaitlin back again.

'I'm just going to have a quick word with Sally,' Kaitlin announced, nodding back to the drinks table. Catching Sally's eye, Zoe waved at her. It took Sally a second, but when she recognised her, she waved back. Half-heartedly, Zoe noticed. She could see by her expression that she wasn't exactly thrilled to see her. Sally and Kaitlin had been friends since childhood, gone to the same schools together. Sally had been miffed when Zoe had come along, an interloper, someone who didn't belong in their circle, and monopolised Kaitlin, forming a close bond with her.

She watched as Kaitlin pressed a kiss to Greg's cheek then twirled around and headed off. Clearly, she wanted her fiancé and her best friend to bond. Zoe wasn't sure that was likely, but she would make an effort for Kaitlin's sake. She didn't have a lot of choice, she thought gloomily, since it seemed he was now a permanent fixture in her friend's life.

'I was wondering where you were from,' she picked up, fishing for at least some basic information about him. 'Kaitlin hasn't told me very much, apart from the fact that you're wonderful, of course.'

'Obviously.' Greg's mouth curved into an amused smile. 'You don't have all the juicy details, then?'

'Not yet, no.' Zoe smiled back. 'We haven't had a chance to talk very much. I'm sure Kait will fill me in, though.'

He nodded good-naturedly, as if accepting that his life was about to come under scrutiny. 'I was based at a fire investigation company in Manchester when I met Kaitlin, but I'm from around here originally. Naturally, with Kaitlin here, I jumped at a transfer when one came up.'

'Really?' Zoe's interest was piqued. 'Small world,' she said. 'Whereabouts?'

Greg hesitated for a second. 'We moved around,' he said vaguely, eyeing her thoughtfully over the rim of his glass.

'You went to school locally then?' Zoe tilted her head to one side.

He appraised her quietly. 'For a while.' He shrugged. Then, 'You ask a lot of questions,' he said, his tone sharp, which took her aback.

'Just curious.' She shrugged in turn and held his gaze.

He glanced down. 'Like I said, we moved around, so ...' He looked back at her, his obvious irritation apparently forgotten and his amiable smile back in place. 'What about you? I take it you're local?'

'Not really.' Zoe scrutinised him carefully, his shift in mood definitely giving her cause for concern. 'I'm a bit of a nomad too. I was brought up in care, so not moving around wasn't an option. I got fostered a couple of times, but it didn't work out. I don't think I settled in school until I was around thirteen, fourteen.'

Greg nodded. 'That's rough,' he said, his expression now inscrutable.

'It was, sometimes. But it toughened me up. At least I know I can fight my corner if I need to.' She wanted him to know that she would fight Kaitlin's corner too, if she had to.

'I'd better not cross you then,' he joked.

'Probably not a good idea.' Zoe smiled. 'So, tell me all about this grand romantic gesture of yours.' She changed the subject, keen to hear from the horse's mouth why he'd taken it upon himself to organise everything without Kaitlin's input. Also, what it was he had organised exactly.

'Ah. The wedding surprise that turned out to be more of a shock, you mean?' Greg winced in embarrassment. 'I think I was probably a touch too impetuous for Kaitlin's liking. Also, thoughtless. I wanted it to be just the two of us, but of course that excluded Kait's family and friends, which isn't what she would want. You are invited now, obviously.' He smiled again, disarmingly.

'I should think so too.' Knitting her brow into a mock scowl, Zoe played along.

Greg laughed. 'I think she'd rather have you there than me, to be honest.'

'I'm not sure it's me she wants to get married to, though,' Zoe pointed out. It was blatantly bullshit, but he was clearly trying to win her over. 'And do I get to know where in Portugal I'm invited to exactly?'

'Vista do Penhasco Falesia,' Greg supplied.

Zoe was taken aback. The Vista do Penhasco was a lovely hotel in a quiet location, with a picturesque setting on top of a cliff overlooking the sea. It had access to a beautiful beach, which she supposed was what he had in mind for the ceremony.

'Good choice. Who did you speak to? I know the manager there. I might be able to get you a discount,' she offered, hoping her fishing expedition wasn't also becoming blatantly obvious.

'Er, can't remember offhand,' Greg replied with a frown. 'Afonso, or Alfonso? I'll have to check the email.'

'Give me a call.' Zoe made sure to give him a bright smile this time. 'Kaitlin has my number.'

'Right.' He nodded and continued to study her.

Zoe noted the narrowed eyes with a flicker of apprehension. Unsure what to say next, she breathed a quiet sigh of relief as she noticed Kaitlin heading back towards them.

'So, how are my two favourite people getting on?' Kaitlin threaded an arm through each of theirs.

'Like a house on fire,' Greg assured her, leaning to brush her lips with his.

'Greg's just been telling me about the hotel he's booked,' Zoe said, noting him unlinking arms and threading his around Kaitlin's waist instead, pulling her close. Did he think Zoe was going to steal her away from him? Would that she could.

'It's gorgeous, smack bang on the beach, isn't it, Greg? So romantic.' Kaitlin sighed dreamily.

'That's right.' He squeezed her impossibly closer.

'We'll have a browse of some pics online tomorrow,' Zoe suggested, fully intending to arrange to meet up with Kaitlin and wanting Greg to know it. 'Talk more in a sec. I just need to pop to the loo. Too much wine.' She smiled at Kaitlin and glanced meaningfully at Greg, whose eyes seemed to harden for a second before he focused his attention on Kaitlin.

'Don't be long. We have to strut our stuff on the dance floor,' Kaitlin said, clearly having missed the look that had passed between them.

Zoe laughed, recalling how they had once strutted with abandon. Oh, to be that carefree now. 'I won't,' she promised, parking her almost full glass on the table behind her. She didn't actually need the loo. She did have a pressing phone call to make, however, which she thought might be best made in private.

FIVE

KAITLIN

Having searched everywhere for Zoe and then double-checked the loos, Kaitlin was heading back to the hall when she noticed her walking past the main hotel doors. What on earth was she doing outside in the drizzle? Making a call, she gathered, as Zoe walked past again in the opposite direction with her phone glued to her ear.

Kaitlin went out after her, wanting to find out what she really thought of Greg. They had seemed to be getting along, though not quite as well as Sally had hinted they might be. 'Zoe seems to have taken a shine to him,' she'd said, her eyes narrowed suspiciously as she'd nodded towards them. Glancing behind her to see Greg and Zoe doing nothing but talking, Kaitlin had ignored her.

Sally had always seemed to dislike Zoe, and Kaitlin could never quite understand why. She'd assumed it was because of Zoe's background, which didn't make it easy for her to open up in front of people. She didn't join in the girlie gossip they were all guilty of then, possibly because she was often the subject of such gossip. Sally had called her secretive. Said it was as if Zoe was working at not fitting in. Kaitlin should probably have reprimanded her for it, pointing out that Zoe was a loner because she'd had to be, but guessing that that might cause more bad feeling between them, she had thought it better to leave well alone.

Zoe had her back to her as she approached her on the drive. 'I have to go,' she said, ending her call and whirling around as Kaitlin's footsteps crunched on the gravel behind her.

'Shit,' she muttered shakily. 'You almost gave me a heart attack.'

'Sorry, I didn't mean to creep up on you. I just wondered what you were doing out here in the rain?'

'Daniel,' Zoe answered, a flash of fury crossing her face. 'He's bloody well stalking me, I swear.' Dropping her phone back in her bag, she hooked an arm through Kaitlin's.

'*Stalking* you?' Kaitlin repeated, shocked, as they made their way back to the hotel foyer.

'He hasn't stopped ringing or texting me since I left Portugal.' Zoe huffed angrily as she pushed through the entrance doors. 'I can't believe I was so wrong about him. He's getting possessive now to the point of aggressive.'

'Aggressive? How?' Kaitlin asked, alarmed.

'Just verbal stuff.' Zoe sighed. 'He's at the airport, on his way here, apparently. Swears he loves me. Says that if he can't have me, no one will. Romantic, hey?'

'Bloody hell, Zoe.' Kaitlin stopped walking and turned to face her. She seemed to be brushing it off, but that was an actual threat. Zoe was just five foot three. Petite. She was tough, yes, but she'd stand no chance if this guy got physical. Recalling what she'd said about his predilection for bondage, Kaitlin was scared for her. 'You should report him to the police,' she said, her own anger rising.

'And say what?' Zoe raised a dubious eyebrow. 'As I said, it's just verbal stuff. I can't see them rushing to arrest him, can you?'

Kaitlin thought about it. 'No,' she conceded with a sigh. 'Do you think he might actually mean you harm, though? Because if so, you really ought to at least talk to the police.'

Zoe knitted her brow. 'No, not really,' she said uncertainly. 'The bondage thing was just a bit of harmless ...' She stopped, alarm crossing her face. 'You won't tell anyone about that, will you?'

'Don't be silly, Zoe. Of course I won't. Why would I?' Kaitlin felt a smidgen of guilt recalling that she had mentioned to Greg when he'd asked whether Zoe was in a relationship that she'd just split up with her boyfriend. She'd told him the man was married and a bit weird, not wanting to go into too much detail for Zoe's sake. She'd asked him not to let on that she'd told him, Zoe having told her in confidence, and Greg had understood.

Zoe nodded, looking considerably relieved. Kaitlin guessed why. She would be crushed if she thought that particular juicy bit of gossip was circulating about her.

'Do you want to come and stay with us?' she asked her.

Zoe smiled wryly. 'I can't see Greg being very keen on that, can you?'

'He won't mind,' Kaitlin assured her.

'I think he might. Three's a crowd in a relationship, after all,' Zoe pointed out.

And now Kaitlin felt awful. It sounded as if Zoe already felt she was being pushed out.

'I'll be fine,' Zoe insisted, leaning to give her a hug. 'Or at least I will when I've been to the loo. I seem to need to go every five minutes lately.'

Kaitlin eyed her friend curiously as they both headed that way.

Zoe caught the look. 'I'm on a diet,' she said. 'Drinking loads of water. Probably not a good idea before coming to a party.'

A minute later, she called through the cubicle partition. 'Are there many of Greg's friends here?'

'He hasn't made a lot of friends in the area yet,' Kaitlin replied, hoping that Zoe wasn't on the lookout for a man to salve her wounds. She suspected that this Daniel had been just that, someone who would help her shore up her flagging self-esteem after finding her previous boyfriend had been cheating on her. 'They're real pains, aren't they, exes?' She changed the subject, not wanting to speculate about why Greg didn't have any friends here. She had wondered herself why he hadn't invited anyone. 'Can you believe Sean's actually pretending interest in Ruby now he knows I have someone else in my life?'

'Sounds like you're the one who might need to hone your self-defence techniques,' Zoe said, eyeing her worriedly as they both emerged from the cubicles.

'I doubt he'll try anything. He's met Greg,' Kaitlin confided. Sean was a coward when all was said and done. He'd been abusive and aggressive to her, and probably would be to any other woman who might have the misfortune to get involved with him. He'd swallowed, visibly, though, when, after calling at her house uninvited, he'd met Greg, who was taller and broader than he was, for the first time.

'Well, Greg certainly looks as if he'd fight for you,' Zoe commented, eyeing her in the mirror as she washed her hands.

Kaitlin smiled. 'He would. Not that I would want him coming to actual physical blows, but I'm confident he would look out for me, yes.'

Zoe nodded and offered her a small smile in return. 'You love him, don't you?' she asked, drying her hands and turning to face her.

'I wouldn't be marrying him otherwise.' Kaitlin glanced at her curiously. Zoe looked troubled, sad, rather than happy for her. She desperately didn't want her to be that. She would always value her friendship; she was a confidante and a shoulder to cry on, just as Zoe could cry on hers. They needed to have a good chinwag, a catch-up, just the two of them. Zoe would soon stop worrying when she realised how happy Kaitlin was. Ruby too.

Zoe hesitated for a second. 'And you are sure this great romantic gesture, wanting to whisk you off abroad and get married, is all it seems?'

Kaitlin searched her eyes, and wasn't sure she liked what she saw there. Zoe was obviously suspicious of Greg's motives, with no justification as far as Kaitlin could see.

'Meaning?' She understood her friend might have concerns. Things had moved quickly, and Zoe hadn't had time to form a proper impression of him, but surely now that she had met him …

'Nothing.' Zoe glanced down, two bright spots forming on her cheeks. 'It's just …' She looked back at her, something akin to guilt in her eyes. 'Nothing. It's nothing, just me being neurotic.'

'Zoe, what?' Kaitlin urged her. 'If you have some kind of a problem with Greg, you really need to tell me.'

Zoe drew in a breath. 'Why doesn't he have any friends here?'

Kaitlin blinked, perplexed. 'He's only recently moved here from Manchester.' Where was this leading?

'Yes, but there must be someone he would have liked to invite – colleagues from work maybe? It seems odd that—'

'It's *my* party.' Kaitlin eyed her incredulously. Was this really the extent of the problem? She couldn't quite believe that Zoe, who she thought she knew better than anybody, was suddenly being so petty. 'One that Greg went to some effort and expense to arrange. *My* friends are here. They're his friends too. Or at least most of them are.'

'But he's local, isn't he?' Zoe persisted. 'Surely he must have old friends he would have wanted to look up. I just don't understand—'

'Nor do I,' Kaitlin snapped, her agitation spiralling as she found herself having to defend the man she was in love with. Instantly regretting it, she tried to calm herself. 'He obviously lost touch with people when he moved out of the area. Men don't usually keep in contact with old school—'

'He must have gone to school locally, mustn't he?' Zoe went on over her, definite suspicion now in her eyes.

'And?' Kaitlin felt her hackles rise. She really wasn't going to let it drop, was she?

Zoe paused before answering, as if she were reluctant to say more.

'Zoe, what?' Kaitlin demanded, frustrated.

'There was a Gregory Walker at the middle school I went to. Someone with exactly the same name, Gregory Mark Walker. He was a friend. This isn't him, Kait,' Zoe said, a worried frown creasing her forehead. 'He doesn't look anything like him.'

'Are you serious?' Kaitlin laughed, astonished. 'Is that really all you can come up with to justify the fact that you've obviously decided not to like him?'

'I haven't decided I'm not going to like him.' Zoe's eyes shot wide in surprise. 'I'm just—'

'Really? It seems that way to me, Zoe.' Kaitlin glared at her. 'For your information, since you insist on knowing everything there is to know about him, he grew up in Hibberton. Would you like me to ask him to write down the details for you?'

'No.' Zoe's cheeks flushed with embarrassment. 'I'm your *friend*, Kait. I'm concerned for you, that's all. I'm worried that this is history repeating itself. That you're in danger of making the same mistake all over again. I think I've got just cause.'

'What *just* cause?' Kaitlin demanded.

'The wedding, for starters,' Zoe shot back. 'When did he book it?'

Staring at her friend in sheer disbelief, Kaitlin didn't answer immediately. 'You went outside just now to call the hotel, didn't you?' she said, her heart plummeting. 'You were checking up on him.'

Zoe said nothing, which told her that that was exactly what she'd done. 'There's something not right about him, Kaitlin,' she murmured eventually, her shoulders dropping. 'I can feel it. He—'

'Right! And you're an excellent judge of men, aren't you, Zoe?' Kaitlin growled angrily across her. 'So bloody adept at reading the signs, you let a married man completely humiliate you! And while we're on that subject, can you imagine what finding you the way she did must have done to this Daniel's wife?'

Zoe stared at her, thunderstruck. 'That's not fair, Kait,' she countered, breathing hard.

'Nor is what *you're* doing,' Kaitlin shouted, her fury spilling over. 'You don't even *know* Greg. Yet you come here, determined to spoil my birthday with baseless *rubbish*. What is wrong with you, Zoe? I can't believe you would be so jealous you would want to ruin everything for me. Why? I don't understand it. *Why* don't you want me to be happy?'

'I'm *not* jealous. I *do* want you to be happy!' Zoe shouted back, tears springing from her eyes. 'I'm not trying to spoil things for you. I'm worried for you, Kaitlin. Little Ruby too. I'm your best friend. I *love* you. You know I do.'

Kaitlin's blood pumped. 'And therein lies the problem, doesn't it? Greg loves me too, and you just can't bear that fact, can you?' The words spilled from her mouth unhindered by forethought.

'It's nothing of the sort, Kait. I ...' Zoe stopped as there was a knock at the door.

'Are you decent in there?' called Greg. 'Sorry to interrupt,' he said, poking his head around the door and glancing curiously between them. 'The band is about to play "Happy Birthday". I think it might fall a bit flat without the birthday girl.'

Kaitlin tore her gaze away from Zoe. She felt dreadful about the things she'd said, but that Zoe would do this, here, now, was beyond unbelievable. It was cruel. 'I think you might do better to leave,' she suggested over her shoulder as she walked towards the door.

'Kaitlin, wait!' Zoe called tearfully.

Kaitlin couldn't turn around. If she did, she was sure she would burst into tears too.

She'd reached the hall doors when she heard Greg speaking to Zoe behind her. 'That was a bit fraught, wasn't it?' he said.

Zoe didn't answer for a second, then, 'You were listening?' she asked, bewildered. 'It was a private conversation. None of your business.'

'It sounded to me as if it was very much my business,' Greg replied tersely. 'Look, Zoe, I know you've split up with your boyfriend, and I get that you're upset, but you should know that I'll do anything to protect Kaitlin. Whatever it takes. Understand?'

Kaitlin's hand froze on the door handle. That sounded almost like a threat. Why had he said that? Why had he mentioned Zoe's boyfriend when she'd specifically asked him not to? She couldn't just leave Zoe like this. She would be devastated.

'Zoe ...' She whirled around, but Zoe was already disappearing through the main entrance.

SIX

'Kaitlin!' She heard Greg shout after her as she flew through the main entrance after Zoe. 'Kaitlin, wait!' She guessed he was coming after her, but she couldn't wait. She couldn't let Zoe run off into the night. Not like this.

'Where on earth are you going?' He caught up with her as she paused a few yards down the gravel drive.

'*Bloody* shoes,' Kaitlin cursed, hitching up the hem of her dress and bending to grapple with the strappy shoes that were impossible to walk in let alone run. 'I have to catch up with her,' she muttered as he reached out a hand to steady her.

'But you have a room full of guests,' he pointed out. 'It's your birthday party. I wanted it to be special for you. You can't just disappear.'

'She's my best *friend*.' Straightening up, Kaitlin almost glared at him, for reasons he clearly couldn't fathom. He looked completely bewildered. 'She was in *tears*, Greg. I can't let her wander around the streets in that state on her own.'

He answered with a short nod. 'She won't have got far,' he assured her. 'You go back in and I'll—'

'Why did you have to say that to her?' Kaitlin cut in, her agitation this time with him.

Greg looked mystified. 'What?'

'All that stuff about protecting me and telling her you knew about her boyfriend. Surely you must have realised she would be upset?'

'Whoa.' He held up his hands defensively. 'I hardly said a word. I thought her breaking up with her boyfriend might be why she was upset, that was all. I didn't realise being sympathetic was a crime.'

'But I didn't want her to know I'd told you.' Kaitlin looked at him in despair. 'It was a confidence between friends. I asked you not to say anything and now she's thinking the whole world knows and that everyone is gossiping behind her back, thanks to *me*.'

'Right.' His jaw tight, he drew in a terse breath, and Kaitlin realised she'd managed to upset him too. Of course he would be upset, having gone to so much trouble to make this an unforgettable evening for her. 'So she imagines you don't share confidences with the man you're about to marry, then?' he asked her.

'It's not that. It's ...' She shook her head and groped for a way to explain. 'She hasn't told anyone else. She wouldn't want people to know. It's personal information, don't you see? She's embarrassed, hurt. She obviously feels like a complete fool being taken in by him. It's the sort of thing a woman would only confess to someone she could trust, her best friend, and now ...' Some friend she'd turned out to be. Recalling the awful things she'd said to Zoe, she blinked her tears back. 'I have to go after her.'

'I'll go. It's about to bucket down. I have my jacket on and I'll be quicker than you, since I'm not wearing my strappy shoes.' He shrugged half-heartedly and gave her a small smile.

Kaitlin hesitated, glancing towards the road. 'Thanks,' she

said eventually, grateful that he realised how much it meant to her, how much Zoe meant to her.

'No problem.' He squeezed her briefly to him. 'Keep your mobile close. I'll call you.'

Kaitlin nodded, now feeling guilty on all fronts. 'Thank you,' she said again as he set off. 'I'm sorry I snapped,' she called after him.

'I understand,' he called back, heading off at a run towards the road.

She watched him go, her stomach churning with anxiety, for Greg as well as for Zoe. She doubted he really did understand. More likely he was confounded by her turning on him after all he'd done. And by what must seem to him a complete overreaction by Zoe. She would have to try to explain why Zoe was feeling so emotionally fragile; how her insecurity would have been exacerbated by her coming home to find her best friend had seemingly shut her out of her life.

She would have to apologise to him and to Zoe. She hoped to God he caught up with her. She hated the thought of her walking home alone.

Going back inside, her shoes in her hand, her emotions fraught, she found Sally waiting for her in the foyer. 'I've had a word with the bandleader,' she said. 'He's filling in with a few slow numbers until you're ready. I'm going to miss wishing you happy birthday, though. I have to go on duty, I'm afraid.' She sighed. 'A policewoman's lot is never done.'

'Oh no.' Kaitlin tried to focus. 'I'm sorry, Sally. I've hardly had time to talk to you.'

'It's your birthday. You're forgiven.' Sally paused. 'I couldn't help noticing the fracas out here. Is Zoe all right?'

'I don't know. She's upset. Man problems.' Kaitlin was reluctant to divulge too much.

Sally sighed and eyed the ceiling. 'It usually is.'

'Greg's gone after her.' Kaitlin glanced worriedly back to the exit. The rain had started, slashing and icy cold, and looked to be set in for the night.

'And you're okay with that, are you?'

Kaitlin knitted her brow, confused.

'After what happened with Sean, I mean.'

Kaitlin's frown deepened. What on earth was she talking about?

Sally looked confused for a minute. Then, 'Oh hell. Kaitlin, I'm so sorry. I thought you knew.'

'Knew what?' Kaitlin's heart boomed a warning. 'Sally, I have no idea what—'

'I should go,' Sally said quickly. 'I'm already late.' Breaking eye contact, she made to move past her.

'*Sally!*' Kaitlin caught her arm. 'What is it I'm supposed to know? I have no idea what you mean.'

'I have to go, Kait.' Sally pulled away, heading swiftly for the door. 'You need to ask Zoe.'

'Ask her *what*?' Kaitlin's stomach twisted with sick apprehension. 'You have to tell me, Sally.'

Sally stopped. 'Sean came to see me,' she said, turning back. 'Just before you were married, he came to the station. He said Zoe had come on to him, that he turned her down and that she'd started threatening him. She told him she would tell you he'd taken advantage of her. He said it was all lies, but he seemed genuinely scared. There was nothing I could do, not without proof, and we all know now what Sean was like, but ...'

Kaitlin stared at her, thunderstruck

'I thought you knew.' Sally's expression was agonised. 'I was sure he must have told you. I'm so sorry, Kait. I wouldn't have dreamed of saying anything if I'd thought you didn't. Talk to Zoe. She'll tell you what really happened, I'm sure. Although ...' she paused, a flicker of uncertainty crossing her face, 'if there was any truth in it ...'

Kaitlin felt a rush of fury unfurl inside her. If Zoe had been trying to split her and Sean up, it had clearly backfired. And now this. Had that been her aim tonight, to try to drive a wedge between Kaitlin and Greg? She'd clearly made up her mind to hate him even before she'd met him.

SEVEN

ZOE

Tears mingling with the rain on her face, Zoe blundered along the waterfront towards her apartment. Realising her phone was buzzing, she fumbled it from her bag, checked the text she'd received, and then squinted at it with a combination of astonishment and crushed disillusionment.

I miss you, Daniel had sent. *Please talk to me.*

She tugged in a tremulous breath. *How's your wife?* she replied succinctly. Then, wiping a hand across her face, she stuffed the phone back in her bag and walked on, anger and hurt churning inside her.

What had possessed her? She'd left her home, her best friend – the only person who'd truly cared about her, or so she'd thought – and her job to make a new life for herself in Portugal, only to find she'd walked away from one cheating, two-faced bastard straight into the arms of another. She'd been brought up in care, for goodness' sake. She was supposed to be streetwise and savvy. Why then had she been stupidly naive enough to fall for his false promises and lies? Because she'd fallen in love with him. Because she'd needed to be loved.

Shivering, she wrapped her arms around herself, and quickened her pace. Why had she blurted those things out to Kaitlin tonight? It was her birthday party. A great big showy affair, all laid on by the man she was about to get married to. She was *engaged* to him, obviously hopelessly in love with him. Was she really likely to have listened to anything Zoe had to say? She probably hadn't told her she was getting married because she knew Zoe would put a damper on things, reminding her that it was too soon after what she'd been through with Sean. She had assumed Zoe was jealous. Zoe was no longer sure. All she knew was that Kaitlin's emotions were compromised. She'd just wanted her to take a step back, think it through before rushing in. And now Kaitlin probably hated her.

She gulped back a sob climbing her throat. Confused and wretched with guilt, she headed miserably on. She would have to call Kaitlin first thing, beg her forgiveness. She might still need to be there for her, if Kaitlin wanted her to be. They needed to be there for each other, though Zoe wouldn't blame Kaitlin if she decided to wash her hands of her.

Approaching the path that would take her down to the riverbank, from where it was a short walk across the footbridge into the dock and on to her apartment, she was about to send her a quick text, at least let her know she was okay – knowing Kait, she would be worried, even if she had decided she wanted nothing more to do with her – when her phone buzzed again. Another text from Daniel, no doubt. Why was he doing this? Having ruined her life, why couldn't he just leave her alone?

Reading it, she blinked in disbelief: *Zoe, I'm sorry. I should have told you about her. I would have left her, but for the kids. I know what I did was unforgivable, but what we have together is special. Please talk to me. Please don't shut me out.* Translation: *Please let me sweet-talk you into not telling my wife the truth about our relationship* – which, in the heat of the moment, she'd threatened to do.

Such a caring daddy. The children are so lucky to have you, she sent back acerbically, all the while wishing she really was that kind of woman, that she could be hard, self-serving and unforgiving. That she could just stop bloody well loving him.

Cursing as the rain turned to an icy deluge, she was almost at the bridge when the phone rang. She knew it was him before she even looked. She had to talk to him. She had to tell him to stop, once and for all. She took the call.

'Zoe, don't hang up,' he said urgently, before she had a chance to speak.

'What do you want, Daniel?' she asked shakily.

'Just to talk,' he said. 'Face to face. To explain, Zoe, that's all I want. Will you give me a chance?'

Face to face? Oh no. Surely he didn't imagine she wanted to see him? 'Where are you?' she asked warily.

A pause, then, 'In the area,' he said. 'I'm actually not that far away from you.'

Her heart flipping, she cut the call. She couldn't meet up with him. There was no way she could be that close to him. Closing her eyes, she recalled how he'd assailed every one of her senses the first time she saw him. Impeccably dressed in a short-sleeved white shirt, tanned, tall and lean, he'd caught her interest as he'd strolled into the Poolside Café, where she'd worked. She'd noticed how gorgeous he was while taking his order, but his expression had been deadpan, his eyes hidden behind impenetrable dark glasses. And then he'd smiled, a disarming smile that had transformed his whole face. She'd fallen for him over the next few weeks, hook, line and sinker. His easy charm, the way he'd romanced her, sending her flowers, beautiful full-scented red roses, leaving little sprigs of lavender outside her apartment door. How could she not? She'd loved him with all of herself, believed he'd loved her. Now, she just wanted to forget about him. To try, somehow, to move on.

She was about to call him back, tell him she would report him to the police if he didn't leave her alone, when she heard the crunch of footsteps behind her. Tentatively she peered over her shoulder, to see someone tall and dressed in dark clothes step out onto the path. She couldn't make out much more; whoever it was had paused in the shadows.

Her heartbeat ratcheting up, she snapped her gaze forward. It was probably just someone else on their way home. So why were they lingering? It was hardly the right weather to be taking in the view. Her blood pumping, she hurried on. Rounding a bend, she held her breath and waited a second, straining to hear through the rain, and then almost jumped out of her skin as the person started whistling, a soft, mournful tune.

Shit! Zoe felt an icy chill travel the length of her spine. If this person meant her harm, she was a sitting duck out here. Her fight-or-flight instinct kicking in, she swallowed back a hard knot of fear and started to run. Her heart lurched as, risking a fleeting look back, she realised they were running too, and that they were gaining ground.

Feeling the hairs rise over her skin as she imagined a hand clamping the back of her neck, she faltered. She was going the wrong way, on the wrong side of the river. If she went much further, she would be heading into the wilder, undeveloped part of the bank.

No. She would *not* let this happen. She would not be frightened. She would not be intimidated. Stamping down her panic, she summoned her courage and whirled around. 'What do you *want?*' she screamed, her stomach turning violently over as she realised they were almost upon her.

'Just to talk, Zoe, that's all.' The voice was calm, kind almost. Zoe wasn't sure she felt relieved as she recognised its owner.

EIGHT
KAITLIN

'Thank you ...' Kaitlin began, and then stopped as a sudden raucous screeching from the microphone drowned her out. Waiting while one of the band members made adjustments, her eyes drifting to the doors in the hope of seeing Greg and Zoe come through them, she tried again. 'I think the mic feedback was more exciting than anything I have to say, but I'll give it another bash,' she joked weakly. 'Thank you all so much for coming to my lovely party, and for your support over the years. That is, for bothering to stay in touch when it appeared I couldn't be bothered.' Her thoughts went immediately to Zoe, who'd always been there for her, night or day, whenever she'd called on her, and she felt her chest filling up with sorrow and regret.

'It's been so amazing to see you all.' She forced herself on. 'I should be thanking Greg for all his tremendous work organising everything – the beautiful venue, the fantastic band ...' She paused, sweeping an arm in the direction of the band members behind her. 'Unfortunately, he's had to slip out, and I, um ... Damn. Sorry.' She stopped again, trying hard not to let the tears escape. 'I'm a bit overemotional, I think.'

'Aw, come here and have a group hug.' Susie, one of the women she'd studied with, beckoned to her, reminding her of how important her friends were to her. She didn't believe what Sally had told her about Zoe. More likely Sean had invented the whole story. Even in the early days, he'd wanted to isolate her.

The band struck up with the birthday song as she stepped off the stage, corks popping and everyone wishing her well. Thanking people individually as she went, she tried to make her way not too obviously to the foyer.

Emerging from the hall, relief crashed through her as she saw Greg coming in through the main door, swiftly followed by disappointment when she realised Zoe wasn't with him. 'Did you catch up with her?' she asked, a hard ball of fear wedged in her throat. She'd tried her mobile. Zoe had been on another call, and then she hadn't answered. Kaitlin had sent her texts. Willed her to reply with the briefest text back, just one word to indicate she was all right, but she hadn't.

Dragging a hand through his hair in frustration, Greg shook his head. He was sopping wet from the rain, droplets running down his forehead to drip from his eyelashes like tears. 'No.' He met her gaze, his look one of wary trepidation. 'I assumed she'd stay on the main road, but I couldn't see any sign of her.'

Kaitlin's heart dropped. 'Did you check the side roads?'

He looked nonplussed by that, and she realised it was a stupid thing to say. It would be an impossible, fruitless task. In any case, Zoe would have no reason to detour off the main road, which would take her straight into the city centre. 'Do you think she might have flagged a taxi?' She looked at him hopefully.

'It's possible.' Greg didn't look convinced. Kaitlin guessed why. There wouldn't be that many taxis for hire passing on a Friday night. If Zoe had called one, she would have had to wait, and Greg would surely have caught up with her.

She checked her phone again, and felt a combination of nausea and nerves churn inside her. There was still no reply to her texts. She tried Zoe's number again, her heart sinking further as it went to voicemail. 'We need to go to her apartment,' she said, fear blooming inside her. Zoe would never do this. She was probably angry with her – she had every right to be after what Kaitlin had said – but she would never leave her to worry about whether she'd got home safely.

'I was about to suggest that,' Greg said. 'If you let me have the address, I'll go straight there and call you once I know anything.'

Kaitlin shook her head. 'No. I should go.' She was grateful to him for realising how worried she was, for supporting her, but as it was him who seemed to be a bone of contention between them, she doubted whether Zoe would want to see him. She might not even answer the door to him. She needed to go personally. She had to apologise to her, beg through the door if necessary for her to open up and at least let her know she was all right.

Greg took a breath, and then nodded, a flash of annoyance crossing his face as his gaze swivelled to the hall doors, where a group of people appeared to be leaving, indicating that the party might be breaking up. Kaitlin couldn't blame him for being annoyed after he'd worked so hard to make it special for her.

'See you soon,' an old school friend said, leaning to give her a hug. 'Thanks for a lovely party.'

'I'll call you.' Kaitlin hugged her back, the lump of guilt in her chest expanding as she met Greg's gaze. He didn't look overly impressed.

'I called a taxi on the way back,' he said, once the group had headed off to collect their coats. 'It should be here soon. Don't worry. I'm sure she's fine. We'll probably find she's already crawled into bed and won't thank us for waking her up. She'd obviously had a fair amount to drink.'

Kaitlin supposed he might be right. She hoped he was. She

hadn't actually seen Zoe drink very much, but a combination of alcohol together with the fact that she was upset might explain why she'd stormed off into the unfriendly night without even a coat. Please God she was home safe and sound.

Greg threaded an arm around her shoulders as her mind conjured up graphic alternative scenarios that caused her stomach to roil. 'She's okay.' He gave her a reassuring squeeze. 'You two will be back to being best of friends and laughing about this tomorrow, you'll see.'

Kaitlin wasn't so sure. She would settle for just friends. Right now, she would settle for Zoe refusing to speak to her at all as long as she was okay.

'I'll get your coat,' Greg said, brushing her cheek with a kiss.

Kaitlin turned her face to his. 'Thank you,' she said, conflicting emotions running through her. Relief that even with the party he'd gone to such trouble to organise ending on an unhappy note, he was every inch the man she'd known he was, thoughtful and caring. Deep sadness that Zoe, without whom she couldn't have turned her life around, seemed convinced he wasn't any of those things.

'No problem.' He reached for her hand, kissing the palm softly. 'I'm here for you, Kait, whatever. I always will be.'

Kaitlin knew he would be. Smiling tremulously, she looked him over, this gorgeous hunk of a man she still couldn't believe was in love with her, despite her quirks and the baggage she carried in trunks.

'Won't be a sec.' He smiled reassuringly back and headed towards the cloakroom.

'Greg, hold on.' Kaitlin squinted as he turned, her eyes snagging on a fleck of crimson on his shirt collar. 'You're bleeding.'

'Am I?' He stopped and tugged the collar up, craning his neck to look at it. 'Damn. Got into a tangle with an overhanging branch.' He sighed, his hand going to the side of his neck. 'Didn't see it while I was running. Not to worry, it'll wash out.'

'Let me see.' Kaitlin moved towards him as he pulled his hand away, peeling his collar down to reveal an angry, raw scratch. 'You should bathe it,' she said, her gaze flicking to his face.

'It's nothing.' He gave her another reassuring smile. 'I'm a big bloke. I won't bleed to death. I'll get that coat before there's a queue.'

Watching him go, Kaitlin felt an icy chill of trepidation prickle her skin. She'd almost begun to believe that Zoe was home safe in her bed, but seeing those specks of blood, stark against the pristine white cotton, had caused her stomach to wrench afresh. What if she wasn't? What if she wasn't answering her phone because she couldn't?

NINE

'She's probably dead to the world,' Greg said outside Zoe's apartment building half an hour later.

Kaitlin felt a cold hollowness spread through her as he said it. 'She isn't,' she insisted. Even if Zoe had been drunk – which Kaitlin hadn't thought she was – she wouldn't have just switched her phone off and gone to bed knowing how worried her friend would be. She wouldn't be lying in bed now ignoring the incessant ringing on the buzzer. She would know it was Kaitlin, and no matter how badly they'd fallen out, she just wouldn't do that.

Scanning the front of the ground-floor apartment, realising there were no signs of life, not even a glimmer of light through the patio windows, she dug her phone from her bag and tried her number again, as she had done several times in the taxi. Again she got her cheery message: 'Hi, you've reached Zoe's phone. I can't get to you right now, but if you leave a message, I'll call you back.'

Why couldn't she get to her phone? *Why wasn't* she calling her back?

'Maybe the intercom system's not working,' Greg suggested.

And maybe she *was* asleep, and maybe she *had* turned all the lights off and switched her phone to silent. But Kaitlin didn't think any of those things were likely. There were too many maybes. The worst maybe of all was that something might have happened to her. She closed her eyes, seeing again the stark crimson stain on Greg's shirt. Quickly she dismissed it. She was buying into the story Sally had told her. She felt as if she was going mad. Why wasn't Zoe *answering*?

She eyed the security gate in frustration, and then made up her mind and jabbed the intercom again. No doubt she would infuriate Zoe's neighbours, but she couldn't just leave it. Couldn't just go home and tuck herself up in bed not knowing where her friend was.

Getting no response, she was about to press randomly on the basis that someone would answer when a voice crackled tetchily, 'Frank, if you've lost your key again, you can sleep in the doorway.'

Kaitlin recognised the voice of Janice, the long-suffering wife of a resident who, she remembered from when she'd stayed here after leaving Sean, regularly lost his key after late-night drinking sessions. 'Hi, Janice, I'm really sorry to disturb you,' she said apologetically. 'It's Kaitlin. I don't know whether you remember me. I'm Zoe's friend, and I—'

'I remember you,' Janice said. 'You were the one young Zoe was worried to death would go back to her rat of a husband.'

'That's right.' Kaitlin swallowed back the knot in her throat, which was growing more excruciatingly painful every time she recalled how worried Zoe had been for her back then. She'd given over her apartment and her life to making sure Kaitlin and Ruby had a safe place to live. She'd never worried about the mess a toddler made, even though she normally liked everything to be scrupulously tidy. 'Zoe was at my birthday party tonight,' Kaitlin went on. 'She was a bit poorly before she left, and I—'

'Alcohol.' Janice tutted over her. 'The devil's nectar. No

good ever comes of drinking too much. You'd better come and check on her.' She sighed and pressed the buzzer, granting them access.

Kaitlin pushed the security gate open and headed straight to Zoe's apartment to tap lightly on the door. 'Zoe,' she called, knocking again when there was no answer. 'It's me, Kaitlin.'

Still nothing. She rapped harder. 'Zoe, if you're in there, please answer. I'm really worried about you.' She waited. There wasn't a squeak from inside, which caused the knot of anxiety inside her to twist itself tighter.

'Do you want me to try and force it?' Greg asked, his voice full of concern. 'I can get a locksmith out tomorrow if it turns out to be a false—'

'No need.' Janice appeared, coming down the stairs from the apartment above, wearing pyjamas and tightly rolled curlers. 'She left a key with me. I'm sure she won't thank us for walking in and gawping at her if she's the worse for wear, but better to be safe than sorry. Make way.'

Inserting the key into the lock, she gave the door a shove as it appeared to jam. 'Post,' she said, peering around it as she squeezed inside. 'I would have thought Zoe would have picked that up.'

So would Kaitlin. Following Janice in, she bent to scoop up the envelopes that must have been posted through the door in Zoe's absence abroad. Her apartment was only small, but she'd always kept it immaculate, because she was proud of the fact that she'd managed to secure a mortgage and buy a share in her own property, albeit nothing grand.

'You'd better check the bedroom,' Janice suggested, though Kaitlin was already walking past her, through the small kitchen that led directly onto the living area, noting the washing-up piled in the sink as she did. A carrier bag had been left half emptied on the work surface, the contents unstowed, something Zoe never did. She'd practically put the shopping away before Kaitlin had brought it in when she'd lived here.

Approaching the bedroom door, she took a breath, tapped once and squeaked the door open. The bed was empty, unmade. Zoe's suitcase was lying on the floor, clothes spewing out from it. This wasn't like her, not at all. Kaitlin had often thought that after her chaotic childhood, Zoe had needed order in her life. She'd tried to relax around her and Ruby, but when Kaitlin had first met her, she'd sometimes bordered on the obsessive about things being in their proper place. It reassured her that she was in control, Kaitlin suspected. This didn't look like her friend in control; quite the opposite. It seemed to Kaitlin that Zoe felt everything was spiralling *out* of control. She was clearly feeling extremely emotionally vulnerable.

Full of remorse at how the things she'd said must have contributed to that vulnerability, Kaitlin reached into the corner of the case for the raggedy old teddy bear Zoe took everywhere with her. He was called Buttons, because he had buttons for eyes, which she had sewn on when she was child. She'd confided – something Zoe didn't do easily – that the moth-eaten teddy was the only toy she could remember having before she'd been placed in residential care. Remembering that now, Kaitlin's throat tightened. 'I'll find her, Buttons, don't worry,' she whispered, swallowing hard as the bear's eyes seemed to look hopefully back at her. 'She'll be home soon.' Placing him on the dressing table, she straightened his little limbs and was about to go back to the living area when her eye snagged on something that caused her breath to catch.

It was a list, the sort of list Zoe had insisted Kaitlin make when she'd thought there was nothing but negatives in her life. She'd told her to write down the negatives and then the positives alongside them, which she had assured her would cancel them out. With trembling fingers, Kaitlin picked it up. She felt as if she were snooping on her friend as she read it.

THE INVITE 63

NEGATIVES
Daniel is married with two children.
I still love him.
He's begging me to talk to him.
I've had to leave my job.
I had to leave my apartment.
I'm lonely.

POSITIVES
I found out before I told him.
I hate him enough to move on.
I'm strong enough to move on.
I still have some savings.
I still have my apartment here.
I have Kait.

Shit. Blinking hard to hold her tears back, Kaitlin snapped her gaze to the ceiling. She should never have let Zoe leave the party. What on earth had possessed her to say the dreadful things she had? Her chest constricted as she pictured Zoe's stricken face when she'd pointed out what finding out about her in the way she had would have done to Daniel's wife. Could she have been more spiteful? She'd accused her of being jealous. Zoe had been hurt, humiliatingly, horribly hurt, and then Kaitlin, her so-called best friend, had turned her back on her. And now she probably thought she had no one.

I'm here, Zoe. You have me. No matter what happened in the past, or why, you will always have me. Going back to the lounge, she glanced over to Greg, who smiled hesitantly as he noted her determined expression.

TEN

Realising how distraught Kaitlin was, Janice wrapped an arm around her as she went into the kitchen. 'She probably called a friend or a boyfriend to pick her up,' she suggested, giving her shoulders a comforting squeeze. 'She'll be back right as rain in the morning, wondering what all the fuss is about, you'll see.'

She was trying to sound reassuring, but Zoe could see she was dubious. Janice was aware that Zoe had broken up with her long-term boyfriend here before she'd left for Portugal. She'd heard the horrendous argument they'd had. Zoe had said the whole neighbourhood must have heard it, that she'd had to go up and apologise to Janice and Frank once he'd left. As far as Kaitlin knew, there were no old boyfriends Zoe would have wanted to call, no close friends in the district she was aware of.

Zoe had never really had that many friends. Because she'd been brought up in care, she'd felt different from other kids growing up, a legacy that had carried over into her teens and on into adulthood. She felt awkward socially, always trying to hide it by being perhaps a little too animated in company for some people's tastes. Kaitlin loved that about her, though, the fact that she spoke out, offering her opinion where others might hesitate, particularly if she thought someone might need the scales peeling from their eyes. That was what made Sally's story so difficult to believe. She couldn't ever imagine that Zoe, in order to peel the scales from Kaitlin's eyes, would have made a play for Sean, and if it were the other way around and Sean had tried to take advantage of Zoe, she would have *told* her. It seemed to Kaitlin that the whole thing was a fabrication to cast doubt on Zoe, who hadn't got an ounce of malice in her body.

She recalled the way Zoe had looked at her once, her cheeks flushed with embarrassment, her eyes scuttling downwards, as if for safety, when she'd admitted that Kaitlin was the only person whose company she felt able to relax in. With Ruby tucked up in her cot in the corner of Zoe's bedroom, they'd been having a girls' night, a good heart-to-heart, curled up the sofa, a bottle of wine between them.

'Why?' Kaitlin had asked her, carefully, because sometimes getting information from Zoe about her childhood was like trying to prise a winkle from its shell.

Zoe had shrugged and glanced reflectively away. 'Because you don't judge me,' she'd said. 'Because you accept me for who I am, a bit moody and scatty, a bit clingy sometimes.'

'And bonkers,' Kaitlin had joked, reaching across to grab her hand and give it a good squeeze. 'You must be to put up with me. You're not clingy, you daft thing,' she'd assured her. 'I don't know what I would have done if you hadn't been there for me.'

It had been true. She'd felt as if she were going slowly insane while she was still with Sean, constantly wondering what it was she'd done to infuriate him. Zoe had never given up on her, even though Sean had tried to stop Kaitlin from seeing her. She'd rescued her, always been there to support her. Yet now Kaitlin had given up on Zoe. Zoe must feel so betrayed. So lonely.

Stifling her tears, Kaitlin ran a hand under her nose and nodded. 'I'm sure she will,' she said, smiling shakily. 'You don't mind if I hang on here for a while, though, do you, Janice?' Her gaze flicked again to Greg, who glanced down, possibly to hide his despair. She was sure he would much rather be home in bed. The night definitely wasn't ending the way she suspected he'd hoped it might. She looked back at Janice. 'I'll make sure to lock up. I'll call back first thing in the morning if she doesn't show up tonight. I still have my key, so I won't need to disturb you.'

'Of course I don't mind.' Janice waved a hand. 'I'll sleep safer knowing you're keeping an eye out for her. She's a lovely girl, always helpful and polite. I'll let you have the new security code,' she added, giving Kaitlin's shoulders another squeeze and then glancing around for a pen and paper. Greg delved in his jacket pocket and offered her his pen, along with an abandoned receipt from the work surface. Janice wrote the number down and handed it to her. 'I'll leave you to it,' she said. 'If you hear any clanging and banging, it will be Frank trying to get in. Don't worry, I'll grant him access.' She headed for the door with a roll of her eyes. 'I usually do.'

Greg waited for the door to close behind her and then walked across to Kaitlin. 'Okay?' he asked softly.

Kaitlin nodded. 'Do you mind if we wait here for a while?'

'I don't have much choice, do I?' He mustered a small smile, despite the fact that he must be terribly frustrated and disappointed.

'I'm sorry, Greg,' she blurted, feeling she owed him an apology. 'I've ruined everything, after all the effort you went to. You must be so fed up. Look, why don't you go home and—'

'Hey, hey.' He threaded an arm around her waist. 'It takes two to tango, you know. It was an argument. Stuff happens. I'll get over it. And so will Zoe. Meanwhile,' he drew her to him, 'there's no way I'm leaving you here on your own. I'm not your ex, Kaitlin. I'm here for you.'

Kaitlin nodded and leaned into him, needing the solidity of him, to be held by him, just for a second. She was looking for someone to blame, but it wasn't his fault. He'd been unthinking, that was all. 'Do you reckon we should call the police?' she asked him, cold foreboding creeping through her as she realised that in making that call, they would be acknowledging that Zoe was missing.

Greg pulled her closer. 'I'm not sure they'll be able to do very much at this juncture. Let's wait and see if she turns up.'

Again Kaitlin nodded, a feeling of helplessness washing through her. She guessed he was right, but with each minute that ticked by, the icy apprehension twisting her stomach grew. What if Zoe was lying injured somewhere, in need of help? She would have come straight home from the party. There was nowhere else she would have gone, Kaitlin felt sure of it.

'Look, why don't you make yourself a coffee?' Greg suggested. 'I'll go out again and have another scout around, check the area around the new-build apartments. You never know, she might have curled up somewhere.' He pressed a soft kiss to her forehead. 'If I can't find her and she's not back in another couple of hours, we'll call the police then. Okay?'

Kaitlin nodded, but a new surge of fear swept through her. Zoe hadn't been drunk. She certainly hadn't been drunk to the point of passing out. She wouldn't have just curled up some-where, particularly so close to home.

'Keep trying her on your mobile. I'll be back soon.' Brushing her lips with his, Greg smiled encouragingly and turned for the door.

Watching him go, Kaitlin felt her heart swell with gratitude. It was pouring with rain out there and he had nothing but his jacket for protection. She knew most men weren't Sean, but she was sure there were those who would have gone home and tucked themselves into bed, telling her to let them know when Zoe turned up. The evening had ended in disaster, and yet he'd brushed it off with a shrug. She didn't know what she'd done to deserve someone who was so genuinely caring. She knew he wasn't just saying what he thought she wanted to hear to win her affections. He loved her. That was why he'd told Zoe he would do anything to protect her. He wasn't being possessive or controlling, which for one dreadful second she'd thought he was.

ELEVEN

A combination of nerves and nausea churning inside her, Kaitlin stepped back from Zoe's front door to allow Sally and the detective accompanying her access. She'd been surprised when the police had turned up so soon. Zoe had only been missing for four hours, but they'd been the longest hours in Kaitlin's life. She was doubly surprised to see Sally, though there was no reason she should be. Sally had been based in Birmingham for a while after her probation period. She'd told Kaitlin she'd grabbed the first opportunity she could to transfer to Worcester, to be closer to home, having moved in with her life partner. They'd split now, sadly. Emelie had also apparently got homesick and had gone back to Paris. Kaitlin felt for Sally. She would have to make some time to talk to her.

'I'm sure she'll turn up. About eighty per cent of people return home or are located within twenty-four hours without police intervention. Try not to worry too much.' Sally smiled reassuringly as she stepped in, her sharp blue eyes darting around, taking in Zoe's meagre furnishings.

Kaitlin felt a smidgen of relief, but it was short-lived. Try as she might to believe what everyone seemed to, that Zoe would eventually turn up, she just couldn't make the cold foreboding in the pit of her stomach go away. 'Thanks for coming so promptly,' she said, her gaze travelling to the detective, a tall, athletic, if slightly jaded-looking man, with soulful brown eyes that seemed to quietly appraise her.

'DI Adam Diaz,' he said. 'We've just called to collect some initial details. We were in the area, so—'

'Thought you must have been,' Greg interrupted, stepping forward and offering his hand. 'I think we might have met. Greg Walker. I work for FFI Fire Investigation Services. Our paths have probably crossed.'

The detective squinted at him curiously. 'Possibly,' he said, his gaze going back to Kaitlin. 'As I say, we're here to collect some initial information. We've set up a missing persons log, and every little helps.'

They'd classified her as officially missing *already*? The knot in Kaitlin's stomach tied itself tighter.

'You said you've tried to call her mobile?' Sally enquired, as Kaitlin showed them to the living area and moved cushions on the sofa to make space for them to sit.

'Constantly. I've texted her too,' she said, her eyes flicking to Greg as she sat on the single armchair. He remained standing, his hands shoved in his pockets and a deep furrow forming in his forehead.

'What about her social media accounts? Might there be any recent posts to indicate where she is?' Diaz asked.

'I've checked those too,' Kaitlin assured him. 'Her last photos on Instagram are of her in Portugal. She's been working out there. She was due to come back for my birthday party, but I suspect she's back permanently now.' She faltered as recollections of their argument and Zoe's devastated face came flooding back. Her heart stalled as the thought crashed into her head that that conversation might have been their last.

'She split up with the man she was going out with,' she

pushed on, glancing at Sally, who she hoped would understand why she hadn't divulged that information earlier. 'He was messing her around, apparently.'

'That's a shame.' Sally glanced down, pulling a notebook from her jacket pocket and scribbling in it.

'She said he'd been calling and texting her constantly since.' Feeling as if she were betraying Zoe's trust all over again, Kaitlin supplied the information nevertheless, because she thought it might be pertinent. Crucially pertinent, if what Zoe had told her was true. 'I think she felt he was stalking her. He texted her to say he was at the airport. He was obviously on his way here, or else he'd already landed.'

Diaz exchanged wary glances with Sally. 'Do you have the man's name?' he asked.

'Only his Christian name. Daniel,' Kaitlin provided. 'I have a photograph of him Zoe sent a while back. I showed it to you when we met up, do you remember, Sally? He was supposed to be coming with her to my birthday party. You said you thought Zoe had landed on her feet.'

'Vaguely,' Sally said with a short smile. 'Could you send us the photograph?' She reached into her pocket for a card and passed it to Kaitlin. 'It might be helpful.'

Becoming more sure that the man must have something to do with why Zoe hadn't come home, Kaitlin nodded.

'Do you have details of her family and friends?' Diaz asked. 'It's possible she may have simply gone to her parents' or a friend's house, in which case she'll no doubt—'

'She hasn't. She doesn't have any parents.' Kaitlin glanced again at Sally. 'That is, none she's in touch with. She was brought up in care.'

'No foster parents?' Diaz checked.

Kaitlin shook her head. 'No other close friends in the area either. Or old flames she would want to keep in touch with. In fact, I'm her only really close friend.'

'I think Kaitlin and her parents became her substitute family, didn't they, Kait?' Sally reminded her. 'You two were inseparable, as I recall.'

'Yes.' Kaitlin caught her breath. 'We were, once.'

'And did she seem worried about anything, Miss Chalmers, when she left the party?' Diaz went on after a suitable pause.

Kaitlin hesitated. She was aware that she might be dropping this bastard Daniel in it, but as far as she was concerned, he bloody well deserved it. 'Definitely the situation between her and Daniel. It was obvious she was heartbroken. She was upset when she realised that Greg and I are living together as well. We ended up arguing, and ...' She trailed off, tears squeezing from her eyes.

'About?' Sally urged her gently.

'She felt a bit pushed out, I think.' Kaitlin glanced at Greg. 'Greg and I are getting married. She wasn't aware of that either. It's all happened quite quickly – we're expecting, you see, and ...' She stopped, a huge lump lodged in her throat that she couldn't seem to swallow. 'Sorry, I, um ...'

Sally stared at her, stunned. 'Wow, congratulations, Kait,' she said, a smile forming on her face. 'That is good news.'

'I thought it was. Zoe obviously wasn't so sure.'

'No.' Sally scribbled another note, while Greg moved to thread an arm around Kaitlin.

'I think Zoe might have been put out because Kaitlin hadn't told her we were engaged,' he said. 'I'd only just proposed, so she hadn't had a chance to tell anyone. It's possible Zoe might have been a bit jealous because of her own circumstances.'

Diaz nodded thoughtfully. 'And had she been drinking?'

'Considerably,' Greg confirmed.

'*No*, not considerably,' Kaitlin protested. Zoe hadn't had that much to drink as far as she'd seen. She certainly hadn't gone off so drunk she couldn't walk straight. 'She'd had a drink, yes ...'

'She said herself she'd had too much wine.' Greg knitted his forehead in confusion.

'She wasn't drunk, Greg. I know her. She wasn't staggering or ranting. If anyone was ranting, it was me. I should never have said the things I did.'

'There's something we need to mention, Kaitlin,' Sally interjected carefully. 'Zoe's bag ...'

Noting the wariness in her eyes as she hesitated, cold goosebumps prickled the entire surface of Kaitlin's skin. 'You've found it, haven't you?' she asked, her throat parched.

Sally nodded regretfully. 'It was handed in at the station.'

Fear crackling through her, Kaitlin stared at her. That was why they'd escalated their report to missing persons. 'But ... how can you know? That it's hers, I mean,' she stammered. 'How can you be sure?' Dreading the answer, the official confirmation that it was actually Zoe's, she swallowed back the hysteria she could feel rising inside her.

Sally paused before answering, glancing at Diaz, as if checking with him. 'There was something inside it,' she went on when he nodded almost imperceptibly. 'A first-trimester scan. It might explain why Zoe was feeling emotional, particularly if she had been drinking.'

Oh God, no. Kaitlin felt the blood drain from her body.

Greg squeezed his hold tighter around her as she turned into him. 'Where did you find it?' he asked, his voice thick with shock.

'On the riverbank, not far from the footbridge,' Diaz supplied.

'Jesus Christ.' Greg gasped out a breath. 'You're not thinking she's ...' He stopped, gathering Kaitlin closer as a guttural sob escaped her.

TWELVE

SALLY

'Diplomatic sort, isn't he?' Adam said, climbing into the car.

'I'm not with you.' Sally glanced curiously at him as they pulled away from the dock.

'That comment he made when I told him where the bag was found. His fiancée obviously filled in the gaps. She looked about ready to pass out.'

'He was holding her up,' Sally pointed out. 'He seems pretty supportive to me. And he looked pig-sick as soon as he'd said it. He probably wasn't thinking. They must both be in a state of shock.'

'I suppose,' Adam conceded.

Sally was still feeling shocked about Kaitlin's news. She'd kept that quiet. Obviously, she hadn't told anyone if she hadn't told Zoe, which was also surprising. Zoe had always been the first person Kaitlin shared her news with, to the exclusion of anyone else. When Sally had realised that Kaitlin had finally seen the light and extracted herself from a marriage that was doomed to failure from the start – Sean Cooper had always been a cocksure pretty boy with nil respect for women – she'd hoped to rekindle her own friendship with her. Now it looked like Kaitlin was going to be too busy nest-building with the new man in her life to have much time for anything else. Sally was happy for her, as long as Kait was happy. She aimed to keep a close eye on this Walker guy, though. Kait didn't deserve to be messed around, manipulated until she couldn't see a way out, not again. Her trouble was, she had a big heart and couldn't see that people were using her for their own ends.

She'd been surprised to see Zoe at the party, flabbergasted when she'd heard the exchange between her and Kaitlin from her cubicle in the loos, and then again when they'd openly argued in the foyer. Zoe clearly had a problem with this Greg, which made Sally wonder whether there might *be* a problem. More likely, though, was that Zoe's nose had been put out of joint. No doubt she'd imagined that they could pick up where they'd left off before she went to Portugal. Kaitlin had been quite blunt with her, which was also surprising.

Sally felt bad when she realised that Zoe too had been pregnant. Kaitlin hadn't taken the news well, clearly blaming herself for her running off like that. She shouldn't. It had been Zoe's decision, a calculated one possibly to get Kaitlin's attention. Sally would have to keep it professional, but she needed to stay close to this. Emelie had thought her being a uniformed response officer was exciting, until she'd realised she couldn't hack the worry that came with it. They'd argued because of Sally's long night shifts, but being a police officer was what she did, who she was. They'd argued constantly in the end. Since Emelie had gone home, claiming that Sally gave all of herself to her job, she'd immersed herself in her work, but she wanted more than this. She wanted detective inspector. She was up for it, but she was on trial here. If she didn't stay on top of this, she was in danger of blowing everything. She glanced sideways at Diaz. She had to impress him, that was paramount.

'It did make it awkward asking Kaitlin for something of Zoe's we could get a DNA sample from, I have to admit,' she said as they headed back to the station. 'She looked worried sick, even though I reinforced that we were just following protocol. Shitty birthday party she's had.'

'Did you see his shoes?' Adam asked.

Sally nodded. 'I saw. They were covered in mud. He did go out searching for her, though.'

'Twice, apparently,' Adam added.

Sally pondered that. Obviously Gregory Walker would be in the frame. He would be whether or not he had mud on his shoes, as would everyone at the party until they could be eliminated, particularly anyone who might be seen to have a problem with Zoe. 'So, are we wondering where it was he searched, exactly?'

'We are,' Adam confirmed.

Sally nodded, relieved. At least now they had somewhere to focus their attention.

'I might be barking up the wrong tree,' Adam said, 'but ...'

'Best to leave no stone unturned,' Sally finished, guessing that was what he was about to say.

He smiled wryly, but Sally noted the tic going in his cheek. Adam Diaz made sure to be thorough in his investigations. Sally gathered it was because of what had happened with his wife. She'd found it paid to familiarise herself with the background of the people she worked with, and had done her homework. Joanne Saunders, who'd kept her maiden name, had been a DI a few years back and apparently hadn't been so thorough when she'd pulled the man she suspected of murdering a sex worker. Making discreet enquiries, Sally had learned that a routine DNA swab taken from the man had matched traces of semen found in the woman's body. It seemed he didn't deny having had sex with the woman, which might have been problematical in court, but Saunders had thought they had a strong case nevertheless. It never made it to court. According to one of her colleagues, whose tongue had loosened over a few pints at the pub, Saunders had been devastated when she'd been dragged over the coals, her DCI bawling her out for the whole station to hear because the principles and practices of the crime-scene investigation hadn't been followed. It turned out that the evidence linking the suspect to the victim included microscopic particles found on his clothing. The original source of the particles, however, could have been from his previous encounters with the woman, or even environmental contamination. None of this had been mentioned in reports, Sally had discovered, but Saunders swore it had all been documented correctly. She'd also reported that a crucial piece of evidence linking the assailant's footwear to the victim had gone missing.

Sally guessed the woman had worked hard to prove herself in what was still a male-dominated world. She'd been sick to her soul, according to those in the know, when a man she believed to be dangerous and violent had walked free, most likely to offend again.

Sally mulled it over while Adam took a call on his phone. From his daughter, she guessed, hearing him promise to be careful, as he did whenever he spoke to her. Sally felt for him. It had to be tough bringing a teenager up on his own, even without the godawful hours.

'Freya?' she asked when he hung up.

'It was.' He smiled. 'She worries, you know.'

'Can't say I blame her,' she said.

Adam nodded and fell quiet.

'Can I ask you something?' Sally ventured after a while.

'As long as it's nothing too technical or complicated,' Adam answered, dragging a hand over his neck. 'I think the brain cells are suffering severe caffeine depravation.'

Sally hesitated, then, 'Your wife.' She glanced at him warily. 'What happened to her?'

'Ah.' Adam drew in a terse breath, and Sally immediately regretted asking.

'Sorry,' she said. 'It's personal. I shouldn't have—'

'She killed herself,' Adam said bluntly over her. 'Drinking and driving is a failsafe way to do that.'

'Shit. I'm sorry, Adam,' Sally repeated. 'I didn't mean to pry. I just—'

'It's okay. It's common knowledge anyway. I'm surprised you didn't already know.' Adam smiled tiredly. 'We weren't doing too well, arguing a lot. Joanne was drinking. Pretty much the whole station heard the last argument we had. She was trying to prove herself over again after a case went belly-up. She wasn't proving anything. She was falling apart. I accused her of being married to the job, not being there for Freya. She accused me of wanting her to be at home like a good little wife. I said I didn't need her, but that Freya did.'

He stopped and kneaded his forehead. 'She walked out. Had a few drinks. Never came home. The thing was, I didn't realise how much I did need her until then. I only wish I'd told her that.'

Sally heard his voice crack. He'd loved her, obviously. 'I'm sorry, Adam,' she said again, uselessly, as he glanced to the side window. 'I really should learn to mind my own business.'

'No problem.' He coughed to clear his throat. 'You need to know who you're working with, I get that. So, do I pass the competence test?'

Sally nodded, feeling extremely *in*competent. 'You do,' she assured him.

'Good.' Adam looked back at her as they slowed in the station car park. 'As long as you're not hiding any deep dark secrets, we should get along fine. Yes?'

She swallowed, feeling suddenly exposed as he narrowed his eyes, scrutinising her carefully.

'Nope, no deep dark secrets or skeletons in my cupboard,' she said, looking away.

THIRTEEN

KAITLIN

'Swim! Zoe, swim!' Kaitlin heard the words emerging from her mouth elongated and slurred. Her limbs flailing ineffectually in the foul-tasting water, she ignored the excruciating pressure in her chest and stretched out a hand, straining desperately to reach her friend. Zoe wasn't moving. Her skin was translucent; the pallor of death.

A strange whooshing, gurgling sound filled her ears. Panic engulfed her as Zoe bobbed further away from her. Kaitlin tried to follow, but the thick mud oozing between her toes, lapping over her feet and sucking slimily at her ankles wouldn't let go of her. She couldn't reach her. 'Zoe, please!' She wasn't fighting. Zoe was a survivor. She'd *always* been a survivor, but she wasn't even trying. She was giving in. *Drowning.* Kaitlin could hear it, a new sound, her baby's tiny heart slowing until it stopped beating.

'Zoe!' Waking with a choking jerk, she pulled herself up, disorientated for a moment, before she realised where she was. Safe. Not in the cruel churning depths of the river. She was at home in her bed, while Zoe ... Terror pierced her chest like an icicle. *Please let her be safe. Please don't let anything have happened to her.*

'Mummy?' Ruby's voice reached her, tremulous and uncertain. 'Mummy ...' Kaitlin felt a movement towards her, a dip in the bed, a small hand on her cheek. 'You were dreaming, Mummy.'

Confusion and fear clogging her throat, Kaitlin gathered her daughter quickly to her. 'I'm sorry, sweetheart,' she murmured, burying her face in her glorious copper hair, inhaling the perfect sweet innocence of her.

Why was Ruby wearing her coat? it occurred to her to wonder. With the cobwebs of her dream still clinging cloyingly to her mind, she struggled to get her chaotic thoughts in order. *Of course.* She remembered through the cotton wool in her head that she'd been at her nana's. It was late. Daylight filtering through the crack in the curtains told her that. She should be up. Panic gripped her, rising rapidly inside her as the events of the horrendous long night before slotted sickeningly into place. Had Greg gone out early to collect Ruby? Had her mother dropped her off?

'Were you feeling tired, Mummy?' Ruby asked, her huge green eyes filled with nervous uncertainty as she eased away from her.

Realising that her little girl was obviously also feeling disorientated – Kaitlin rarely slept late, if ever – she arranged her face into a reassuring smile. 'I think I must have been. I was so fast asleep I didn't even know you were here. Did Nana bring you home?'

'Uh huh.' Ruby nodded. 'Greg phoned her. He said you were poorly. I think Nana was worried, because she let me come home in my jimjams.' Pressing her chin into her neck, she pulled her coat open to reveal her Peppa Pig pyjamas underneath. 'Are you really poorly, Mummy?' She studied Kaitlin, her little forehead knitted into a troubled frown.

'I'm fine, darling.' Kaitlin reached to cup her face in her hands. 'We didn't get home until very late. I'm just tired, honestly.'

Ruby processed that. Then, 'You'll have to go to bed early tonight,' she said with an assured nod, 'or you'll be too tired for the park tomorrow.'

Though she felt as if her heart were tearing apart inside her, Kaitlin couldn't help but smile at her daughter's grown-up expression. 'I will,' she promised, aware that Ruby always looked forward to their Sunday trip to the park, which was sacrosanct time spent together. Uninterrupted time when they could relax together and reinforce the family unit, something Ruby had never had until Greg had come into their lives. Greg relished it too, clowning around on the swings and the round-about like a big kid himself. She would have to make that happen. Somehow she would have to force herself to play foot-ball in the park, to be there for her little girl.

She should have been there for Zoe. Her stomach twisted excruciatingly.

'Why don't you pop back downstairs and wait with Nana while I get dressed?' she suggested, pressing a kiss to Ruby's forehead and climbing out of bed, though she actually felt like staying there, cocooned under the duvet, until the nightmare was over, until Zoe was safe at home.

Might she be? Her heart jolted as she realised she hadn't checked her phone.

Her eyes flicking to the clock, which showed that it was well after eight, she grabbed the phone from the bedside table and pulled up her messages. An icy dagger of foreboding pierced her chest as she saw no returned texts or calls from Zoe. Perhaps she just wasn't talking to her? She clung to that hope for a second as the memories came flooding back, the unfeeling things she'd said to her. Zoe had been shocked, hurt. Tears streaming down her face, she'd run off into the cold, unfriendly night because of *her*. Even then, though, Kaitlin could never imagine she would leave her to stew in her worry. She wasn't like that. If Zoe had something to say, she simply said it. She believed that life was too short to waste time on negative emotion. Where was she? She would have contacted her by now, Kaitlin was sure she would ... *if* she could. Nausea rose hot inside her. Please God, don't let her dream have been some kind of prophecy.

'Nana said I'm to wait here until she comes up,' Ruby said, sliding to the edge of the bed, where she sat with her feet dangling, her hands tucked under her thighs. 'There's a man downstairs. I think it might be Daddy.'

Sean? What the *hell* was he doing calling here uninvited? 'Nana's right,' Kaitlin said, her chest tightening. He was here to cause trouble, obviously. Come to claim his rights to see his daughter, as if he'd ever cared a damn about her. 'Stay right here, sweetheart. I'll just pop down and see what he wants. Nana will be up in a second, don't worry.'

'Okay.' Ruby nodded hesitantly. 'Mummy,' she said behind her as Kaitlin flew to the door, 'he doesn't want to take me away, does he?'

Kaitlin stopped in her tracks and whirled back around, a part of her dying inside as she noted her daughter's wide, worried eyes. 'No, cupcake. He probably just wants to see how you are. But that's all, promise.'

Her baby was scared. Of her own father. God, that *bloody* man.

Ruby's gaze flickered nervously down and back. 'He told Greg he had a right to see me,' she said, her voice small. 'That I should visit him at his home. Do I have to, Mummy?'

She was close to tears. She'd never been anything but tearful whenever that bastard was near her. Fury pumping through her veins, she hugged the little girl hard to her, and then eased back to lock her eyes firmly on hers. 'No, Ruby,' she told her forcefully. 'You never, ever have to do anything you don't want to. Not *ever*. Do you hear me?'

Ruby studied her for a second, her eyes still wary. 'Uh huh.' She nodded, looking slightly more confident.

'Good girl.' Kaitlin gave her another tight squeeze. 'Now you wait here while I go and have a word with him, and Nana will be up in a flash. Okay?'

Again Ruby nodded and managed a smile.

'I won't be long,' Kaitlin promised, grabbing her dressing gown and flying to the landing.

Sean was in the hall, Greg standing between him and further access to the house, her mum to the side of them, her face fraught with worry. 'In which case, you won't mind producing some legal documentation to prove it, will you?' Kaitlin heard Greg say, his tone palpably angry.

Exchanging knowing glances with her, her mum flew up the stairs as fast as Kaitlin had come down them.

Sean eyed her mockingly. 'You're looking a bit rough,' he quipped. 'Long night?'

Pulling her dressing gown belt tight, Kaitlin ignored his comment. 'Outside,' she said.

'What?' He screwed up his forehead in confusion. He wasn't used to her giving orders.

'I said outside.' She walked past him to hold the front door open. 'I don't want you in my house, Sean, or anywhere near my daughter.'

Sean gawked, incredulous. '*Your* daughter.'

She didn't rise to the bait.

'You heard the lady.' Greg nodded him towards the door.

'What fucking lady?' Sean muttered. Then, seeing Greg's furious expression, he obviously decided his interests might be best served by doing as he was told.

Greg waited on the doorstep while Kaitlin followed Sean out, his arms folded across his chest, his eyes thunderous. Sean looked him over, his lip curled in contempt, then turned back to Kaitlin. 'I want to see Ruby,' he said. 'I have a right to be involved in her life. You know I do.'

Kaitlin resisted the retort that the only involvement he'd ever had was as a sperm donor. That would be sinking to his despicable level and was sure to incite argument. She had no intention of arguing with him. She simply wanted him gone. 'In which case, you'll need to hire a good solicitor,' she warned him, 'because I will fight you every step of the way, right through the courts if I have to. I'm already looking at getting an injunction taken out against you.' She was lying. She hadn't gone that route because he'd never been interested in seeing Ruby. She'd thanked her lucky stars for that and tried to move on. Now it seemed he wasn't going to let her do that.

He shook his head. 'You always were an unreasonable bitch,' he sneered.

Greg stepped forward, and Kaitlin cast him a glance, urging him not to react. She didn't want this escalating with Ruby upstairs. 'Go, please,' she instructed Sean.

Sean stayed where he was, his gaze travelling between them. 'I will see her, Kaitlin. You can't stop me,' he said, smirking as he turned to leave.

Over her dead body he would. 'Sean, wait,' she said, moving after him.

He stopped and turned back, a knowing smile on his face. Clearly he thought she was about to backtrack and give in to his demands, as she always had. He'd underestimated her. She would never give him access to Ruby, no matter what he threatened.

'Did you go to the police with some tale about Zoe?'

He looked baffled. 'Did I do what?'

'Sally Hanson said you went to see her at the station, that you said Zoe was coming on to you, that she threatened to tell me you assaulted her. Did you?'

'Oh, that.' He nodded thoughtfully. 'That's right, she did. It was bullshit, of course. She was obviously pissed off because I didn't fancy it. I told you your friends didn't give a shit about you, didn't I? That I was the only one who ever would.'

Kaitlin surveyed him coolly, saw the look of triumph in his eyes. 'Are you sure about that, Sean?' She called his bluff. 'Because if you did, you'd better have your facts straight. The police will want all the details now she's gone missing.'

'Missing, as in ... *missing*? Jesus.' Sean baulked. 'It's nothing to do with me,' he said shakily. 'Look, what I just said, it's not true. I didn't go to the police. I was winding you up. I can't even remember this Zoe. Or Sally, whoever she is. Don't you go blabbing rubbish to the law, Kaitlin, just to get back at me.'

He realised she had good reason to want to get back at him then. Did she believe him? She studied him hard. She wasn't sure. Never in a million years could she trust anything Sean had to say, but one thing she did know was that something here wasn't right.

FOURTEEN

Hot and aching with exhaustion, Kaitlin avoided Greg's questions until she could think properly and went straight upstairs to check on Ruby. Finding her absorbed in an interactive story with her mum, she grabbed the opportunity to jump in the shower and attempt to pull herself together. She'd barely stepped in when she heard Ruby calling her from outside the door. She sounded worried.

'Hold on a second, sweetheart.' Kaitlin stepped out again, grabbed a towel and opened the door.

'There's a man and lady downstairs. I think they might be policemen,' Ruby said, her expression a mixture of anxious and awe-filled as she looked up at her. 'Nana said they needed to talk in secret.'

Kaitlin's heart somersaulted. She obviously meant in private, but why on earth hadn't Greg come to fetch her? Surely he must know she would want him to. That she would be worried out of her mind not knowing why they were here. Her head a whirl of confusion, she hurriedly pulled her pyjamas and dressing gown back on.

'Has something bad happened, Mummy?' Ruby whispered as Kaitlin emerged onto the landing.

'No, sweetheart.' She crouched down in front of her. She had to spare her baby this, at least until she had no choice but to tell her something. She prayed she would never have to, that the police had come bearing good news. Ruby adored Zoe, who'd saved her daughter's sanity as well as her own when she'd taken them in, always making time to talk to her and to listen to her; to reassure her. She would be heartbroken if ... Images of her friend lying bruised and broken in some cold, lonely place assailing her, Kaitlin felt the breath leave her body.

'It's fine, lovely.' Her voice was strained as she tried to reassure her. 'Someone lost something last night,' she went on, a hard lump expanding in her chest as she realised how much *she* might have lost. Sally had been right. Zoe was almost part of her family. Why had she treated her so badly when she'd only been trying to look out for her? She would never forgive herself, not ever, if ... *Please bring her home safe.* She prayed hard again, the knot of guilt twisting itself tighter.

'Is that why the police are here? To find it for them?' Ruby asked innocently.

'That's right.' Attempting to focus, Kaitlin nodded encouragingly.

Ruby thought about it. 'Did they lose some shoes?' she asked.

Kaitlin frowned curiously. 'I'm not really sure,' she answered carefully. 'Do you think it was shoes?'

'Yes,' Ruby replied confidently. 'The man asked Greg for his shoes. When I asked Nana why they wanted them, she said they were only borrowing them. Do you think he's lending them to the person who's lost their shoes in case their feet get cold?'

Kaitlin felt the hairs rise over her skin. 'I, um ... Yes,' she managed past the constriction in her throat. 'I expect that would be it.'

Straightening up, she took hold of Ruby's hand and headed for the stairs. She breathed a sigh of relief when she met her mum coming up them.

Her mum gave her a cautious look as she reached the landing, then smiled for Ruby's benefit. 'I thought I might treat Ruby to a trip to the Cupcake Café, since she's been such a good girl,' she said. 'What do you think, Ruby?'

'Yay!' Ruby clapped her hands and did a little jig. 'I'm going to have ...' she paused to consider, 'Heavenly Melting Chocolate!'

Nana laughed. 'But possibly not in your jimjams.' Arching her eyebrows, she looked her over amusedly.

Ruby's face fell. 'I could just button my coat up,' she suggested hopefully.

'And sit inside the café with your coat on? *You'll* end up melting. Come on, little lady.' Nana stepped forward, urging Ruby towards her bedroom. 'You need to get washed and dressed in double-quick time if we're to get there before all the best cupcakes have gone.'

'Eeek!' Ruby twirled around, heading swiftly off to do as she was told.

'Thanks, Mum.' Kaitlin smiled gratefully once Ruby had disappeared into her room.

'It's no problem,' her mum assured her. 'I'm always happy to look after her, you know that. What on earth's going on, though, Kait?' Her gaze flicking after her granddaughter, she lowered her voice. 'First Sean shows up, and then the police. Greg said something about Zoe being missing.'

There was fear in her voice, in her eyes, too, exacerbating the terror that had taken root inside Kaitlin. Something dreadful had happened, she could sense it. She could *feel* it, a hard knot in her stomach that kept tying itself tighter and tighter. 'We argued,' she said, swallowing back the tears that were too close to the surface.

'Argued?' Her mother stared at her with a combination of incredulity and shock. And no wonder. Kaitlin and Zoe had never had a serious disagreement between them. Her mum was aware of how supportive Zoe had been when Kaitlin had needed her. Last night, Zoe had needed *her* – to be the friend she should be. How could she have been so furious with her for simply caring? So unthinkingly hurtful, causing Zoe to flee without even having a chance to tell Kaitlin her news. They'd been as close as two women could be for years, yet Kaitlin had broken the bond between them as if it meant nothing.

'She left the party upset. It was my fault,' she admitted wretchedly. 'I said some awful things to her. She ran off and ...' Stopping, she breathed in hard. 'I don't know where she is. I have no idea. She seems to have just vanished, and ... Oh Mum, what if she's ...' Tears sprang to her eyes.

'Oh my darling ...' Her mum's face softened, her sharp emerald eyes full of sympathy as she pulled her into a hug. It made Kaitlin want to sob. She didn't deserve sympathy. Would Zoe ever forgive her? Would she even be around either to reproach or to forgive?

'Go on, go on down.' Easing back, her mum caught hold of her shoulders, her gaze holding hers meaningfully. She was telling Kaitlin that she needed to stay strong – for her daughter, for the baby growing inside her – Kaitlin hadn't been able to wait before sharing news of her pregnancy with her, for Greg. Most of all for Zoe, who must have needed her so badly. 'You go and find out what's going on down there. Ruby will be fine with me. We'll slip out as soon as she's dressed. I have my mobile. Call me when you're ready.'

Closing her eyes, Kaitlin took a tremulous breath. 'Why do they want Greg's shoes?' she asked, glancing over her shoulder to make sure Ruby hadn't emerged.

'I've no idea.' Her mum knitted her brow. 'Something to do with foot marks, I think. They're probably just trying to eliminate him from their enquiries. You go down. Best to find out what's happening while they're still here.'

Kaitlin nodded, and moved towards the stairs. 'But what about Dad?' She hesitated. 'Weren't you two supposed to be shopping today?'

'Do you honestly think he won't be overjoyed at an excuse not to?' Her mum rolled her eyes good-naturedly.

Kaitlin was sure he would be. He was a rare breed, her mum always said, a man who'd actually enjoyed shopping until the car accident robbed him of the use of his legs. Wheelchair access was still a huge problem in the smaller shops he liked to mooch around in. Her dad tried to hide his frustration, her mum not so much. It would be her dad rolling his eyes and smiling wryly when she insisted on doing battle for him.

'Go.' Her mum nodded her on. 'We'll be fine. Ready, Ruby?' she called, heading off to her bedroom.

Bracing herself, Kaitlin hurried down the stairs. The washing machine was on; she could hear it spinning clunkily. The dishwasher, too. Everything seemed normal, as if she hadn't woken up to find herself in a living nightmare. Her heart thumped as she heard Greg's voice from behind the closed lounge door. 'As I've already mentioned, I went out looking for her,' he was saying, his tone measured. 'So obviously I was in the vicinity, yes.'

'You did go down to the riverbank then?' Sally's voice, her question sounding like an accusation to Kaitlin's ears.

Greg paused before answering. 'Depends where you mean exactly. My mind was more on searching for her than noting the landmarks.'

'The area directly after the footbridge,' Sally expanded. 'About twenty yards beyond it. You must have been aware where the bridge was relative to where you were. It's quite a sizeable structure.'

Hearing the definite innuendo in Sally's voice, Kaitlin's

heart skipped a beat and she reached to thrust the door open. DI Diaz and Sally were standing. Greg was sitting on the sofa. She noticed his pale complexion. 'Greg? Has something happened?' Panic spiralling inside her when he didn't answer, her gaze swivelled to Sally, who glanced at Diaz as if she should take her cue from him. 'Have you found something?'

'Footwear marks. Fresh imprints, it looks like,' Diaz provided, and then paused as the sound of Ruby chattering excitedly as she came downstairs with her gran reached them.

Once the front door had closed behind them, Sally spoke. 'They might provide useful evidence of who was on the river-bank, should we need it.'

Kaitlin shook her head in confusion. 'Couldn't there be thousands of trainers or shoes with the same patterns on the soles?' Her stomach churned with anxiety as recollections of Sean being questioned after a break-in at Zoe's flat while she'd been staying there rushed jarringly back. His shoe prints had actually exonerated him – those found on the window ledge had turned out not to be his – but she knew a little about the complications of identifying footwear.

'Undoubtedly,' Diaz answered. 'Sole patterns can distin-guish shoe types from each other, though. They can also be linked with certain brands of shoes. We have forensic databases holding such patterns that can help narrow it down.'

'But how can you link the shoe to the wearer?'

Diaz considered, his eyes narrowed for a second. 'There can be individual characteristics specific to a particular shoe,' he explained. 'Wear marks, damage to the sole, for instance. Seized footwear is used to produce marks of the same type as the recov-ered prints. We make comparisons, try to compare like with like.'

'But why are you taking Greg's shoes?' Kaitlin asked, his explanation only having increased her anxiety. 'He went out looking for Zoe. He's said so. I don't understand why you would be questioning him.'

'We're not questioning him, Ms Chalmers.' Diaz offered her a small smile, which she assumed was meant to be reassuring. 'We're just trying to ascertain what Mr Walker's movements were.'

'But why, if he's already told you—'

'Hey, hey, it's okay.' Greg spoke at last, standing to walk across to her. 'They have a job to do, Kait,' he said, placing a hand on her arm, as if to still her worries. 'Like the detective said, they're just trying to eliminate me from their enquiries.'

Kaitlin scanned his face. There was something in his eyes. Guardedness? Concern? Sorrow? She couldn't read it. 'What enquiries?' Her mind ticking feverishly, she looked back to Diaz. 'You think she's dead, don't you?'

Terror settled like ice inside her as she noted Diaz glancing quickly down. 'We're following every possible lead,' he answered vaguely, his expression carefully neutral.

Kaitlin felt the blood drain from her body. They did. They truly thought … Greg was there, catching her, as the floor ripped itself violently from beneath her.

FIFTEEN

Greg was crouched in front of her, holding her hand as she sat immobile on the sofa. She could feel his worried gaze on her. She couldn't look at him. There were a thousand questions buzzing like demented wasps in her head, but her mind was too stultified, her throat too parched to ask any of them. It felt as if the world had stopped turning, the clock on the wall silent, its hands frozen; her heart was frozen, turned to stone in her chest. And then it hit her, shock, like a tidal wave crashing through her, dragging her down, sucking her under, pulling her back to when they were young and carefree, although Zoe had never been able to truly be that. She laughed and she sang and she danced. On the surface she was confident, but underneath she was as vulnerable as the five-year-old child who'd been taken into care, no possessions to her name but Buttons, her raggedy teddy bear.

In her memory, they were in Kaitlin's mum's lounge, stuffing their faces with cheese and pepperoni pizza while watching *Pretty Woman* on the brand-new DVD player. Zoe had decided Kaitlin would fit the part of Vivian, the free-spirited prostitute played by Julia Roberts. 'You look like a Vivian,' she'd said, causing Kaitlin to spit out her Coke as she tried to work out the implication. Zoe was her big-hearted friend Kit De Luca, they'd decided, worldly-wise and sassy.

Later, they were the main attraction at a family wedding – at least they'd thought they were – doing the whole *men's shirts, short skirts* thing on the dance floor. Zoe's gesticulations had bordered on the obscene. She hadn't cared what anyone thought. *A girl's gotta have a little fun* was her motto. Where *was* she?

As Kaitlin had waited with her at the airport before she'd flown off to Portugal, Zoe had squeezed her to within an inch of her life. 'Miss you already,' she'd whispered, tears welling in her eyes, and then she'd spun around and sashayed off to departures, waving a hand nonchalantly behind her. She hadn't looked back because she hadn't wanted Kaitlin to see her crying. She was a survivor. *The bad shit just makes us stronger*, she would often say, shrugging off the painful things she'd had to endure in life.

But she hadn't survived. Kaitlin's throat closed. The detective's face had given nothing away, but she'd seen it in his eyes; there'd been a flicker of commiseration there as he'd left. In that second, Kaitlin had known: they didn't think they would find her alive. A confusion of raw emotion assailed her. Anger. Acrid grief, rising so fast it almost choked her. Guilt, weighing so heavy she didn't think she could bear it.

'Kaitlin, talk to me.' Greg's voice reached her as if from some faraway place. 'Kait ...' He squeezed her hand. 'I'm here for you. Please don't push me—'

'*No!*' A jolt of pure rage shooting through her, Kaitlin jumped to her feet. 'She's *not* dead!' She pressed her hands over her face, trying to stifle the moan that seemed to come from her soul. 'She's *not*! She *can't* be.'

Greg was next to her, trying clumsily to hold her. She pulled away from him. 'She's not!' Her chest heaved with impotent fury. 'She can't be! I can *feel* her.'

'Kaitlin, please calm down. Please let me help you. You're upset. In shock. Let me get you something. Some tea, or—'

'Calm down? Tea?' She laughed, eyeing him with absolute incredulity. 'Do you honestly think *tea* is going to make me feel better?'

Greg ran his fingers through his hair. 'No, I ... I'm sorry. I don't mean to trivialise—'

Kaitlin's tears exploded with confusion and anger. 'Why weren't any of your friends there?'

'What?' Greg squinted at her, confused.

'At the party, why didn't you invite any of your friends?' Zoe's worries kept going around and around in her head; her hurt expression when Kaitlin had snapped at her, defending him, accepting his explanation that he hadn't made many friends in the area yet. 'Your family? There must be someone you would have liked to invite.' She pushed it even though Greg was looking at her in shocked bewilderment. He would never hurt anyone, she'd never seen a single sign of aggression in him, yet he was right there on the riverbank. She had to know. She had to fill in the gaps. No, *he* had to. She was already doing that, and it was terrifying her.

He nodded, pushing his hands in his pockets and glancing up at the ceiling. 'It's a fair question. I'd hoped to avoid telling you, but ...' He looked back at her. 'Do you think we could sit and talk quietly?'

Kaitlin stayed standing. She felt like screaming.

Again Greg nodded. He drew a hand over his neck, then turned to drop heavily onto the sofa. 'My family ... My parents ...' He faltered, then dragged in a long breath and blew it out slowly. 'I haven't seen them in a while. A long time, actually. I got out as soon as I could and I never went back.' He stopped as if to take stock. 'They were abusive,' he said finally. 'Both of them.'

'Abusive?' Kaitlin repeated, stunned.

'They did drugs, booze,' he went on awkwardly. 'Classic co-dependency between two people in a toxic relationship, according to the counsellor I eventually found. That was hard, confiding in someone. I know I'm a big strapping bloke now, but ...' He paused. His eyes were filled with deep humiliation. 'It's the abuser who seems too big to fight when you're just a little kid,' he carried on with a defeated shrug. 'The thing is, you're still that little kid even when you're an adult, you know? No matter how strong you might appear on the outside, inside you're scared, carrying the wounds. You feel ... weak, I guess, as if you were somehow responsible for the shit that blighted your life.'

Kaitlin stared at him, shocked to the core. She'd been there, suffered at the hands of an abuser. She could feel every single one of his emotions: the pain that was evident on his face, the embarrassment, the self-recrimination and the guilt. Yet he hadn't trusted her enough to tell her, to realise that she would understand. Why?

'I should have told you.' He answered her unasked question. 'I ... just couldn't at first.' He glanced towards the window, looking anywhere, Kaitlin felt, but at her. 'And then as time went on, it didn't seem important, but now ...' He looked at her at last. 'I'm sorry. I should have said something. I thought I might lose you, and now I'm wondering whether I have.'

Kaitlin had no idea what to say. She wanted to go to him, to reassure him, but she was struggling to process why he wouldn't trust her. He knew her well enough to know she would be nothing but understanding. Didn't he? Did *she* know him? She'd thought she did, but ...

Sighing heavily, he closed his eyes. 'You think I have something to do with Zoe's disappearance, don't you?' he asked, taking her by surprise.

'No. I ...' Kaitlin hesitated. 'I'm confused. I ...' She recalled the stark crimson stain on his collar, and her emotions reeled. 'There was blood on your shirt.'

'From the *foliage*.' Greg was adamant. 'I'm not lying, Kait. I omitted to tell you something, but I've never lied to you. Surely you don't think I'm capable of hurting anyone?'

She looked back at him. He had tears in his eyes, which shook her. 'No.' She swallowed. 'I don't. I just ... I need to think things through, that's all.'

'I've broken your trust, haven't I?' He smiled sadly. 'Not telling you something so fundamental about me was bound to, I suppose.'

'No,' Kaitlin shook her head, 'I *do* trust you. I ...' She hesitated, feeling hot, and now horrendously nauseous. *Did* she? Truly? Was she suspicious of him because of her own insecurities? 'I just need a little time to myself. I should have a shower. Get dressed.'

Greg nodded and got to his feet. 'Ironic, isn't it?' he said. 'I was worried that Zoe was trying to plant doubt in your mind, and now I've managed to do that myself.'

He'd overheard. He couldn't have failed to hear their argument in the toilets. Even before that, though, every time she and Zoe had been alone, he'd appeared. *Because he was concerned.* She searched his face. He looked heartbroken. 'She cares about me, Greg. I care about *her*. I ...' She stopped, swiping at the tears that spilled down her face.

'Of course you do. I care about you too, though, Kait, remember that. More than anything.' He studied her for a long, searching moment. 'I'll go to the office for a while. I have paperwork to catch up on. I'll call you later.' Hesitating for a second, he pressed a soft kiss to her cheek, then turned to the door.

Kaitlin wanted to go after him. To tell him she didn't doubt him and that everything was all right; to have him tell her that everything would be. But she couldn't, because things felt far from all right.

SIXTEEN

ADAM DIAZ

'You sure you don't want me to drive?' Adam asked as he and Sally headed from the station to take another look at the suspected crime scene – which in Adam's mind had become such as soon as the missing woman's bag had been handed in. Studded with crystals, some of which were encrusted in blood, it was obviously an evening bag, and had been found on the riverbank, where there were obvious signs of a struggle. It didn't look good.

'No problem,' Sally assured him, going round to the driver's side. 'Something about keeping my eyes on the road lulls my brain into doing some actual thinking. Plus it will give you chance to answer some of those texts and calls I've heard pinging on your phone.'

She gave him a look somewhere between inquisitive and amused as she climbed in, and Adam's mouth curved into a rare smile. He supposed she was wondering whether they were personal. They would all be work-related or from Freya, checking up on him. If Sally imagined his life beyond work was remotely exciting, she might be disappointed. There was nothing about him that was remotely exciting. He had no vices, apart from his workaholic tendencies. No particular aspirations, other than to be the best father he could be to his daughter – and to do his job to the best of his ability. In short, he was nothing to write home about, though his daughter disagreed, telling him he was selling himself short and that he should join a few dating apps and put himself out there. He'd smiled wryly, imagining what kind of field day his colleagues would have with that.

Freya had given him her considered opinion just the other day, looking him over critically. 'You're not bad-looking. A bit moody and broody, but my mate fancies you. Mind you, she does wear glasses.' Adam had chuckled at that. Joanne might have disagreed with the 'not bad-looking' observation. He recalled how she'd once described him as 'reasonable', a teasing smile playing at her mouth as she'd eyed him in the bathroom mirror he was attempting to shave at. 'Not bad between the sheets, though,' she'd added, giving his rear end a tweak and disappearing smartly back into the bedroom.

They'd made love that morning; spontaneous, uninhibited sex against the bedroom door – at Joanne's instigation, because that was the kind of person she'd been, impulsive, free-spirited, before she'd allowed the job and all the shit that went with it to get to her, grinding her down. Christ, he missed her. He sucked in a breath as a wave of grief crashed ferociously through him, leaving him winded in its wake. Since her death three long years ago, he'd learned to cope with the routine everyday grief of her absence. These unexpected episodes, though, raw emotion rushing to the surface no matter how hard he tried to keep it at bay, almost knocked him sideways. He wondered whether it would ever stop.

Climbing into the passenger seat, he drew in a deep breath, held it and then breathed slowly out. He could still hear it, the plaintive wail of the siren that had drowned out everything but the terrified thud of his heart. He could taste the petrol fumes thick on the air, searing the back of his throat as he ran towards the road traffic accident just one road away from the station. Every time he closed his eyes, he could see it, her car, nothing but mangled metal, the front so concertinaed he knew in a blood-freezing instant that no one could have survived. The light fading from her eyes as he'd crouched down next to her, desperately pleading with her not to let go – that was what haunted him most. He'd had counselling. He'd had no choice after his boss had reminded him that it was protocol when an officer had witnessed the death of someone close. The counsellor had told him he needed to forgive himself. Adam had made all the right noises, ticked all the boxes, got himself signed off as fit for work, but he could never stop blaming himself.

'So what do you reckon to this Walker bloke?' Sally asked him, jarring him from his thoughts.

Adam buckled up as she pulled away. 'Not sure.' He sighed contemplatively. 'He seemed a bit twitchy, but then most people are when we pay them a house call.'

'True. Could be our prime suspect, though,' she suggested. 'In the vicinity, mud on his shoes ...'

'Maybe.' Adam was reserving judgement for now. The guy had gone out searching for the woman. It was something he himself would have done under similar circumstances. 'What about motive?' he asked her.

Sally shrugged. 'Kaitlin said she and Zoe had argued. Walker reckoned Zoe was jealous. He might have caught up with her, tried to reason with her. If Zoe had been drinking, she might have not been in a listening mood.'

'And things escalated, you reckon? Could be,' Adam conceded. 'Unfortunately, we need evidence,' he reminded her, which was something they had precious little of. He had no doubt a crime had been committed, but there was no body, meaning the level of response wasn't classed as high priority. He wasn't holding out much hope that the powers-that-be would sanction a search team including divers with so little to go on.

Analysis had yet to confirm who the blood on the evening bag belonged to, but he was guessing it was Zoe's. If so, there might well be blood on her assailant's clothing. They had nothing on Walker, though, other than that he'd been on the riverbank searching for her – as corroborated by his fiancée.

'Do you reckon we should have another chat with him?' Sally asked.

'I intend to. We don't have much to justify bringing him in, though. The man's squeaky clean. No prior. No warnings.' Adam had already done the usual checks. There was nothing on the database, not even an unpaid parking fine.

'Apart from the shoes,' Sally reminded him, 'which might place him more specifically in the area.'

'Possibly.' Adam nodded, reaching for his seat belt as they approached the dock. 'Collecting evidence can also be a process of elimination, though,' he pointed out. 'Let's find out if making casts of the foot marks on the bank is viable and take it from there.'

Once they were parked and kitted out in the requisite clothing, they made their way down to the riverbank. On learning from the crime-scene coordinator that there was a good chance of getting some usable casts, he breathed a sigh of relief. His jaw clenched as he re-examined the area. There were definite signs of a struggle near the water's edge, but as yet, nothing to give them any leads as to what had happened and why. He had to get a fingertip search under way asap.

Straightening up, he headed back along the bank. He was climbing out of the suffocating forensic gear when a uniformed officer attracted his attention from the footbridge. 'We have a witness, sir,' he shouted. 'At the station. Says he saw an attack on a woman taking place around the time Zoe Weller would have been walking home.'

Damn. Adam almost fell over his feet in his haste. 'Tell them to offer him tea, coffee, anything,' he yelled back. 'Just make bloody sure he doesn't leave until I get there.'

'On it.' The officer gave him another wave and turned away.

Hurrying up the incline to the dock, Adam's blood pumped, a surge of adrenaline coursing through him as he realised he might now be able to move things forward. This kind of thing made him sick to the pit of his stomach. As she'd taken her last breath, he'd promised Joanne he would keep their daughter safe. He couldn't rid the whole world of scum, but locking up the kind of human flotsam that scoured the streets preying on young women was a step closer to doing that.

SEVENTEEN

KAITLIN

Wretched with worry and suffering overwhelming morning sickness that wouldn't go away, Kaitlin wandered aimlessly from room to room, wondering what she should do. With Ruby at her mum's for the rest of the day, she felt lonely, bereft, alternating between anger and guilt about the conversation she'd had with Greg. He hadn't confided in her – she still couldn't quite believe that. She hadn't reacted the way she instinctively would when he had told her about his dreadful childhood. In normal circumstances she would have gone to him, held him, assured him that she loved him, the man he was. Instead of which, she'd doubted him, questioning him about his friends, his family, asking him about the blood on his shirt, accusing him of ... what? She couldn't even bear to contemplate the unthinkable. Why hadn't he denied it more stringently? Why hadn't he been angry that she would doubt him, even for a single second? Why hadn't he rung her?

Going into the kitchen, she opened the fridge and closed it again. She should eat, but she had no appetite. She should rest, but she simply couldn't sit still. She felt exhausted, but taking a nap was out of the question, though she craved sleep, deep, dark and dreamless, where her nightmares couldn't haunt her.

Trailing back towards the lounge, she stopped, placing her hands over her bump as she felt little limbs flail frantically against her tummy. It was as if her tiny foetus was distressed too. Was she doing her baby harm? Her heart ricocheted against her ribcage as her thoughts swung to Zoe, the baby *she* carried. She could see her, her hands protectively over her tummy, trying to keep her child safe. It froze her heart inside her.

Hollow tears of hopelessness rising, she prayed with all her might that Zoe would come home, that she was somewhere safe. Why hadn't they found any trace of her? She recalled her friend's stricken face, the hurt and bewilderment in her eyes. *I'm your* friend, *Kait. I'm concerned for you, that's all*, she heard her say. Actually heard her, she was certain she did, a frightened whisper above the rain relentlessly lashing against the window.

'Zoe?' She spoke out loud, her voice echoing around the house that seemed suddenly too empty.

I love you. You know I do, Zoe answered. In Kaitlin's heart, in her mind, she answered her. She *couldn't* be dead. How could she possibly be? How would Kaitlin live without her? Without knowing? With the knowledge that Zoe might have been utterly petrified, in incomprehensible physical pain, because of her? She would *have* to live, somehow she would have to survive, smile and go through the motions for her daughter, for the child growing inside her, but part of her would be missing. She would feel the cold emptiness inside her for the rest of her life. 'I love you too, my darling. Please, *please* forgive me,' she begged.

She gulped back her own excruciating pain, born of the knowledge that she didn't deserve that forgiveness from someone who'd been a better friend than she herself could ever be. She should have listened to Zoe. She'd been right. She should have given herself more time to discover who she was. Even after leaving Sean, she'd continued to view herself through the eyes of the man she was with, constantly questioning herself because her husband had undermined her.

She *had* to be more assertive. She'd sent Greg a text asking him to call her. He hadn't. She'd hurt his feelings – undoubtedly she'd done that, appearing not to trust him, but trust was a two-way road. She didn't need the added worry of whether she might have damaged their relationship. She *couldn't* worry any more. He must see that. Determinedly she grabbed her phone up from the coffee table and called him. His phone went straight to voicemail, sparking a kernel of anger inside her. Had he decided *not* to answer her calls? No, he wouldn't do that. He wasn't prone to sulkiness or childishness as Sean had been, manipulative behaviour that had always made her want to fix whatever he was upset about; a relationship that could never be fixed.

Aware that the company Greg worked for operated around the clock, she decided to ring them direct. Someone would be able to locate him or get a message to him if he'd simply muted his phone. 'FFI Fire Investigation Services. Emma speaking,' a young woman trilled brightly after a second. 'How can I help you?'

'Hi.' Kaitlin took a breath. 'My name's Kaitlin Chalmers. I'm Gregory Walker's fiancée,' she said, trying for some level of calmness. 'I wondered if I could have a quick word with him?'

'Gregory Walker?' Emma repeated, sounding puzzled. 'Hold on a sec.'

Kaitlin waited, stroking a hand softly over her tummy as her baby did another little flip. What if he really didn't want to speak to her? She didn't feel she could cope with any more upsets.

'Good afternoon,' another chirpy voice said a minute later. 'Rachel Johnson, Chief Administrator. How can I help?'

'I'd like to speak to Gregory Walker, please,' Kaitlin repeated patiently. It was possible he'd been called out, she realised, which might explain why he hadn't been in contact. 'If he's at a fire scene, do you think I could leave him a message to call me back when he comes in?'

'No, he's not ...' Rachel paused. 'Sorry, who am I speaking to?'

She sounded wary. Kaitlin felt a chill prickle her skin. What on earth was going on? Why was she being passed around? 'I'm Kaitlin, his fiancée,' she said. 'It's just his phone is switched off and I really need to have a word with him as soon as possible.'

'I, um ...' Again Rachel hesitated. 'I'm afraid Mr Walker isn't in today.'

'But ...' Kaitlin shook her head, now very confused. 'Are you sure? He did say he was coming in today to catch up on some paperwork.'

'I'm sure,' Rachel answered. 'We have a skeleton staff on at weekends but there's no one else in the building.'

Kaitlin's stomach turned over. 'Might he have gone out to a fire scene?'

Rachel fell silent for a second. 'He doesn't attend fire scenes,' she said eventually. 'He works in the finance department.'

Kaitlin felt as if she'd been hit by a thunderbolt. That wasn't right. It couldn't be right. 'I see,' she managed, her voice strained.

'I could leave a message on his desk if that would help?' the woman offered. 'As I say, he won't be in until Monday, but—'

'No,' Kaitlin said quickly. 'I'll see him before then. Please don't worry.' Her heart palpitating wildly in her chest, she ended the call.

He'd lied to her. Deliberately. She pictured Zoe's fearful expression as she'd tried to warn her. *There's something not right about him, Kaitlin.* What else had he lied about?

EIGHTEEN

'Just have a bite or two.' Kaitlin's mum was trying to encourage her to eat, but she just couldn't face food. Her nerves were in shreds since realising Greg had been lying to her. When her mum had suggested she and Ruby stay the night, she'd left him a note telling him her mum and dad were upset about Zoe and she wanted to be with them. She couldn't be at home with him, not tonight.

'But you have to eat, Mummy, or the baby might get hungry,' Ruby pointed out, a worried little V forming in her brow.

Kaitlin glanced at the box filled with delicious cupcakes that Ruby had picked especially for her, and felt her little girl's disappointment. 'I will,' she promised, opening her arms and beckoning her into them.

Giving her a firm hug, she kissed the top of her head and reinforced her promise to herself never to let anything hurt her daughter ever again. She *would* be hurt, though. Greg was part of Ruby's life. Yet how could she allow him to be, knowing he'd been dishonest? And what about Zoe, the blood on his collar?

Could she really believe his explanation as to how it had got there now?

'Mummy, the cupcakes.' Ruby tugged on her sleeve.

Kaitlin forced a smile. 'Why don't you pop them in Nana's fridge?' she suggested. 'I can have one later, when baby's finished his gymnastics.'

'Is he gambolling again?' Ruby asked with a world-weary sigh, and Kaitlin felt her heart sink as she remembered how overwhelmed Greg had been when he'd felt those miraculous first kicks. The movements had come early because it was her second baby. Greg's baby, the man she'd trusted implicitly. The man she'd agreed to marry. A man who might have had something to do with what had happened to Zoe. Acknowledging that thought, a fresh wave of nausea swilled through her.

Her mum obviously noticed. 'Sit,' she instructed, catching hold of her arm and steering her to a seat at the table. 'Pop those in the fridge, would you, Ruby sweetheart, while I get Mummy a nice cup of tea and a biscuit.'

Seeing her mum's worried expression, Kaitlin nodded. She needed sustenance, even if she didn't want it.

'Should I ask Gramps if he wants a cupcake, Nana?' Ruby asked, lifting the box from the table.

Almost as if he'd heard, her grandpa's voice drifted up the hall. 'Not putting the kettle on by any chance, are you, Jayne?'

Her mum's eyes drifted amusedly in Ruby's direction. 'I think we might have to offer him one now that we've been caught red-handed.' She laughed as Ruby immediately put down the box and skidded out of the kitchen, eager for the wheelie her grandpa would give her along the hall.

'Hey, sweetheart. Up we come.' Kaitlin heard her dad, no doubt about to indulge her. 'Hold on tight.'

A second later, accompanied by a whoop of delight from Ruby, the two of them appeared in the kitchen doorway, Ruby clinging tight to her grandpa's neck while he lowered the front wheels back to the ground. He lifted her up and swung her down onto her feet. 'So, does that earn me a cupcake?' he asked her.

'Um …' Pressing her finger to her chin, the little girl made a great show of considering it.

'I might need one for energy,' he added, wearing his best doleful eyes.

'Yes, okay.' She beamed him a smile and twirled back to the table.

'Don't forget you need to cancel the restaurant booking, Richard,' Kaitlin's mum said over her shoulder as she made the tea. 'We were going to treat ourselves,' she added, glancing at Kaitlin, 'but under the circumstances …'

Kaitlin had no idea what to say. They obviously wouldn't want to go out now. Her mum and dad had known Zoe as long as she had, after all, working hard to make her feel part of the family whenever she was here. She could tell from the look in her mum's eyes that her heart was quietly breaking inside her, just as her own was.

'Already done,' Richard assured her, wheeling himself through the doorway.

She *had* rushed into things. Believing that at last she could have the solid relationship her mum and dad had, that Ruby would have a reliable, caring father figure in her life. She'd defended her decision, defended Greg, at the cost of her friendship with Zoe, and possibly Zoe's life. That thought hit home, and grief and guilt sliced through her like a knife.

'You look a bit pale,' her dad said, gently taking hold of her hand.

Tears clouding her vision, Kaitlin looked at him, taking in his still handsome features, the concern and kindness in his eyes. Grief clogging her throat, she dropped her gaze and squeezed her eyes closed, desperate for her daughter not to see her crying.

'Come on, little Ruby, let's go and see if we can find a film we can all watch, shall we?' her mum said intuitively.

'Paddington!' Ruby exclaimed gleefully as she followed her into the hall.

'That should be entertaining for the hundredth time,' Richard said quietly. Seeing him roll his eyes good-naturedly, Kaitlin choked out a laugh that turned into a sob.

'Come here.' He held out his arms, and Kaitlin leaned into them, hugging him hard.

'How do you feel about Greg, Dad?' she asked him, her voice ragged.

Richard was quiet for a moment. Then, 'I take it you might be having some doubts?' He studied her worriedly as she eased away from him. 'All I can advise you to do is listen to your instincts. It vexes me to admit it sometimes, but a woman's instinct is rarely wrong. Don't tell your mother I said that, though,' he added. 'I'll never hear the last of it.'

Wiping a hand under her nose, Kaitlin smiled tremulously. 'Do you mind if I pass on the film and use your PC for a while?' she asked him.

'Is this pertinent to the subject?' her dad asked, gauging her carefully.

Kaitlin nodded.

'Use my study,' he said. 'Take your time. It's a long film.'

Grateful for his diplomacy in not asking too many questions, Kaitlin settled in front of his computer and set about googling Gregory Mark Walker and checking social media accounts. Somehow she wasn't surprised to find that her Gregory, as she'd once fondly thought of him, had no such accounts. There was no reason he should have – some people preferred not to spend time on social media. Kaitlin had been tempted to opt out herself. But for the WhatsApp parent group, which was useful, she might have. Now, though, she couldn't help wondering why there seemed to be no online trace of him.

Finally, in a last attempt to find something, she pulled up the latest Facebook posts by people with the same name. Flicking through them, she came across one that stopped her with a jolt.

A huge shout-out to everyone who attended the reunion and fundraiser at Park Hill Middle School last night. We raised over £2,000 to help redecorate the local children's hospice. How cool is that? Look forward to seeing you guys again next year. Meanwhile here's some photos from yesterday, plus some historic year pics to make you cringe.

This was Zoe's old school. The post must be from the Gregory Walker she had spoken of. It definitely wasn't the Greg Kaitlin knew. Tentatively she clicked on the photos, and found herself looking at a year photo, the girl just off centre in the front row unmistakably Zoe. She had hardly changed. Her hair was darker, light brown instead of the copper colour it was now, but she'd worn it in a similar elfin cut back then, her huge amber eyes wide under her trendily long fringe. Her nickname had been Bambi. She looked like a little deer, lost and lonely even in a crowd. That was how she'd looked before she'd fled from the party last night, lonely, bewildered that her best friend had turned on her.

Where are you, Zoe? Why did I say those awful things to you?

Closing the search down, she accessed her email account. The last contact they'd had before they'd seemed to drift apart for a while was via email, and she desperately wanted to touch base with her. She soon found the email Zoe had sent, attached to which was a photo of Daniel.

I've been taking in the local sights, she read. *What do you think? Hot or what? You can't see much of his face behind the shades, but he has a smile that could melt hearts from fifty paces. And his eyes! Imagine the deepest crystal blue of the ocean. I swear to God they sent a jolt of electricity right through me. He's quite tall, toned – and tanned obviously. In short, ticks all my boxes. Best of all, he's not wearing a wedding ring. I'm meeting him later. Don't worry, I will be undertaking extensive research regarding his status and suitability.*

Kaitlin had laughed when she'd read it. Zoe had told her before she left for Portugal that she had her 'bastard antennae' on red alert. Clearly, though, this man with his heart-melting smile and electrifying blue eyes had already broken through her defences. She remembered thinking at the time that she could see why. He was classically good-looking, tall and dark, as was Greg. She'd just hoped his charms were more than skin deep.

Be gentle with him, she'd replied jokingly. *And make sure to report back.*

Zoe hadn't, other than a quick one-line text: *Sex orgasm-inducing,* she'd sent, with a panting emoji face and a thumbs-up. Had *he* been gentle with *her*? Kaitlin wondered now. Had he loved her, as Zoe had plainly loved him – enough to want to have his child? Or had had he just been seeking the thrill of illicit sex behind his wife's back?

NINETEEN

ZOE

Portugal: Before the party

A thousand jittery butterflies taking off in her tummy, she nodded her consent, then watched mesmerised as relief flooded Daniel's features. 'Did I tell you how much I love you?' he whispered throatily.

He had. He'd said he wanted to be with her, that he couldn't stop thinking about her, losing his train of thought even at crucial moments when he was closing a property deal because his mind was full of her and the mind-blowing sex they had together.

'Not just the sex, I hope?' She'd smiled uncertainly.

'Not just the sex,' he'd assured her, locking his gaze intensely on hers. 'I love all there is to love about you. Your spontaneity, your infectious enthusiasm, your laugh, which always makes *me* laugh, your beautiful amber eyes – like finest liquor. I love you, Zoe. I want to be with you. I want you. Here. Now. Always.'

She held her breath as he climbed off the bed, moving to the end of it to gently but deftly tie her ankles with the ropes that had sent a shudder of apprehension through her when he'd first produced them. Making sure they were secure, he kissed each of her toes, lingering at her ankles, and then wordlessly worked his way upwards, pausing at the insides of her thighs to tease and tantalise just long enough to send a jolt of pleasure through her.

'Shh.' He pressed a finger to her mouth as a moan escaped her, and then, brushing her lips with his, eased her arms upwards, snapping first one wrist and then the other in place with the handcuffs she also hadn't been sure of.

'You're beautiful,' he said, his eyes holding hers as he positioned himself over her.

Zoe wasn't beautiful, she knew she wasn't; certainly not like this, all of her imperfections embarrassingly on display. Seeing herself through his eyes, though, she could almost believe that she was, that she might even compete with the perfect Barbie doll her previous boyfriend had left her for.

'Don't be nervous,' he urged her, clearly sensing her anxiety. 'Just go with the flow.' He eased back to scan her face. 'Okay?' he checked, and there was such tender concern in his eyes that she knew she was safe. She always knew.

His smile one of tangible relief as she nodded, he took a breath and pressed himself into her, slowly at first, as careful of her as if it were her first time. Zoe couldn't help but love him for that. 'Perfect. Every inch of you,' he murmured, thrusting more deeply a second time. And again. Slowly increasing the pace, his eyes on hers, building the momentum, until she felt as though he filled her to the brim. She whimpered as he picked up the tempo, thrusting still deeper, fast, sure strokes, until she undulated under him, raising her hips to meet him, matching him thrust for thrust, pushing her tongue deep into his mouth, biting his lips, breathing into him. She felt wanton, uninhibited, for the first time ever. All her self-consciousness gone.

He sought her breasts, urgently nipping and sucking as she bucked beneath him, her muscles clenching around him in one flowing contraction, her climax exploding with such ferocity she sobbed out his name.

His eyes smouldering above her, he thrust one last time, and then, with a throaty moan, he came too. She felt his release. Felt a drop of sweat fall onto her forehead. His breathing was ragged. He closed his eyes, exhaling hard, his beautiful dark eyelashes brushing his cheeks.

'I love you too,' she whispered, her own eyes closed as she floated deliciously down from the kind of orgasm she'd never imagined she could achieve.

Feeling cool air brush her skin as he moved quickly away from her, she craned her neck to look for him. 'Dan?' She frowned, puzzled, as she realised he was gathering his clothes from the chair, his shoes from the floor.

His gaze shot to hers. 'Shit!' Dropping a shoe, he bent hurriedly to retrieve it, then snapped his eyes across the room towards the door.

Icy fear tightening her stomach, Zoe followed his gaze, and her heart almost shot out of her mouth. 'Daniel?' A strangled murmur escaped her as the wild-eyed woman standing in the open doorway took a step into the room.

'So this is what you've been doing behind my back, is it?' The woman's voice shook with anger. 'Fucking some cheap little gold-digger?'

'No.' Daniel's face paled visibly. 'I—'

'How long has it been going on, Daniel?' the woman snarled over him. 'How long have you been cheating on me, not giving a damn about what this will do to our children?'

She was his wife? Seeing the tears cascading down the woman's face, Zoe knew with heart-stopping certainty that she was. Nausea swilling inside her, she yanked on her wrists. Panic almost choked her as she realised she had no hope of freeing them.

'Nothing's going on,' Daniel insisted. 'This isn't what—'

'Do not lie to me!' the woman screamed. 'At least have enough respect for me not to add insult to injury, you bastard!'

'It was a mistake,' Daniel yelled back. 'A one-off, I swear. Please, I can explain.' Scrambling into his trousers, he headed, half stumbling, half hopping, towards the door.

'A prostitute, then?' the woman surmised, obvious disgust in her eyes as they pivoted back to Zoe. 'Why am I not surprised? Been here before, haven't we, Daniel?'

'No!' Daniel exclaimed. Then, 'Yes,' he said throatily. 'I'm sorry. I ...'

What? Zoe felt as if he'd just punched her, a low, painful blow to her pelvis.

'Get out,' the woman seethed, lifting her chin as she stood aside to allow him to pass.

Thinking she might actually be about to be sick, Zoe jerked hard on her wrists. 'Daniel!' He wavered, but he didn't look back.

'As for her ...' the woman growled, looking murderously back at her, 'she can fucking well stay here until I decide what to do with her.'

'I didn't know,' Zoe whispered, fear and deep humiliation churning inside her. 'He didn't tell me.' She stopped, her throat tightening, her insides turning over, as the woman stepped back, crashing the door closed behind her.

TWENTY

KAITLIN

Half an hour later, Kaitlin was parked on Hibberton's tiny high street, which consisted largely of pretty cottages and barn conversions, the village shop and the pub nestled amongst them. On the opposite side of the road was the parish church and the local primary school. Climbing out of the car, she tried to think what to do next. She could hardly go knocking on doors asking where Greg's family lived, particularly when all she had was their surname. Her gaze drifted back to the shop, which was still open, and she gathered her courage and headed in that direction. She might come up blank, but it was worth a try.

Stepping in, she hung back behind the queue at the checkout for a second, and then caught the eye of the man behind the counter. 'Excuse me.' She waved. 'I have a parcel delivery for someone by the name of Walker. I'm not sure the address is right. Couldn't tell me where they are, could you? Save me going around in circles.'

'Up on the Trench Road, my lovely. Number five.' The man gave her a smile and turned back to his customers.

Kaitlin went back to her car. She'd never dreamed it would be that easy.

It didn't take her long to find the road, a small turning off the main road alongside the canal. Parking by the kerb, she climbed out and located number five, which appeared to be in a sad state of disrepair. Bracing herself, she approached it with some trepidation and knocked on the door. She waited a minute, glancing up at the upstairs windows, where the curtains were half-closed, then knocked again. Still there was no answer. She was about to turn away when she heard a movement from inside, and the front door swung open.

A man about her father's age eyed her curiously. He didn't speak, presumably waiting for Kaitlin to introduce herself and tell him why she was calling.

'Sorry to bother you,' she managed, mustering up a smile. 'My name's Kaitlin Chalmers and ... Is this Gregory Walker's address? I mean, are you his father? It's just—'

'What?' The man squinted at her. 'Why?'

Kaitlin faltered under his unwavering gaze. 'I'm his fiancée,' she said, her tongue feeling suddenly too big for her mouth. 'I was passing, and—'

'You've got the wrong address,' the man said tersely, and made to close the door.

'No. He definitely said Hibberton,' Kaitlin said quickly. 'There can't be two families by that name in such a small village, surely?'

The man looked thunderstruck, as if she'd punched him.

'I just wanted to have a quick word,' she stumbled on, wondering now why she'd come, what she hoped to achieve. 'It's just that Greg seemed to find it difficult to—'

'He's dead!' the man barked, his gaze now burning with something close to fury.

Kaitlin felt the blood leave her body. 'Dead?' She stared at him, uncomprehending.

The man glanced behind him and then stepped out, almost pushing her out of the way as he did. 'Dead,' he repeated, his voice an angry hiss. 'He died when he was four years old. Now, I have no idea what the *hell* you think you're doing, coming around here upsetting people, but—'

'James,' a woman called from inside. 'Who is it?'

The man sucked in a breath. 'Just some joker,' he answered, his eyes never leaving Kaitlin's. 'She's leaving.'

'I thought I heard Gregory's name mentioned,' the woman said, coming to stand next to him. 'I was sure I heard her say ...' She trailed off as he took hold of her hand, squeezing it hard. Her eyes were full of confusion, Kaitlin noticed, as if she didn't quite know where she was, and swimming with tears. She'd opened their wounds. Unthinkingly, selfishly, she'd blundered in and ...

'I'm sorry,' she whispered, her mouth dry. 'So, *so* sorry.'

TWENTY-ONE

SALLY

Sally held her breath as she waited for their eyewitness, Andrew Taylor, to confirm the timing of what he'd seen from his apartment window.

The man thought about it. 'I honestly can't be sure,' he said at length. 'We were watching a film on Netflix, me and the missus. I must have fallen asleep, I usually do after a few beers, and she went off to bed and left me there. She gets annoyed, see, watching stuff on her own, but working on a building site is knackering, you know? Plus we have the babby now, waking at all hours.'

Sally buried a frustrated sigh and smiled understandingly. The time would have been useful. It might have substantiated that Walker was there or thereabouts. 'But you're sure it was after midnight?'

Taylor nodded. 'Well after. We sat down to watch the film at about eleven. When I woke up, the credits were rolling.'

'And you looked out of the window because?' Adam prompted him.

'No reason in particular.' Taylor shrugged. 'I heard a shout. I didn't think anything of it really. Kids often hang about down there, vaping or smoking weed, causing a general bloody nuisance. There's nothing much you can do about it, but I had a nosy anyway.'

'And?'

'I think it was a couple arguing. We do get couples down there, kissing and canoodling, you know, especially after club chucking-out time.'

Sally wrote it down. 'And you're sure it was a couple? A man and a woman?' she asked. Adam seemed to be keeping an open mind about Walker, though Sally was doing her best to get him to focus on him. She'd never been particularly close to Zoe, but overhearing what she had at the party, she wasn't very enamoured of this Walker bloke either. Kaitlin didn't need another controlling prick in her life.

'Well, one was tall, wearing trousers, the other was short and was wearing a dress,' Taylor answered. 'So, yeah, I assumed it was.'

'Right.' Adam nodded. 'And was there any intimate body language between them?'

The man raised an eyebrow.

'Did the person you assume to have been a man try to put his arm around her, that sort of thing?' he clarified.

'As in trying to get her to stop stropping off like a silly cow sort of way, you mean?' Taylor asked.

'Something like that,' Sally answered, a despairing edge to her voice despite her best efforts to remain impassive.

'No, nothing like that,' he went on, oblivious. 'He put his arm around her all right, but since it was around her neck, I doubt he was trying to pacify her or coax her to come back.'

'The shout you heard,' Adam asked, 'was it a male voice or female?'

'Female. Definitely her, I'd say. "What do you want?" she asked him. It was actually more a scream.'

'Can you take me through what happened next – in your own words?'

Taylor frowned thoughtfully. 'Well, like I said, I heard this scream, a woman shouting, "What do you want?" She sounded pretty upset, so I looked out my lounge window, trying to see what was going on. It's quite dark out there, there are no lights after the footbridge, but I could see two people on the riverbank.'

'Could you tell me more about the clothes they were wearing, how they were dressed? Could you see? Formally? Casually?'

'Not much,' Taylor answered with a shake of his head. 'The bloke, the taller figure, had his back to me. His clothes were dark, though, black jacket and trousers maybe? Could have been blue.'

'A uniform possibly?' Adam suggested, and Sally's gaze shot sideways. What was his thinking here? Hurriedly she scribbled a note – *Security guard?* – on her pad and slid it towards him. He shrugged, meaning he considered it might be. Fair enough. He was doing his no-stone-unturned thing. Walker was in the frame, though. He'd been wearing a black dinner jacket when they'd gone to Zoe's flat, and he was tall. He definitely fitted the description.

Taylor considered Adam's question. 'Might have been. It was difficult to tell. Like I said, she was wearing a dress. Couldn't tell you what colour it was. She had short hair, I think. A bit like yours.' He nodded at Sally. 'She was definitely quite small. I remember thinking she looked ... petite. Yeah, that's the word. Tiny, you know?'

Sally encouraged him with a smile.

'There was a sort of stand-off, I suppose you could say. They were facing each other, maybe a couple of yards apart. I couldn't make out much of what they were saying, but I did hear the woman yell something about the bloke wanting to keep someone to himself because he was jealous.'

'And the bloke didn't answer?' Adam checked.

'Nope, not from what I could hear. He just stood there. Then, as she turned to walk away from him, he lunged for her, wrapped his arm around her neck, had her in a headlock.' Taylor's face darkened. 'He was obviously not about to let her go anywhere.'

'And then?' Sally asked, her adrenaline pumping. Adam had to be thinking it was Walker now.

'He dragged her backward, forced her to the ground and then he, er ...' Taylor broke off, looking unsettled as he reached for his glass of water, 'he stamped on her.'

Adam jolted to attention. 'Stamped on her?' He stared at the man incredulously.

'That's what it looked like from where I was standing.' Taylor placed his cup back down, twirled it around, studied it for a second and then looked uncomfortably back at them. 'He started punching her then, repeatedly. I mean really walloping her. She was face down, and he was just laying into her, punching the back of her head, her back. I thought, he'll bloody well kill her in a minute.'

'Jesus Christ.' Adam's face drained. 'Kyle Roberts,' he muttered to Sally. 'The case that went belly-up.'

The case that had derailed his wife. Sally got the gist. 'Same MO?' she asked, her eyes flicking cautiously to Taylor, though as he was yawning his head off, she doubted he was taking much notice.

'The same,' Adam confirmed, visibly shaken.

TWENTY-TWO

KYLE ROBERTS

Six years ago

'Not pretty, is it?' Eyeing him with ill-concealed disdain, DI Joanne Saunders shoved the photographs of Melanie Ryan under his nose yet again.

Kyle felt nausea roil inside him. It definitely wasn't pretty. The woman's flesh, tinged greyish-blue, was clearly dead flesh, and her body, bloated and nibbled at, had obviously been fish bait. Face down in the water, and even with half her clothes missing, he recognised her from the ugly black rose tattoos adorning both of her shoulders. He hadn't coughed up to knowing her, not at first. Using the services of a sex worker wasn't an easy thing to admit to, especially to a woman. He'd had no choice but to, though, once the police had taken DNA swabs establishing he'd had sex with her.

'See those?' Saunders jabbed a finger at an enlarged photograph showing livid purple bruising on her upper back. 'Fist marks,' she reminded him tersely. 'Delivered forcefully. Yours, Kyle?' She paused, her expression carefully neutral.

Kyle could see the contempt in her eyes, though. He could feel it. 'No comment.' Now feeling sick to his guts, he answered as instructed by his solicitor, who was ready to interrupt should he need to.

'We have your shoe impressions, Kyle.' The detective leaned closer. 'At the point she went into the water.'

Kyle shifted uncomfortably. Still he said nothing.

'Whoever did this must have been angry. Furious, I'd say, wouldn't you?' Saunders waited.

Kyle scratched his forehead with his thumb, looked away, looked back at her. He was trying to stay calm, to not react, which would do him no favours, his solicitor had warned him. Inside, though, he was shaking. They were building a case against him. Little by little, they were stacking up the evidence. They'd taken his clothes, for Christ's sake, turned his parents' house upside down, causing his old man to go ballistic. Kyle was sporting some vicious bruising of his own as evidence of that. A trickle of sweat ran the length of his spine as he considered that whichever way he turned, he would be under physical threat. The husband was an aggressive bastard, shouting abuse every time they dragged him in. Catching him outside the station, he'd already knocked seven shades of shit out of him before the coppers hauled him away. Kyle didn't fancy his chances if he were to meet the man again any time soon in some secluded location.

'Melanie's injuries were consistent with her being punched repeatedly in the back. Also the back of her head,' DI Saunders continued, her tone subdued. 'She was stamped on, and then strangled with a ligature before being dumped in the water.'

She waited again, allowing Kyle to digest her words. He could feel every violent blow.

'Stamped on *hard*, judging by the shoe print left on her

body.' She scanned his face, a flash of something close to hatred crossing her own.

Kyle closed his eyes, then jumped as she shouted, 'We have your boots, Roberts! We found your semen in her body! We have CCTV footage of you picking her up, eyewitness statements! Why don't you just stop messing about and—'

'I didn't kill her! I *told* you!' Kyle yelled. He knew the shoe print on the body was a partial, his solicitor had told him that. Also that they hadn't been able to substantiate a definitive match to his footwear. Even so, they seemed determined to make sure he went down. He had to get out of here. He couldn't breathe. He couldn't do time. He pretended he was hard, talked the talk, but suffering his old man's violence all his life hadn't toughened him up as the bastard was fond of telling his mother it would; it had just made him shit-scared of shadows, even his own. He *couldn't* go to prison.

'Did she try to overcharge you, is that it? Taunt you in some way? Humiliate you?' Saunders softened her tone, her look now one of near-maternal understanding. *Bullshit.* 'Why don't you just tell us what happened and put her family out of their misery, hey? It will help your case if you tell us now. We can—'

'I think that's enough, Detective Inspector Saunders, don't you?' Kyle's solicitor intervened. 'As you're aware, my client is reserving his right to—'

'Why did you have sex with her?' Saunders spoke over him. 'Regularly, I mean. You'd obviously formed some kind of a relationship with her.'

Because I fuck up every normal relationship I have. Kyle folded his arms tight across his chest. He could feel his heart banging, panic spiralling so fast inside him he was sure it would choke him.

'I think a short break might be in order. My client is obviously struggling.' His solicitor smiled shortly and began to collect up his papers.

'With his conscience?' DI Saunders muttered, stopping the tape nevertheless.

'On the other hand …' Checking his phone, the solicitor paused. 'You might want to reconsider your case, DI Saunders. I've just been alerted by our forensics experts that there's nothing to specifically link particles found on Mr Ryan's clothing to the crime, rather than to environmental contamination. He's admitted having contact with her, hasn't he?'

TWENTY-THREE

ADAM DIAZ

Seeing Gregory Walker's car pull up outside Kaitlin Chalmers' house as he turned into her road, Adam pressed his foot down hard on the accelerator.

'Bloody hell, don't mind my whiplash.' Sally, who was barely awake, having slept badly, shot him a surprised glance as she braced herself against the dashboard. 'Talk about a man on a mission.'

'Sorry.' Adam glanced apologetically at her. 'I want a word with Walker before he decides he might have urgent business elsewhere.'

'I gathered.' Sally unbuckled her belt and reached for her door as Adam parked the car at an angle across the front of Walker's.

Shoving the driver's door open, he climbed out, meeting Walker as he emerged white-faced from his own vehicle. 'After-noon.' He greeted Walker with a brief smile.

Walker's expression was wary. 'Are you here to see Kaitlin?'

'No,' Sally informed him. 'It's actually you we wanted to have a word with. We wondered if you wouldn't mind having a chat down at the station.'

'If you're not too busy,' Adam added with forced politeness.

Walker's apprehensive gaze travelled between them.

'We can always come back later,' Sally suggested when he hesitated.

Nets were twitching at neighbouring windows, a front door diagonally opposite inching open, as they tended to in situations like this. There was no movement at Kaitlin's windows or door, though. Adam was relieved. He didn't want her little girl witnessing any of this. Or Kaitlin herself, come to that, not if she didn't have to.

'Is it okay if I take my own car?' Walker asked.

'No need.' Sally twirled around to open the passenger door of their car. 'You can have a nice comfy ride with us and do your bit to save the planet. Don't want all those unnecessary fuel emissions spewing into the atmosphere, do we?' She waited, smiling flatly.

'No. I suppose not.' Walker smiled back, although not very enthusiastically, and then walked towards the car.

Twenty minutes later, Adam assessed Walker's body language from the viewing room. The man was twitchy, running his hand repeatedly through his hair and over the back of his neck. Finally he leaned back in his chair, laced his hands tightly on the table, and glanced towards the camera. Was he just nervous? Or had he been here before? The latter seemed unlikely. They hadn't been able to find so much as a blemish on him on the national database.

Hoping this wasn't a waste of time, Adam sighed and headed towards the interview room, meeting Sally outside the door. 'Shall we?' he asked her.

'Let's.' She nodded. 'I've got his coffee, strong and with exactly half a teaspoon of sugar and a splash of milk, just like he asked for. Nothing but the best service here.'

Adam smiled wryly as she held the polystyrene beaker reverently before her, her pinkie finger extended genteelly.

Walker's gaze shot up as they entered the room. 'Do I need a solicitor?' he asked worriedly, half on his feet.

'No,' Adam assured him with a convivial smile. 'It's just a few questions, Mr Walker, to make absolutely sure we got your version of events in regard to Zoe Weller correct.'

Walker relaxed back into his chair, looking relieved. 'So this is definitely an informal interview then?'

'It is.' Adam offered him another small smile, his eyes sliding towards Sally's as she straightened up after setting his cup down. Sally's look said *guilty bastard if ever I saw one*. Adam just wasn't sure. They needed evidence, irrefutable evidence.

Sitting opposite Walker, he leaned back in his chair. He didn't want to be seen to be doing anything that might be deemed intimidating. He watched, interested, as Walker reached to take a sip of his coffee. His hand was shaking, he noted. 'According to what you told us,' he began, 'you didn't see Zoe on either occasion you went out after her?'

'Looking for her,' Walker corrected. He held Adam's gaze for a second, as if searching for a clue as to what this was all about, then glanced away.

'Looking for her,' Adam acknowledged. 'Yet it would appear your footprints were at the location Zoe Weller was last sighted.' He chose his words carefully. The footwear marks were similar, possibly the same brand of shoe, but they hadn't had corroboration yet of any specific characteristics that would identify them as Walker's.

'Last sighted?' Walker was definitely looking worried now.

'Did you see her, Mr Walker? Did you talk to her?'

'No. I would have told you if I had.' His tone was adamant. His eyes, though, told a different story. Adam noted the dilated pupils, the slow swallow sliding down his throat. He waited. 'Okay.' Walker heaved in a breath, blew it out slowly and looked away. 'Okay, yes, I did see her.'

Adam's insides jerked. He didn't move, not a muscle.

'But only from a distance,' Walker clarified quickly, palpable panic now in his eyes as he looked between Adam and Sally.

'Yards? Feet?' Sally scribbled on her notepad.

'I don't know. I can't say exactly.' Walker grabbed the cup. Took a large swig of coffee, swallowed hard.

Again Adam waited. He should have listened to Sally. He'd thought she was over-keen, but she'd been on to this bastard from the outset.

'I offered to help her. She's Kaitlin's best friend. I was only doing what anyone would do,' Walker went on, wiping his mouth with the back of his hand. 'She was drunk, upset. Not making much sense. She basically told me to fuck off.'

'Basically?' Sally attempted to keep her voice neutral. If she scribbled any harder, though, she'd be through the notepad onto the table.

Walker shrugged awkwardly. 'She said she didn't need any help. Like I say, she'd had a fair amount to drink. She was obviously pissed off.'

'With you?' Adam asked.

'At a guess, with all men. She's had a rough time apparently, recently split with her boyfriend.'

Adam nodded. 'And you didn't approach her?'

Walker shook his head. 'No.'

'So there was no physical contact between you?'

'No!' Walker stated categorically. 'Absolutely not. She carried on and I walked away.' Adam noted the sweat beading his forehead. The man was lying. He wasn't likely to admit he'd approached her.

'And left her on the riverbank,' Sally confirmed icily, her sympathy for the man clearly nil.

'Not there, no.' Again Walker shook his head. 'I don't know what sighting you have of her, but she wasn't on the riverbank when I left her. She was approaching the path leading to the footbridge. I thought she'd just go on across it and she'd be home safe. I *was* on the bank earlier. The first time I went out looking, I checked there, but when I saw her, I was nowhere near it.'

'And you didn't tell your fiancée any of this?' Sally enquired.

Walker eyed her levelly. 'Not in detail, no. And then when you turned up, I thought I might have been the last person to see her alive. I made a bad judgement call, I know, but under the circumstances ... I'm sorry. I just panicked, I guess.'

'Understandable.' Sally smiled congenially, but the contempt in her eyes was off the scale. 'Just one more thing, Mr Walker. Would you mind very much if we asked you to undergo a DNA test?'

TWENTY-FOUR

KAITLIN

Leaving Ruby with her mum and dad, who'd promised her a trip to McDonald's once they got back from the park, Kaitlin checked her phone, hoping against hope that Zoe might have picked up her messages. Seeing that she hadn't, she drove home, sick to the pit of her stomach with worry. She'd told her parents that Greg had lied about his job, but she couldn't bring herself to pile more worry onto their shoulders and tell them he'd possibly lied about his whole life. There were no other families by the name of Walker in Hibberton. As far as the owner of the village shop knew, there never had been. It couldn't be a mistake. Greg had quite clearly told her he'd grown up in Hibberton. She remembered commenting what a pretty village it was.

She'd tried all day to call him. He hadn't answered his phone. She had no idea whether he would be at home, or what she would say to him if he was. Would he have an explanation? She almost laughed at the absurdity of that thought. The people she'd spoken to were the parents of a little boy called Gregory Walker, who should have grown up in the tiny village. The man she knew didn't exist. If he had stolen that child's identity, there was nothing that could explain his reasons away.

Her dad had suggested she stay with them for a while, just until they knew more about what might have happened to Zoe. 'It would be good for Ruby, with things so uncertain,' he'd urged her. Kaitlin had noted the troubled look in his eyes and, pressing him about it, had learned he'd become concerned about Greg when he'd seemed evasive about his past, cutting the conversation short when Richard asked him about his family, all of which confirmed her own suspicions. Her dad didn't say as much out loud, but Kaitlin gleaned he didn't trust him. When she'd asked her mum for her opinion, she'd said she'd always liked Greg, that he was wonderful with Ruby, courteous and helpful. Kaitlin had seen a flicker of apprehension cross her face and sensed there was a 'but'. It turned out that she too had had concerns, mostly about their relationship moving so fast, but seeing how obviously in love they were, she'd been reluctant to mention it. Zoe had been wary of him. The look in her eyes hadn't been one of jealousy. She'd been scared, for Kaitlin, and now ... 'Where are you, Zoe?' she whispered.

Blinking back the tears that were perpetually threatening, she tightened her grip on the wheel and focused on the road. She had to stay in control of her emotions, for Ruby's sake, for her unborn baby's sake. For her parents' sake. She couldn't fall apart and expect them to pick up the pieces. They'd always been there for her. Even when she thought she knew better and ignored their advice, they'd been there when she needed them. She needed to be there for them too.

Pulling onto the drive minutes later, she surveyed her modest semi-detached house, the house she'd hoped to be living in with Greg as man and wife. He'd moved in at her invitation, but then hadn't she suggested it when he'd told her how dingy the properties he'd been looking at were, how extortionate the rents? It had seemed sensible for him to move in with her, but if she were honest with herself, hadn't she felt the tiniest bit compromised?

Her heart leaden, she climbed out of the car, pulled her phone from her bag and tried Zoe's number for the millionth time as she walked to the front door. It didn't ring out, a monotone voice informing the number she'd dialled wasn't in service. Kaitlin's hope dwindled painfully inside her. She'd been praying that the police might be able to locate Zoe's phone, that some miracle would occur and that they would then locate Zoe herself, perhaps back in Portugal. It had been a forlorn hope. They hadn't found the phone in her bag. There'd been no money or bank card. As they hadn't found a bank card when they'd searched her flat either, they'd assumed the items had been stolen. They hadn't said as much, but Kaitlin guessed they suspected the phone might have been thrown in the river.

Imagining it sinking into the muddy depths, her photos and memories erased, the light fading from the screen as surely as the light that had always danced in her eyes, Kaitlin felt a wave of grief crash so ferociously through her, it forced the air from her body.

Trembling, she paused on the doorstep and drew in a tremulous breath. It seemed to stop short of her chest. Zoe wasn't dead. She *couldn't* be. A sharp sob escaped her. That was what her instinct was screaming at her. Yet everything was pointing to the opposite. What had been Greg's involvement? What else had he lied about?

Pushing through the front door, she selected his number, calling him as she turned to close the door, then almost leapt out of her skin as his phone rang directly behind her.

'Greg?' Fear coursing through her, something she'd never imagined she would feel in his company, she whirled around to face him as he stepped from the kitchen. 'Where were you? I've been trying to call you. I ...' With no idea what to say to him, she trailed stumblingly off.

'At the police station,' he replied.

'Why?' She scanned his face. His eyes were full of anguish.

'They just wanted to ask me a few more questions about Zoe. Make sure they'd got their facts right. I answered them as best I could.' He glanced down, taking a breath and rubbing the thumb of one hand against the palm of the other.

Staying where she was, close to the door, Kaitlin waited, a thousand questions crowding her head.

'There are some things we need to talk about, Kait,' he said after an agonisingly long pause. 'Things I should have told you. Before I do, though, I need you to know that I love you, that I'm here for you. I'll always be here. Even if things were to fall apart between us, I would always look out for you. You know that, right?'

Kaitlin squinted at him. But I don't know *you*, she wanted to scream.

'Kait? Say something.' He moved towards her and she stepped instinctively back.

He smiled, a sad, almost fatalistic smile. 'I have to talk to you, Kait,' he said. 'Will you hear me out?'

Kaitlin's heart thudded. Was he about to tell her? It was something big. It had to be if he didn't think she would want to hear it. His expression was apprehensive. His eyes dark and uncertain. 'Is it something to do with Zoe?' She held his gaze.

He sighed and ran a hand through his hair. 'No. I don't know where she is, Kait. If I knew anything at all, I would tell you. Please trust me.' He took another step towards her.

He wasn't going to tell her, not the truth anyway. He was just going to keep right on lying. 'I have to go.' Kaitlin backed away.

'Go where?' Greg looked alarmed. 'Where's Ruby?'

'At Mum and Dad's. I need to be there for a while.'

'But why? That makes no sense.' He raised his eyebrows

quizzically. 'I've just told you I'm here for you. I realise you're distraught, but—'

'My best friend is *missing*,' Kaitlin cried. 'She was part of my family. I have to be there for—'

'*I'm* your friend,' Greg said over her, a desperate edge to his voice. 'For Christ's sake, Kaitlin, *we're* family. Please don't leave. We need to sit down and talk ... Kait? What's wrong?'

A sharp pain had shot through her abdomen, causing her to clutch for the wall behind her. She held her breath, waited for it to pass. 'It's nothing. Indigestion probably, that's all.'

'Come on.' Greg threaded an arm around her. 'Come and sit down, and I'll get you some tea.' His tone was full of concern as he guided her towards the kitchen.

Kaitlin allowed him to lead her. The pain was intense.

'You've had a massive shock,' he told her, an almost paternal scolding look in his eyes as he pulled out a chair and helped her into it. 'That can impact on you physically. You need to take care of yourself, for your own sake, as well as little Bump's. Do you want me to call a doctor?'

'No. It's fine,' Kaitlin assured him. 'It's passing now.'

'You're sure?' Greg caught her hand as she placed it protectively over her tummy, bringing it to his face and pressing a soft kiss onto the palm.

'Positive.' Kaitlin forced a smile. *Who* are *you?*

'Did I mention I love you, Kaitlin Chalmers?' he asked throatily, brushing her lips with his. She resisted the urge to push him away and run, keep running from the nightmare her life had suddenly become.

'Tea,' he said, easing back with a smile. 'Strong and sweet, for energy.'

She watched him walk across the kitchen. Putting the kettle on, taking charge of things. She'd found that comforting once, felt that she was being cared for. Now she didn't know what she felt, other than terrified and utterly bereft. 'What do you think happened to her?' she asked him, wishing he would face her so she could read the look in his eyes. But she couldn't, could she? She never had been able to.

He poured water into the mugs. 'I honestly don't know any more than you do, Kait.' He sighed heavily. 'I'm not sure it's a good idea to speculate until we know more.'

Kaitlin pushed on anyway, desperate to know what the police had asked him, about the lies he'd told. 'Do you think she was attacked?' she asked, a tremor running through her as she waited for his answer.

Turning around, Greg looked her over sympathetically. 'I don't know what to think,' he said softly. 'I do think we need to let the police do their job. We'll know more eventually.'

'But do you?' she persisted. 'She's not here. Disappeared. There can't be any other explanation, can there? She would have contacted me. I *know* she would. She's a caring person. She wouldn't leave me to worry like this.'

Greg took a long breath, turned back to fish the tea bags out and add milk. 'It's possible she was attacked,' he conceded at length. 'Although ...'

'Although what?' Kaitlin studied his face as he placed the mugs on the table.

His gaze flicked to hers, his blue eyes growing stormy as he seemed to wrestle with how much he should say. 'I might be way off the mark, but ...' he hesitated, 'I wondered whether she might have jumped.'

'What?' She stared at him, stunned. 'From *where*?'

'The bridge.' He shrugged awkwardly. 'She had been drinking,' he pointed out. 'She was broken-hearted, for obvious reasons, and ... I don't know.' He wavered as Kaitlin continued to study him, confounded. 'She seemed very volatile, to me anyway. She was definitely acting irrationally.'

Kaitlin almost laughed, something close to hysteria bubbling up inside her. 'She didn't *jump*,' she said, disbelieving. 'She *wouldn't*!'

She was positive Zoe wouldn't have done that. She'd been upset when they'd argued, traumatised by Kaitlin turning on her. She was clearly more devastated than she'd let on about her failed relationship, but she would never end her own life and that of her unborn child. *Never*. She was a positive person, always looking for the up side. *I will survive* was another one of her catchphrases. It was Zoe's positivity that had helped Kaitlin pick herself up and rebuild her life.

'She wouldn't,' she repeated, catching a ragged breath in her chest.

'Christ, Kaitlin, don't.' Greg moved quickly to place his arm around her. 'I shouldn't have said that. It was insensitive. You know her better than anyone. I'm sure they'll find her.' He gave her shoulders a squeeze. 'She's probably just gone off somewhere and doesn't want to be in contact.'

That was the hope that Kaitlin had been nurturing, that she would eventually turn up. Knowing that the police would have checked flights to Portugal, though, that Zoe's phone was missing, her hope had been fading.

'Drink your tea,' Greg said, sliding it towards her. 'You're tired, distraught. Why don't you have a lie-down and I'll collect Ruby? We need to try to get back to some sort of normality.'

Kaitlin tried to make sense of the thoughts rushing pell-mell through her head, her conflicting emotions. Surely he didn't really think she should just get back to normal, accept that Zoe had gone and pick up their routine as if nothing had happened?

TWENTY-FIVE

Having gone upstairs on the pretext of resting, as Greg had suggested, Kaitlin was collecting a few belongings together for her and Ruby when she heard the doorbell go, followed by urgent knocking on the front door. 'Who on earth ...?'

Heading for the landing, she peered over the rail. She'd left Greg in the kitchen. Why wasn't he answering?

Hurrying down as whoever it was knocked again, she pulled the front door open. Her heart leapt into her mouth as she found DI Diaz and Sally standing on her doorstep. 'Is it Zoe?' she asked, her throat so tight she could barely get the words out.

DI Diaz's look was apologetic as he produced his identification, which surprised her, since she'd already seen it. 'We're obliged to ask for permission,' he said, 'but I must advise you that we have a warrant to search the premises.'

Kaitlin looked from him to Sally, who was holding a legal-looking document. 'But why?' She scanned Sally's face. Her expression was impassive, which sent a wave of apprehension through her. She looked back to Diaz. 'Why didn't you just ask? I would have granted you access.' She studied him, puzzled. 'Is this something to do with Greg?' It had to be. 'Something to do with his shoes?'

'Is he here, Kaitlin?' Sally asked. 'If so, we'd like to talk to him.'

'In the kitchen. But haven't you already spoken to him?' Kaitlin shook her head in confusion, and then moved back as Diaz stepped in.

'We just need to clarify a few things,' he answered vaguely. 'We'd like to take a look at the clothes he was wearing on the night of the party, assuming that would be okay with Mr Walker.'

Kaitlin felt her stomach turn over. 'Why?' she asked, but she knew. 'You think he had something to do with Zoe's disappearance, don't you?'

Diaz broke eye contact, glancing past her to the kitchen. 'Could we have a word with him, do you think?'

Icy fear constricting her throat, Kaitlin stood frozen to the spot for a second. Then she jolted as there was a crash behind her.

Gulping back her racing heart, she turned to the kitchen, but Diaz was faster, sprinting along the hall, while Sally muttered, 'Shit!' and flew through the open front door.

Panic climbing her chest, Kaitlin followed Diaz through the kitchen into the back garden. He was at the gate leading to the side entrance. Dazed, Kaitlin watched him bang his hand against it in frustration as he found it locked.

'Fuck it,' he cursed quietly, turning around to scan the garden. But Greg wasn't there. There was nowhere for him to hide. The garden was still unplanted; nothing but open lawn, and a shed leaning dismantled against a side fence, waiting to be erected.

Diaz doubled back, his eyes meeting Kaitlin's briefly as he squeezed past her, in them a confusion of regret and fury.

Heading to the hall, Kaitlin following him, he stopped as Sally came back through the front door. 'Anything?' he asked her.

'No.' Blowing out a heavy breath, she shook her head. 'You?'

'Nothing. He must have scaled the gate.' Diaz's face was taut. 'I didn't think it was worth going after him, since you were already out front.'

Kaitlin's head reeled. What was happening? Had they come to arrest him?

Sighing wearily, Diaz turned back towards her. 'We need to take a look around,' he said, his eyes narrowed as if assessing her, as if imagining her guilty. Of *what*? Helping Greg to run? Her stomach lurched. Her throat closed, tears rising so fast she couldn't stop them.

'Is your daughter here?' His tone was softer, his expression concerned, which only made her want to cry harder.

Unable to trust herself to speak, she shook her head. She felt dizzy; the ground seeming to be shifting, everything spinning out of control. What had Greg done? How could she have trusted him? What had *she* done? Nausea churning hotly inside her, she pressed a hand against her forehead, feeling now distinctly woozy.

'Would you like to sit down?' she heard Diaz ask, as another sharp pain ripped through her, causing her to wince. 'Ms Chalmers?' His voice reached her as if through a tunnel. '*Shit!* Sally, could you get some water?'

Kaitlin sensed him move towards her, felt his arms supporting her as her legs turned to butter beneath her.

Sally held the glass for her as she sat disorientated on the sofa a minute later. She had no idea how she'd got there. Presumably Diaz and Sally must have helped her. 'Slow, small sips,' Sally advised.

'Sorry,' Kaitlin murmured, taking the glass with trembling hands, her teeth clinking against the rim as she tried to drink.

'Don't be,' Sally said. 'The baby probably moved suddenly. Same thing happened to my sister. Just take your time.'

Kaitlin nodded, feeling shaken and utterly bewildered. 'Why did he run?' Her gaze went from Sally to Diaz, whose look was now one of compassion rather than suspicion. 'You think it's him, don't you? You think he ...' She clamped her hand to her mouth, attempting to suppress the sob climbing her throat. 'It's my fault. All of it. I wouldn't listen to her. She tried to tell me, and ...'

'Kaitlin.' Sally sat down next to her as she choked out another sob, pulling her into an embrace. 'It's not your fault. You mustn't blame yourself. Wouldn't Zoe be the first person to tell you not to?'

Kaitlin breathed, and nodded. Sally was right. But that didn't change the facts. If she hadn't been so ready to leap to Greg's defence, in so doing alienating her friend when she'd needed her, Zoe would still be here.

'Would you like us to call your GP?' Sally asked gently.

Kaitlin shook her head hard. 'No,' she said, heaving in another breath. 'I'll be fine. I've not been sleeping, that's all it is. Please don't worry.' She needed to think. She couldn't do that with people fussing around her. Her mind flew to Ruby. What would she tell the little girl about the man who'd become a father figure to her, a man Kaitlin had allowed into her life, a man she clearly didn't know at all?

Diplomatically, Diaz waited a moment, then, 'The clothes he was wearing, Kaitlin, do you think you could show us where they are? It would save us having to bag everything up.'

Kaitlin nodded, remembering how Greg had insisted her birthday party was a special occasion, calling for formal dress. 'His dinner jacket and his dress shirt. He ...' She faltered, her heart pelting wildly. 'The shirt ... It had blood on it.' She recalled the first time Diaz was here, the washing machine she'd heard going through the spin cycle as she'd paused in the hall. 'I think he might have washed it.'

Diaz sucked in a sharp breath. 'Bag it anyway,' he told Sally, his expression terse. 'And the suit.'

Sally nodded. 'I assume the suit's in the wardrobe?' she asked Kaitlin.

'I'll show you.' Kaitlin got shakily to her feet. She had to pull herself together. Somehow she had to function, put on a brave face for her daughter, whatever happened.

She wavered as a thought occurred. It might not be relevant. If they'd been here to arrest Greg, then it obviously wasn't, but ... 'Can I ask you something?' She glanced at Diaz. 'Are you still looking for Daniel?'

TWENTY-SIX

ZOE

Portugal: Before the party

'Go away, Daniel!' Zoe shouted, determined not to let him into her apartment. 'We have nothing to talk about.' Gulping back her tears, she flew to the bedroom adjoining the hall, yanking drawers and cupboards open and stuffing things randomly into her case.

'We have to talk about us, Zoe,' he pleaded through the door. 'For God's sake, I'm sorry. I love you. Please believe me. Please let me in.'

'There *is* no us!' Zoe yelled. 'There never was any us. It was all bullshit!' And she'd fallen for it. Convinced herself he actually did love her – common little Zoe, brought up in a care home, as if she could ever compete with a woman who, even when she was spitting and snarling and hurling obscenities, was every man's fantasy. Next to his wife, with her lithe tanned figure, full breasts and perfectly groomed blonde hair, Zoe looked like just what she was, a cheap little working girl hoping her white knight would whisk her away to a fairy-tale ending.

Ha! Great analogy, Zoe. Kaitlin would love that. Snatching up a carrier bag, she marched to the tiny bathroom, swiping contents arbitrarily into it, and then marched out again, leaving half the toiletries and cosmetics she'd paid far too much for to impress him where they'd spilled on the floor.

'I want to be with you, Zoe,' Daniel persisted. 'I can make it happen.'

'I don't want you to make it happen! You're a liar, Daniel, and a cheat!'

'I didn't mean to lie to you. I didn't want to. I—'

'Just wanted a quick shag. Got that, Danny. Loud and clear.'

'No!' he protested. 'It was never that. We have something special, Zoe. You must know we—'

'Do you think if I wanted you I couldn't make it happen?' Zoe's voice rose. She didn't care. Let everyone hear. She'd already been humiliated more than she'd thought possible. She'd lost her job, her hopes, her dreams, and still he had the nerve to stand there and apologise, as if that could undo what he'd done. 'I'm pregnant!' she cried, spilling the secret she'd planned to surprise him with, news she'd been sure he would be delighted with. 'I'm carrying your baby! Do you think if I shared that with your wife, she wouldn't throw you out in an instant?'

Daniel said nothing. Wiping the tears from her face, Zoe laughed scornfully. Where was the 'I love you, I want to be with you' now? Bastard. Did he really think she would want to be with a man who would cheat on his wife, break his children's hearts?

'Perhaps I'll tell her anyway,' she said, composing her voice to something less than hysterical. 'You'd have a hard time explaining that away, since it was a "one-off" with some insignificant little trollop.' She swallowed hard. Held her breath to stop the damn tears. 'You forgot to pay me, by the way.'

Still Daniel was quiet. Probably contemplating his fate if she did tell, imagining the luxurious lifestyle funded by his wife snatched away. What would he do then? Zoe doubted very much that moving into her one-bed apartment in the grey UK would appeal.

'Don't do that, Zoe. It would destroy me, but not for the reasons you might be thinking. Please don't do anything rash. We can work something out, can't we?'

And there it was. He was offering to pay her after all. Maybe she should pursue that. Keep his child in the manner to which Zoe would very much like it to 'become accustomed'.

'Piss off, Daniel,' she said, sounding braver than she felt, wishing fervently that Kaitlin was here – the only person who knew her well enough to know that the one thing Zoe wanted above all else was simply to be loved. She wasn't a gold-digger. She didn't want a man who'd clearly never cherished her, never loved her, never known what was in her heart. 'Just go away and leave me alone, will you?'

TWENTY-SEVEN

DANIEL

'Can you put another one in there?' Daniel signalled to the barman, pushing his glass towards him and nodding towards the whisky behind the hotel bar.

The barman arched an eyebrow. 'You sure?' he asked him. 'You're notching up quite a hefty bill.'

Daniel guessed he was. The man probably thought he had a drink problem. 'I can afford it,' he assured him with a wry smile. Rather, his wife could, the woman who'd wasted no time running off to her solicitor father after the violent argument they'd had about his 'pathetic sexual perversions', which most of Portugal must have overheard. No doubt Daddy would have wasted no time either, making sure the prenuptial agreement Daniel had reluctantly signed was watertight.

Jessica had had him exactly where she'd wanted him way before his property company had gone under, and she knew it. He'd hoped to get her to inject more funds into the monthly account she'd set up for him, which he figured she owed him. It had been her who'd been the driving force behind the scheme to sell properties off plan. She'd encouraged him every step of the way. Her bloody father, too, who'd insisted he use the building company he'd recommended – the owner was one of his golfing buddies – which had gone spectacularly bust, leaving Daniel with half-built villas he couldn't sell on. He'd been an idiot, going into a venture with Jessica that would allow her a share of the profits but leave her with none of the debt. That was all his. He'd been stuffed. No choice but to live in fear of being found out if he tried to leave her. He didn't love her. She'd killed any love there might have been. How did a man love a woman who constantly reminded him that without her, he would be nothing? Her father was fond of reminding him that he'd used his considerable wealth to tempt another one of his golfing friends to wipe his slate clean for him so he could make a fresh start. As long as it was with Jessica, that was. Jessica always got what she wanted.

He had loved Zoe, who was everything Jessica wasn't, natural and honest. She didn't have much to call her own, he'd sussed that out immediately, therefore she had no airs and graces. She'd had no agenda either, or so he'd thought. She seemed to like just being with him, preferring long walks on the beach and eating at beach huts rather than fancy restaurants.

He'd been stunned when she'd told him she was pregnant. Shocked when she'd hinted she would tell Jessica. He'd had no way to explain why his life would be destroyed if she did that. He doubted very much that she would want anything to do with him then. But she didn't want him, did she? In her eyes, he was the biggest bastard that ever walked the earth. She was right. That was exactly what he was. Pathetic, too weak to take the risk that Jessica's father would find a way to leak information about him if he walked away from his daughter.

Zoe would never have come near him if she knew his history. He had no idea why he'd followed her to the UK, practically stalking her. He'd watched her walking through the town centre, shopping for the cute blue dress she'd worn to the party he'd said he would accompany her to. Even looking heart-wrenchingly sad – nothing like the woman he knew, whose bubbly laugh was infectious – she'd turned heads. He'd watched her, his gut churning at the thought that she might meet someone at the party. He'd hoped to convince her of how he felt about her, persuade her to at least see him occasionally. She hadn't wanted to listen. She'd been scared, yet all he'd wanted to do was hold her, talk to her.

Jesus Christ, what had he done? He felt regret crash through him to the depths of his soul. Petite and delicate-featured, Zoe had seemed so fragile, so vulnerable when he'd first met her. He'd sworn he wouldn't hurt her, all the while knowing that he inevitably would, and now ...

Sick to the pit of his stomach, he planted the glass on the bar, wiped a hand over his face and headed for the lift. Weaving along the corridor to his room, he paused at the door to grope his key card from his pocket. Dropped it, inevitably. Bending to retrieve it, he almost keeled over as the door swung open from the inside.

She was here! How?

TWENTY-EIGHT

JESSICA

'You haven't called me, Daniel.' Stepping back, Jessica folded her arms across her breasts and eyed him coolly. 'I was concerned about you, as naturally a wife would be.'

'How did you know ...?' Daniel shook his head, clearly confused. He'd told her he was seeing an old business acquaintance in London. He was no doubt wondering how she knew where his slut lived.

She smiled knowingly as he stared at her, confounded. 'You're using your credit card, Dan,' she informed him, arching her eyebrows in wry amusement. 'It didn't take me long to find out where. If you're wondering how I got into your room,' she went on as Daniel closed the door behind him and attempted to collect himself, 'the young man on the bar was quite helpful once I'd shown him some identification and pointed out that it was a joint account. You did remember there's a cap on the amount you can spend on it, didn't you?'

'Yes.' Eyeing her coldly, Daniel headed past her to the mini-bar. 'Since you're so fond of reminding me, I'm not likely to forget, am I?' Extracting two miniature whiskies, he grabbed a tumbler from the tray on top of the fridge and turned to look at her scathingly.

'You've been drinking,' she observed flatly.

'Correct.' He unscrewed one bottle, sloshed the contents into the glass, and then topped it up with the contents of the second.

'It might be a good idea to stop,' she suggested, strolling over to the window to glance out at the view. 'You might need a clear head,' she added, turning back to run an unimpressed gaze over him.

Clearly uncertain what she meant, he studied her, compounding her humiliation as he ran his eyes over her. No doubt he was comparing her to his precious little Zoe, who'd been everything Jessica wasn't: pretty and petite, natural. Jessica could never be considered petite, though she dieted constantly. Next to Zoe Weller, she'd felt gangly and ungainly. Nothing she did made him look at her with love or affection in his eyes. The breast implants, endless visits to the salon, where her blonde hair was sleeked to perfection, gruelling workouts with her personal trainer – none of it made any difference to how he viewed her, with indifference. He would never have looked at Zoe Weller that way.

'You've spoken to her then?' she asked him.

Daniel's gaze faltered. He looked shocked for an instant, as he no doubt gathered she'd been keeping tabs on him, then looked away.

Jessica walked across to him. 'There's no point denying it, my love,' she purred, cupping a hand softly over his cheek. 'I know you did.'

'Christ,' Daniel grated, pulling away from her and taking another large slug of his whisky.

'You didn't think I wouldn't know where you were before you even stepped off the plane, did you, darling?' Jessica blinked languorously. 'I *always* know, Daniel. I have you followed.

Surely you must realise that by now?' She held his gaze as his eyes came back to hers, his look one of pure contempt.

'Tacky little dress she was wearing.' Swallowing her hurt, she turned abruptly. 'I quite liked the colour, but a ruched minidress? I mean, really.' She paused to pluck a grape from the bowl in the middle of the table before turning back to him. 'I imagined you choosing someone with a little more taste.'

Daniel took a second to assimilate. He looked like he'd been hit by an express train when the penny finally dropped. 'You were there?' he asked, his face visibly draining.

'I think your business here is finished now, darling. Don't you?' She smiled enigmatically, popped the grape between her teeth and bit down hard on it.

Closing his eyes, Daniel said nothing.

Jessica felt a degree of satisfaction mingled with deep regret as he turned and walked defeatedly away. 'Don't be long,' she called after him as he headed to the bathroom, closing the door quietly behind him.

Hearing the shower running, she picked up the TV remote and settled down to wait. She would be here for him. She would help him pick up the pieces. She always had.

'It looks like your little slut has made the regional news.' She nodded at the TV as Daniel emerged, having attempted to sober himself up. A photograph of Zoe Weller stared back at them. *Worcestershire woman reported missing* read the ticker across the bottom of the screen. At least she'd got her fifteen minutes of fame, Jessica supposed. She actually felt sorry for her for a fleeting moment, until she reminded herself that she'd had her claws into her husband.

'Jesus.' Daniel reeled on his feet, shocked to the core, quite obviously, and then dropped heavily down on the bed. Jessica allowed him a minute to collect himself and contemplate what the consequences might be if he decided he no longer wanted to be with her. They had to leave, though, and soon. Her father had travelled over with her. They would be safe at their UK property until he'd had time to organise his private plane to fly them back to Portugal.

'Did you speak to her?' Daniel asked at length, his throat hoarse with emotion.

'You need to pack,' Jessica said, avoiding his question. Clearly he was concerned about what his little tart might have told her.

Daniel didn't argue, nodding instead and pulling himself shakily to his feet to retrieve his clothes from the wardrobe. His hands were shaking, Jessica noticed, watching him stuff clothes into his bag. Not quite the relaxed, confident image he'd presented to Zoe Weller, who must have imagined he was the answer to her dreams. She'd obviously been in love with him. Would she have fallen so easily, though, if he'd been honest with her, told her about his past, the fact that he was married, a father to two children whose hearts he would break? But then that wouldn't have mattered to someone determined to improve her status.

'Lost something?' she asked him as he glanced around the room, a puzzled look on his face. She resisted the urge to remind him what he could lose if he didn't stay where he belonged, with his wife and children. She would rather have him with her because he wanted to be, because he loved her, but she wasn't fooling herself. The thing was, she would have him at any cost. It meant little to him, but she could never stop loving him.

When she'd first met him – hopelessly attracted as she'd watched him working on the extension to her father's property in the UK – she'd fallen for him completely. She'd accepted what he'd done prior to their marriage, though it had hurt more than he could ever know. She'd accepted that he might have the odd fling. He was a good-looking man; women were drawn to him like bees to honey. Even as she'd waited for his affair with Zoe to fizzle out, she'd loved him. Their children adored him.

They were always carefree and laughing around him, because Daniel made time for them, never afraid to get messy with them playing games on the beach. Jessica was relying on that to make him see that a life with his children, with her, was better than the alternative. He really wouldn't cope trapped like an animal, having lived the high life. He liked his creature comforts too much.

'My passport.' He answered her question, his forehead creasing as he walked across to check the table, and then the desk.

'I have it. Safe and sound,' she assured him, patting her handbag. 'A little insurance,' she added, knowing that Daniel would know exactly what she was implying. Without his passport, he would be stuck here, and he really wouldn't want that, under the circumstances. 'You won't need it for our trip. You certainly won't need it where you'll end up if you decide you'd rather not come with me.' She held his gaze meaningfully. 'Will you, Daniel?'

She heard him curse under his breath as he went back to the wardrobe, and felt a mixture of sadness and sympathy. She couldn't blame him. Being a kept man was bound to undermine his masculinity. She wished he would understand, though, that she would have cut him off in an instant if she didn't care for him. That everything she did was for him.

Following him, she placed the flat of her hand on his back, tracing the firm contours of his torso beneath his shirt. Her heart sank as she felt his body tense at her touch. It was clear he couldn't bear her anywhere near him.

Breathing a deep sigh, she bent to pick up his shoes from the wardrobe floor. 'I would have thought you would have put these out to be cleaned,' she said, regarding them with a frown. 'Probably a good idea not to have done, though.' She carried them across to his case on the bed. 'We'll dispose of them when we get back. We can always get you new ones.' She glanced over her shoulder with a smile, and her heart plummeted to the depths of her stomach. Daniel's eyes as he turned towards her were filled with hatred almost, and something else: fear.

She didn't want him to feel like that. She didn't want him to hate her, to mistrust her and be afraid of her. Alas, that seemed to be her only way of keeping him. Swallowing back the tight lump of emotion in her throat, she averted her gaze and fixed her smile in place.

'I'll just check the bathroom,' she said, picking up her bag and blinking back her tears. Once there, she pulled the antidepressants she'd been prescribed from her bag. She had to stop taking them. Together with the sleeping tablets, they dulled her thinking. They didn't stop the despair, the anger and the rage that swept through her, though. Why did he insist on hurting her so much when she'd stood by him? Couldn't he see that all she wanted from him was affection? For him to realise that all the material things she was surrounded by meant nothing. That underneath the make-up, the confidence, the image she maintained, she was scared too. That she was a woman still deeply in love with the man she'd married and desperate for him to love her back.

TWENTY-NINE

KAITLIN

Opening the front door, her mum took one look at Kaitlin's face, and then gave her a firm hug and shepherded her along the hall. Once in the kitchen, she guided her to the table and made sure she sat. 'Have you eaten?' she asked, diplomatically avoiding the question she must have been burning to ask.

Kaitlin shook her head and breathed in hard. Once DI Diaz and Sally had gone, she'd sobbed until she'd retched and couldn't cry any more. What good would crying do? Tears wouldn't bring Zoe back. Wouldn't bring back the child whose name she was sure Greg had stolen.

What had Greg done? How could he have?

'When you want to talk ...' her mum said softly, wrapping an arm around her shoulders.

Kaitlin placed a hand over her mum's and squeezed hard. 'I'm okay,' she lied, striving for the strength she would need to try to keep everything normal for the sake of Ruby, who would sense her distress in an instant. For the sake of the child growing inside her. Greg's child, the man she'd thought perfect and who'd turned out to be a monster.

'I'll put the kettle on,' her mum said, nodding towards the

hall, where sounds of Ruby emerging from the lounge reached them.

Kaitlin made herself smile as she heard her calling excitedly back to her grandpa, 'Mummy's here!' The next second, she was flying through the kitchen door, her face delighted.

Kaitlin swept her up, hugging her hard and breathing in the special smell of her. 'Have you been good for Nana and Grandpa?' she asked, her voice catching.

'Uh huh.' Easing away from her, Ruby nodded adamantly. 'But Grandpa hasn't,' she added gravely. 'He's been bad, hasn't he, Nana?'

Her mum glanced over her shoulder. 'Very,' she concurred with a serious nod.

'Oh no.' Kaitlin widened her eyes in mock alarm. 'What did he do?'

Ruby's brow knitted into a frown. 'He went up the snakes as well as the ladders. That's cheating, isn't it, Mummy?'

Kaitlin couldn't help but smile at her five-year-old's earnest expression. 'I think it probably is.'

'You'll have to teach him the rules again, Ruby. I think he's getting a bit forgetful in his old age,' her mum said, coming across with tea and a slice of home-made coconut cake covered in white frosting, which she knew Kaitlin would feel bad saying no to. Kaitlin, though, was sure she wouldn't be able to swallow a morsel.

'I heard that,' her dad said, a scowl on his face as he wheeled himself into the kitchen. 'I'll have you know I'm in my prime, woman.' He smiled for Ruby's benefit, but Kaitlin could see the deep concern in his eyes as his gaze settled on her.

'Is Greg coming here to stay too, Mummy?' Ruby asked innocently – and Kaitlin felt herself reel inside.

'No, sweetheart,' she answered as casually as she could. 'He's on a work course, I'm afraid.' With no idea what she would tell her daughter in the long term, she lied, hating herself for it, hating herself more for never dreaming she might have to. *You can't really know him that well yet, can you?* Zoe's whisper was the soft brush of a butterfly's wings across her mind.

'Oh *Mummy*.' Ruby looked crestfallen. 'He was going to play Danger Mouse on CBeebies with me. He promised.'

Kaitlin's heart fractured another inch. She had no idea what to say to her.

Her mum stepped into the breach. 'How about we take a look?' she offered, gathering Ruby from Kaitlin's lap and swinging her down to her feet. 'I'm probably not the world's greatest at computer games, but I'm betting you're expert enough to teach me. What do you think?'

Ruby pressed a finger to her chin. 'Well, okay,' she decided, glancing uncertainly up at her. 'But you have to concentrate really hard and not fall asleep like Grandpa does, or you'll miss all the fun.'

'From the mouths of babes, hey, Richard?' Jayne gave him an amused glance as she headed off with a placated Ruby to the lounge.

'You do realise men's egos are fragile things?' Richard called after her.

'*Oh* yes,' Jayne called back. 'This is why we women tiptoe around them.'

'Not that you'd notice.' Richard smiled and rolled his eyes, and Kaitlin had to look away, her tears too damn close to the surface again.

'Would you like some cake, Dad?' she asked him, willing herself to keep it together as she got to her feet.

'How about I have some if you have some?' her dad bargained, nodding towards her uneaten slice.

Kaitlin paused halfway across the kitchen. Heaving in a huge breath, she held it until she felt her chest might explode.

'You might have to bend down to my level, but I'm sensing the need for a serious hug,' her dad said softly.

Kaitlin blew a breath out, and though she tried hard to suppress them, her tears escaped with it. 'Oh Dad.' She flew into his open arms. 'I'm so sorry.'

Her dad held her for a long moment. 'You have nothing to be sorry for,' he assured her, gently patting her back. 'Bad judgement isn't a sin, Kait. If it was, your mother and I would be guilty too, wouldn't we? We had reservations, but we trusted him. You have to concentrate on yourself now. Your children.'

Kaitlin knew that must have been difficult for him, to include her unborn child. She didn't think it was possible to love her dad more than she did right then. If he couldn't restore her faith in men, he would try to restore her faith in herself. He always had. Giving him a firm squeeze, she straightened up and dragged her bedraggled hair from her wet face. 'I let him into my daughter's *life*,' she whispered wretchedly.

Richard smiled sadly. 'I rest my case. We did the same, Kaitlin. There's no point reproaching yourself. It can't change anything. Let's have that cake, shall we?' He pivoted his wheelchair around and aimed it at the fridge. 'If you pass out from lack of food, I might struggle to pick you up.' It was his way of saying he was worried about her.

Kaitlin walked back to the table and picked up her bag, about to check her phone for the millionth time. As she did so, it rang. Hurriedly she dug it out of her bag and checked the caller number – and then froze.

Her dad was behind her. 'Him?' he asked, his voice terse.

Kaitlin nodded, every sinew in her body tensing as she considered whether to answer.

THIRTY

RICHARD

Richard cursed the day he'd decided to let his daughter make her own mistakes. He'd thought that being openly disapproving of her involvement with Sean Cooper would only make her more determined to continue seeing him. He'd kept it low-key instead, hoping she would realise in good time that the man was controlling, appearing to want to have her all to himself. He'd been moody about her going out on girls' nights, apparently upset if she didn't call him when she'd said she would. He commented on her appearance: her make-up, her hair, the clothes she wore. Kaitlin wasn't dressing to please him; she was dressing to not *dis*please him, and that rang alarm bells loud in Richard's head, but Kaitlin either couldn't see it or didn't want to.

When Richard had subtly pointed out that Sean seemed to be monopolising her, he'd prayed that Kaitlin would pause for thought. He should have known better. Barely out of her teens, she'd been strong-willed, insisting that she could make her own decisions. She'd accused him of being overprotective. She wasn't his little girl any more, she'd told him. Richard had realised she wouldn't understand that in his mind she would always be his little girl, that his natural inclination would always be to protect her. He'd backed off, simply because he'd thought he might lose her.

He suspected that now she had a child of her own and another on the way, she understood the primal instinct that would drive a parent to lay down their life for their child. Richard would in an instant. He'd come close to death once. The accident, which had been his own stupid fault, driving distractedly while rushing to a work appointment, had left him paralysed from the waist down but with a renewed passion for the simple things in life. He smelled the flowers more often now. It had also left him with a certain clarity. Sean Cooper had done his best to crush his girl, controlling her every move, robbing her of her confidence. Without Zoe – Richard felt his chest constrict painfully as his mind conjured up a graphic image of what might have happened to her – she would never have found the courage to leave him.

Richard bore the physical scars of his accident. For Kaitlin, the scars Sean Cooper had inflicted weren't visible. Her judgement had been impaired. Gregory Walker had appeared in her life, and on the surface he was everything Sean wasn't: attentive, considerate of her feelings, caring, both of Kaitlin and of little Ruby. Richard guessed he loved his daughter, but in his experience, love came in many guises – possessive, obsessive, unrequited – which could drive people to all sorts of madness. Walker fell into the besotted category. He seemed too eager to please, to do and be everything he thought Kaitlin might want. It was too much, in Richard's mind, but it had seemed ridiculous to point it out as a fault. Richard had had a niggling doubt, though, and again he'd trodden carefully, something he now bitterly regretted. Coming so close to death had terrified him, but not enough to make him any less determined. He would protect those he loved: Jayne, Kaitlin, Ruby, his unborn grand-child. If necessary, he would do it with his life. It was that simple.

'Would you like me to speak to him?' he asked Kaitlin as her phone rang again.

Kaitlin glanced hesitantly at him, then shook her head. 'I need to know what's going on.' She looked back to her phone. 'I need to hear it from him.'

Richard breathed in hard as she took the call. He would rather she didn't, that she would alert the police instead, but he could see from her body language that her guard was up, which reassured him a little.

'What do you want?' he heard her ask, her tone devoid of emotion, though there was a defeated edge to it that pained him.

He held up a reassuring hand as Jayne poked her head around the kitchen door and glanced worriedly in their direc-tion. Getting the gist, she nodded and returned to the lounge, closing the door behind her.

'Ruby's fine. She's here with me,' Kaitlin said. 'I'm fine too,' she went on after a pause. Then, 'What do you want, Greg?' she repeated.

Her gaze travelled to Richard as he answered, her eyes wary. 'Here?' she asked, her expression shocked. 'No, absolutely not,' she said adamantly. 'I don't want Ruby brought into any of this.'

Again she paused, and then, 'Wait,' she said.

Covering the phone, she spoke to Richard. 'He wants to talk. He's here, parked down the road.'

Now Richard was shocked – by the absolute nerve of the man. 'Do you want to talk to *him*?' he asked, as calmly as he could.

'I'm not sure.' Kaitlin seemed uncertain. 'I think I should. I need to read what's in his eyes,' she added, her free hand straying to her stomach.

'In which case, I'll be coming with you,' he said, his tone brooking no argument.

THIRTY-ONE

KAITLIN

Sick trepidation washing through her, Kaitlin watched as Greg climbed out of his car, scanning the road both ways. Clearly he was worried a police car might arrive at any minute. What had he done? Her stomach turned over. Would he tell her? Was that why he'd wanted to talk to her face to face? She clung to the hope that he might have at least enough respect for her to do that.

'Kait ...' He smiled as she and her dad reached him, looking as if he was actually relieved to see her. Kaitlin could hardly believe it. 'How are you?'

He'd already asked her that. She said nothing. He knew how she was. Then again, perhaps he didn't. Perhaps he truly thought she would recover from all of this and that their relationship was salvageable. To do the things he'd done, he must surely be out of touch with reality. That thought, and the fact that she'd been so blind to it, terrified her.

His gaze went from her to her dad. For a second, Kaitlin thought he was going to reach out to shake his hand, as he generally did. He obviously thought better of it. 'Richard.' He nodded a short greeting instead.

Her dad didn't respond. A grim expression on his face, he studied him intently.

'What do you want?' She repeated what she'd asked him on the phone. 'Why have you come here, Greg?' *Apart from to torture me? To devastate my child and my family?*

Greg looked hesitantly back at her. 'To make sure you were okay,' he answered with an awkward shrug. 'To tell you I love you. To ask you to trust me.'

Trust him? Kaitlin stared at him, uncomprehending. Why was he doing this? Did he really not realise how badly he'd hurt her, that he'd killed any scrap of trust she'd ever had in him? She needed the truth. She needed him to tell her how deep his lies ran, what despicable things he had done. Did he not realise *that*? Biting her tears back, she worked to keep her emotions in check. She would not break down. She would *not* cry or scream at him. It would achieve nothing.

'How are things at the fire investigation company?' she asked him, summoning her strength and opening the door for him. 'Rachel Johnson filled me in on your crucial role there.' *Please talk to me*, she silently begged him. Where was her friend, the part of her heart that was missing? What had he *done* to her?

Greg sucked in a breath, ran his hand through his hair, appeared not to know how to answer.

'Your parents in Hibberton,' she locked her gaze on his, 'how are *they*, Greg?' A toxic mixture of disgust and raw anger unfurled inside her. He'd stolen a four-year-old child's identity. 'You're not who you say you are, are you?'

His face filled with shame and he dropped his gaze. 'I lied to you,' he said, his voice guttural, a pleading expression in his eyes as he looked back at her. 'You obviously know I did, and I'm sorry. I'm truly sorry, Kait.' He took a step towards her. 'Please let me—'

'*Don't.*' Shooting him a warning glance, Kaitlin stepped

away from him. She couldn't have him near her. If he touched her now, she wouldn't be responsible for her actions.

'Kait, please, just listen to me. Please let me explain.' Greg tried another step.

'I wouldn't go any closer if I were you.' Her dad stopped him, his tone full of implicit meaning.

'Why?' Kaitlin choked the word out. 'Why did you lie to me? Why did you do that to those poor people? You've been living the life their *child* should have lived. They were crushed! Why would you do something so utterly despicable?'

'I had to!' Greg shot back.

'*Had* to?' Kaitlin shook her head in shocked astonishment. Did he honestly believe there was some justification for all of this?

'I had no choice,' he went on imploringly. 'If I'd realised where this would all lead, I ...' Trailing off, he glanced at the sky. 'It's complicated.' His expression was agonised as his gaze came back to her. 'I promise you I would never have lied to you if it hadn't been necessary.'

'*Necessary?*' Kaitlin stared at him, stunned.

He massaged his forehead. 'There were reasons,' he offered lamely. 'I want to explain, really I do. I will, if you'll give me the chance, but not here. I need to talk to you alone. Please give me a chance, Kait. Please don't turn your back on me.'

Now Kaitlin was dumbfounded. 'You ran from the police.' She reminded him of the all-important detail he appeared to think was inconsequential. He'd lied about everything. Who he *was*. Did he think she would just shrug, collect Ruby, and they could all go home to play happy families together? Was he a complete fantasist?

There's something not right about him. Again Zoe's warning rang loud in her head.

'I had to. I ...' He faltered, his expression desperate.

Had he run out of lies? After everything she'd suffered

herself, Kaitlin had never imagined herself being consumed with such overwhelming anger that she would want to hit someone, but she had to work to control her urge to lash out now.

He swallowed hard, glanced away and back. 'I had nothing to do with what happened to Zoe, Kaitlin. I swear I didn't,' he said, clearly aware that she thought he absolutely did. 'When the police turned up, I thought they were going to arrest me. I couldn't let that happen. There's something I haven't told you, about my past. I need to. I really need to talk to you, Kaitlin. We both need to sit down and—'

He was insane. Talking complete gibberish. 'Where *is* she?' Kaitlin screamed.

'I don't *know*!' He moved again towards her. Kaitlin moved further away. 'For Christ's sake, Kaitlin ...' He stared at her, bewildered. 'You don't honestly think I would have hurt her. That I would hurt—'

He stopped suddenly. Physically restrained by her dad, he had no choice but to.

'Back off,' Richard warned him, tightening his grip on his arm. His upper body was strong, Kaitlin knew, his muscles toned from pushing his chair and regular workouts with his weights. 'If Kaitlin wants to talk to you, she'll do it in her own time,' he went on, his tone quiet, belying his tangible fury. 'Meanwhile, since Jayne was calling the police as we left the house, I suggest now would be a good time for you to leave.'

Greg glared at him, a flash of anger in his eyes, then he wiped a hand over his face and nodded defeatedly.

'I didn't have anything to do with Zoe's disappearance,' he called shakily after her as Kaitlin turned away. 'I *didn't*, Kaitlin. But you clearly don't believe me. What's the chance anyone else would then, can you answer me that?'

Astounded, Kaitlin whirled around. 'There was blood on your shirt! You went out after her and you came back with—'

'I didn't hurt her! I didn't go anywhere *near* her! For Christ's sake, Kait, you—'

'Who *are* you?' she screamed.

'Kait, *please*.' Greg gripped his forehead. 'I can explain. I want to. I *need* to, but not here. Not ...'

Kaitlin turned away. She couldn't do this.

'Kait!'

Her heart folding up inside her, she kept walking.

THIRTY-TWO

Kaitlin couldn't sleep for the noise in her head, thoughts tumbling over each other, making no sense. Nothing made any sense. He'd stolen someone's identity. A *child's* identity. *How?*

Untangling herself from the duvet, she crept across to check on Ruby. She was sleeping, thank goodness. Sweetly dreaming and safe. She had to keep her safe. That was her priority. Careful not to disturb her, she tucked her duvet higher over her, pressed a soft kiss to her forehead and crept downstairs to her father's study.

Googling 'false identities' gave her nothing but a string of sites about how a person would create a fake identity to carry out criminal activities, whether it be on social media or in the real world. After reading about combining social security numbers with fake addresses, and credit card theft, none of which Greg could have possibly done – the identity he'd stolen was that of a *four-year-old boy*, she was none the wiser. Half of it was beyond her ability to comprehend.

Weary with fear and confusion, she buried her head in her hands. She was close to weeping. She couldn't do this. She had to tell the police what she'd found out. She should have done it immediately, but ... Had she really been hoping Greg had wanted to meet her to confess, that he would tell her the truth? The man was a pathological liar.

There must be something, she thought, frustrated. She had a whole world of information at her fingertips. There *had* to be something that would give her a clue about how and why he would have lived his whole life as someone else. Taking a breath, she had one last go, typing in: *children's names used for false identities* – and her breath caught in her throat.

With trembling fingers, she clicked through the sites that came up, including newspaper reports revealing how dead children's identities were used for activities she could never have imagined in her wildest dreams. All unbeknownst to the parents. She pictured the woman in Hibberton again, her expression a mixture of bewilderment and heartbreaking sorrow. Felt her palpable grief, the man's justifiable anger. She'd opened wounds that would never heal in her attempt to search for the truth. And now here it was, staring her in the face. Yet she couldn't believe it.

How could this be possible? Her chest constricting, her tummy twisting painfully, she browsed site after site, all telling the same story, presenting irrefutable facts, even testimony from some of the people involved. Shocked, she pushed herself away from the keyboard. She had to corroborate it. How could she? Was there likely to be anyone who could help? Sally! She had to talk to Sally.

Quickly she headed back upstairs for her phone, checking Ruby was still sleeping soundly. She hesitated as she crept back down. It was the middle of the night, but Sally was probably on duty. She would help her. She was a police officer. She would at least be able to confirm that Kaitlin wasn't going completely insane.

Pausing in the hall, desperate not to wake her parents and worry them out of their minds, she shoved her feet into her mum's wellington boots, grabbed her coat from the hook and eased the locks on the front door. The property opposite was empty and under renovation, so hopefully she wouldn't disturb anyone.

Bracing herself against the biting wind whistling mournfully through the trees, she hurried a short distance along the dimly lit road, then stopped and searched for Sally's number. Trembling now with a combination of nerves and cold, she was about to hit call when a branch snapping loudly right behind her caused her to freeze. She didn't have time to coordinate her thoughts before an arm snaked around her, pinning her arms and gripping her tight.

'I can't let you call anyone, Kaitlin,' a voice she recognised whispered close to her ear. 'Please don't scream,' he added, sending a jolt of terror right through her.

THIRTY-THREE

Kaitlin struggled, to no avail, as he dragged her backward. He was much stronger than her, powerfully built. She couldn't scream. Couldn't breathe, the hand he had clamped over her mouth making it almost impossible. *Ruby*, was all she could think. *Please don't do this to her. Please don't rob her of her mummy.* She gulped back the tears threatening to choke her as he manoeuvred her around a corner. The road here was more secluded, with absolutely no signs of life. Fear sliced through her like ice.

'Please don't try to attract attention, Kait. There's no need to be scared,' Greg said quietly. 'I'm not going to hurt you. I just want to talk to you, to explain. Please try to understand. I can't share this with anyone else. It's only you I can trust, do you see?'

Quickly, she nodded. She had to reassure him, placate him. She had to get back to her baby. Her parents.

Greg waited a beat, as if unsure, and then, mercifully, he relaxed his grip.

Kaitlin spun around. *Don't run*, she willed herself, though all her instincts screamed at her to do just that. Ruby was alone.

Her dad would die to protect her, her mum too, but they would be no match for Greg.

'I'm sorry, Kait. I had to see you on your own. I knew you wouldn't want to see me, but I had to—'

'Who *are* you, Greg?' she demanded, courage from some-where rising to the surface.

His gaze flickered down. 'Not who you think I am, clearly. My love's real, though.' He looked back at her. 'If you doubt everything else about me, never doubt that that's the truth.'

'You need to *tell* me,' Kaitlin insisted, her throat thick with fear. 'Why did you steal that little boy's identity? Is it something to do with the police? I've been doing some research. I know,' she added quickly, 'some of it. Please don't lie to me.'

Greg heaved in a breath, hesitated for a second, and then nodded defeatedly. 'I'm a copper. Undercover. That is, I was.'

Kaitlin tried to digest the information. It tallied with what she'd read, but ... 'So why did they try to arrest you? Why did you run? I don't understand.'

'I didn't have much choice.' He shrugged. 'Diaz wouldn't have known who I was. It's classified intelligence. No one on the regular force would even know I exist. I had to get out, give myself some time to think what to do. I did lie to you, and I'm more sorry for that than I've ever been in my life. You have to believe me. I can't lose you, Kait.'

Was *this* a lie? Kaitlin's head swam with confusion. However much he claimed he loved her, surely he must realise that whatever he told her, there could be no future for them now. 'How?' she asked, her voice quavering. 'The child, how did you come to take his name? To live his *life*, Greg. How did that happen? How was it condoned?'

Greg pinched the bridge of his nose and sucked in another tight breath. He seemed to be girding himself to answer her. Kaitlin had to do the same to hear it. If he was about to sully the memory of that little boy further, she couldn't help thinking he deserved to be struck down where he stood.

'I wasn't aware of it at the time, but apparently the national birth and death records are searched for suitable matches,' he provided. 'It's a way of allowing undercover officers to create aliases that check out. All legal documentation was put in place, National Insurance number, driving licence.'

'So you could work undercover?' Kaitlin eyed him narrowly.

He nodded, shamefaced. 'I'd been deep undercover for years. I was investigating organised inner-city crime, infiltrating drugs rings. The operation got bigger, more complex, and I had to immerse myself in the criminal world, become one of them in order to be believable.'

'So are you saying you're a drug user?' His behaviour had been bizarre, unforgivable, but she'd seen no evidence of drugs.

'No.' He shook his head adamantly. 'I managed to align myself with a hard drinker at first in order to get away with not snorting the coke that was offered, which is when you first came on my radar.' He stopped and looked away.

A sour taste popped in Kaitlin's throat. 'Sean?' she murmured, incredulous.

He answered with another uncomfortable nod. 'He was running errands for heroin bosses. I'm sorry, Kaitlin. I got out eventually, I had to. I couldn't live with the fact that the parents of the boy whose name I was given would still be grieving. I felt as if I was desecrating his grave. I began to fear for my sanity in the end; for my life when one major player didn't buy that I steered clear of drugs because of a medical condition. I didn't expect to fall in love with you, but I did, and ... Christ, I am *so* sorry, Kaitlin.'

Kaitlin tried to process what he'd told her. Was he trying to convince her that as a police officer, he couldn't possibly have had anything to do with her best friend's disappearance? To clear his conscience? She had no idea. No idea whether she believed any of it. 'And the fire investigator story?' she asked him.

'It was part of my cover. A way to hide in plain sight. I got carried away.' He sighed heavily. 'I wanted to impress you, I guess.'

Kaitlin studied him a second longer. Whether or not it was the truth, it was still an intricate web of cruel, heartless lies. 'Why, Greg? You must have known how much you would hurt me. What this would do to Ruby.'

'I didn't mean for it to get this far. I love Ruby, Kaitlin. She's like my own flesh and blood. I thought I could find a way ...' He stopped abruptly, his gaze shooting past her. '*Shit!* I have to go. I'll call you.'

THIRTY-FOUR

Kaitlin's blood ran cold as she saw the patrol car approaching at speed, the flashing blue light and screaming wail of the siren chilling her to the bone.

Her heart stalling, she snapped her gaze back in Greg's direction, but he was gone, racing towards the footpath that laced through the new estate backing onto her parents' house. These weren't the actions of an undercover policeman. They were the actions of a guilty man.

Her heartbeat a rat-a-tat in her chest, she watched as the car screeched to a halt, two officers spilling out and giving chase. Would they catch him? Her free hand went to her tummy as a spasm of pain gripped her. Would he lie to them? Perpetuate this torture? She pressed her hand to her mouth. Still a sob escaped her. Why was he doing this? If there was a scrap of truth in anything he'd told her, why was he running?

Fear clawing at her chest, nagging pain low in her abdomen, she walked, disorientated, back to the house. She had no idea what to think, what to feel. Her emotions seemed to be frozen solid.

Her mum pulled the front door open as she reached it, her

face pale and etched with palpable worry. Kaitlin felt a surge of guilt. What had she done, becoming involved with a man who would knowingly tear so many lives apart? He must have known the truth would come out, whatever that truth might be; that those closest to her, who had taken him into their lives, would suffer. That Ruby would suffer. Zoe ... how might she have suffered?

'Mummy,' Ruby drew her attention to where she stood at the bottom of the stairs, her cockapoo cuddle toy clutched to her chest, 'why did the policemen turn their siren on?'

'They were chasing a burglar, cupcake. That's all it was.' Jayne took hold of her hand, her gaze flicking meaningfully to Kaitlin as she did.

Seeing the anxious frown on her daughter's face, Kaitlin crouched to wrap her arms reassuringly around her. 'That's right, darling,' she whispered, her throat tight with tears she couldn't, *wouldn't*, shed in front of her. 'They were just warning people to get out of the way so they could chase him.'

The furrow in Ruby's brow deepened. 'Will they catch him?' she asked, her eyes sprinkled with uncertainty.

'I'm sure they will,' Kaitlin assured her.

'How about we go and put a film on while I make your mum a nice cup of tea?' Jayne suggested. 'I expect she could use one after all the excitement.'

Ruby's gaze drifted to Kaitlin. Still she looked uncertain.

'I bet you could use a drink too, hey?' her nana cajoled. 'How about ...'

'Chocolate milkshake?' Ruby suggested hopefully.

Jayne smiled. 'Chocolate milkshake it is,' she said. 'As soon as we've put the film on.'

Minutes later, with Ruby installed in the lounge, her mum joined Kaitlin and her dad in the kitchen. 'What on earth was that all about?' she asked her.

'Greg protesting his innocence,' Richard growled. 'Lying through his fucking teeth, I've no doubt.'

'Richard ...' Jayne stared at him, shocked. Kaitlin didn't wonder why. Her dad didn't swear. She'd heard him use the word 'damn' occasionally, but bad language was something he detested.

'Sorry.' He drew in a terse breath. 'But after hearing what Kaitlin's just told me ...'

A troubled frown forming in her brow, her mum turned to Kaitlin.

'He's been lying through his teeth, Mum,' she confirmed tearfully. 'About his job, everything.'

Her mum looked stunned. 'Did he admit it?'

'Is that supposed to make a difference?' Richard laughed in bemused astonishment. 'He fed her a complete cock-and-bull story about being an undercover policeman! The man's in fantasy land. He's running from the police, Jayne. He frightened our daughter to death out there. He quite clearly had something to do with Zoe—'

'Richard!' Jayne cut in sharply.

He drew in another breath, heaved it out slowly. 'I'm sorry, Kait. I didn't mean to be so insensitive.' He glanced at her apologetically. 'I'm just stunned by the audacity of the man.'

Kaitlin nodded, managing a small smile. 'How did they know where he was, the police?'

'We rang them. Your mum checked on you, found your bed empty, the front door unlocked ... I assume they located him via his phone signal.'

Kaitlin wrapped her arms around herself. He'd said he wasn't going to hurt her. She didn't think now that he would have. But at the time ... A shiver shook through her.

Jayne came to her, placing her arm gently around her shoulders. 'Do you believe him, Kait?' she asked. Her tone was sympathetic, but Kaitlin could see that she was desperately worried. Believing him was one thing, though. Allowing him back into her life was quite another. Her concerns here were for Zoe – deep visceral anger swirled inside her at the thought that he would have mentioned her name, having harmed her. Had he? Did she truly believe him capable of that?

I'm scared for you, Kait. Surely you can see why I would be? Her stomach twisted afresh as Zoe's voice whispered again through her mind. 'I ... don't know,' she answered her mum falteringly. She'd loved this man, trusted him implicitly. God, how naive had she been, kidding herself that lightning couldn't strike twice, that she was wise and experienced enough now to read the signs. She, above all people, should know that abuse came in many guises. That there weren't always physical bruises. Had their whole relationship been a lie?

She recalled how she'd woken the morning after their first night living together to find his arm wrapped protectively around her. The way he'd been so gentle and caring when they'd made such sweet love together. The love she was sure she could see in his eyes as he'd locked his gaze softly on hers. Was all that just a clever lie told to a woman who'd needed to hear it? The romantic wedding arrangements – arrangements that Zoe had been dubious about. Was there any truth to any of it? Had he wanted to marry her but not wanted it registered in the UK? She almost laughed at the absurdity of that notion, imagining that he did actually care for her. Given what he'd just told her, wasn't it more likely that he was simply trying to maintain his lie? He'd been hiding in plain sight with her, hadn't he? Living a normal existence as a family man. Using her. Using her innocent five-year-old daughter.

Her tummy contracted sharply, the low abdominal pain she'd felt earlier coming back with a vengeance as she realised she'd arrived at the truth. No matter what he'd said, what he'd thought, or even felt, he could never have truly loved her. Would a man who loved a woman as much as he professed to, a woman who was carrying his child, cause her so much insufferable pain?

Weary with exhaustion, she wished dearly that she could curl up in bed and stay safely cocooned there until the nightmare that was her reality went away.

'You look peaky,' her mum said, looking her over, concerned. 'Why don't you go and sit with Ruby? I'll alert you if you're needed.'

Feeling definitely wobbly, Kaitlin nodded. Ruby was an intuitive child. She would be aware that something was wrong and need reassuring. 'Thanks, Mum.' She gave her a small smile. Wanting her dad to know how grateful she was for his support too, she leaned to kiss his cheek and then headed towards the lounge.

Reaching the hall, she started as her phone alerted her to a text. And then almost jumped out of her skin as someone banged on the front door behind her. The police, it had to be.

A small shred of hope inside her that the text might be from Zoe, she quickly checked it as her mum emerged from the kitchen to answer the door. Her heart stalled as she read it, a short message, sent from an unknown number: *He's not who he says he is.* But ... she was already aware of that. Who would send this? Who would know what she knew and how to contact her?

'Kaitlin?' A familiar voice spoke behind her.

Diaz. Trying to still her frenetic heartbeat, Kaitlin turned apprehensively towards him.

'We need to have a chat,' he said, stepping in as her mum stood aside. 'I'm wondering why you wouldn't have contacted us when ...' He stopped, the suspicion in his eyes giving way to unease. 'Are you all right?' she heard him ask as another sharp stomach cramp gripped her. 'Do you need ... *Christ,* someone call an ambulance!'

THIRTY-FIVE

ADAM DIAZ

'I'm assuming you're not the father,' Amy Kelly, one of the A&E consultants, asked Adam as she came through from the cubicles.

'No.' Shaking his head, Adam gave her a small smile.

'I just wondered.' Amy glanced at him in amusement. 'You're doing an awful lot of pacing out here.'

Adam accepted the joke with good grace. He and Amy had known each other professionally for years. He was aware that humour was often a coping mechanism when the going got tough in the department. She never missed an opportunity to rib him, telling him he should get back out there, even pointing out women who were single and available and who wouldn't kick him out of bed. He would swear she was in league with his daughter sometimes. 'I was there when she doubled up,' he explained. 'I followed her in.'

'A white knight, hey?' Amy looked impressed. 'Careful, Detective Diaz, you'll have hearts fluttering all over the show. They'll be queuing up in the corridors.'

Adam very much doubted it. 'Then I'll probably disappoint them. I'm married to the job, Amy, remember?'

'Foolishly,' Amy huffed. 'Your colleagues are not going to be there to comfort you in the small hours, are they?' she pointed out. 'Unless there's something I don't know about, of course?'

'Don't hold your breath,' Adam advised her. He wouldn't know how to begin to start dating again. Definitely wouldn't know how he would cope with losing someone he loved again as much as he had his wife. He still missed her. The guilt didn't help, the argument they'd had before she'd walked out floating constantly back to haunt him. He'd accused her of being married to the job. His counsellor had suggested he might be punishing himself in picking up where she'd left off, thereby denying himself another intimate relationship. He supposed she might be right. He didn't have time to give it much thought. He made sure not to.

'How is she?' he asked. He still needed to speak with Kaitlin, but under the circumstances, he didn't think that would be very considerate.

'Devastated, as you can probably imagine,' Amy said. 'Her father's furious, adamant that it has something to do with the stress she's been under. I've assured him it isn't, that these things sometimes just happen, but to be honest, it can't have helped. She's obviously not living a healthy lifestyle right now, not eating properly, not sleeping well.'

Adam's gut twisted. He didn't know Kaitlin well, but he did know she would be distraught, as Joanne had been when she'd miscarried their second child a week into her second trimester. His heart had been broken. It had broken all over again watching Joanne's heart break. 'Do you know what might have caused it?' he asked, though he knew what the percentages were, that often the cause couldn't be identified, as had been the case with Joanne.

'A weakened cervix, I suspect,' Amy supplied. 'We'll know more once she's been to surgery. Not having much luck, is she? Poor thing.'

Adam felt his heart hitch. 'No,' he agreed tightly, his anger at Greg Walker mounting steadily. The guy had denied outright that there had been physical contact between him and Zoe Weller, but Adam would bet his life there had. He certainly hadn't been searching for her out of the goodness of his heart. He'd been looking for her to shut her up. And the reason for that was becoming abundantly clear, after hearing what Kaitlin's father had told him about the bullshit Walker had tried to feed Kaitlin. The man was older now. He'd changed his appearance somewhat, darkened his hair, bulked up his physique, but Adam was sure he was who he thought he was. Joanne would have known in an instant. He needed to get back to the station, chase up the footwear results. There was a slim chance of getting DNA from the shirt. He needed Walker in custody.

'She's tired, but well enough to have a quick word if you need to,' Amy said, her eyebrows raised in that way that said, 'Do you *really* need to?'

Adam shook his head. 'I won't disturb her. I've got all I need for now from her father. Thanks for filling me in.'

'No problem,' Amy assured him. 'And well done, Adam.'

He eyed her curiously. 'On?'

'On not getting so jaded by the job you don't give a shit about people.' Her smile was warm this time. 'It really is a shame you won't think about dating again, you know,' she couldn't resist adding. 'Such a waste.'

Adam shook his head in amusement. 'So you and Freya keep telling me.'

'You should listen to her,' Amy called after him as he turned to leave. 'Daughters always know what's best for their fathers.'

'Yep, she keeps telling me that as well.'

He was almost at the exit when he noticed Kaitlin's mother walking along the main corridor towards him with little Ruby. She'd taken her to the café presumably, judging by the ice lolly the girl was holding.

Guessing she would be pretty devastated too, Adam debated whether to make a discreet exit. But then, realising she'd seen him, he waited. 'Hi.' He smiled hesitantly as she approached. 'How are you?'

'I've been better,' she said, looking him over cautiously. Adam couldn't blame her for that. 'I hope you're not thinking of talking to Kaitlin right now, because she's really not up to it.'

'No, absolutely not,' he assured her. 'I was just, er ...' He ran a thumb over his forehead, wondering why he had hung around exactly.

'Are you here to arrest my mummy?' the little girl asked, her eyes wide over her lolly.

'No, I'm not here to arrest her,' he assured her with a warm smile. 'I just wanted to make sure she was okay before I left.'

Ruby dropped her gaze. 'She's sad,' she said, her voice small.

Adam swallowed a lump in his throat. There was nothing he could say that would convince her otherwise. Kids were astute. 'She'll be needing some cuddles then,' he said, as he crouched down to her level. 'I know I did when I was sad. My daughter sensed that and gave me lots of cuddles. And I realised that giving her cuddles back made me feel better. Do you think that might be a good plan to help your mummy?'

She thought about it, a small V forming in her brow. 'Uh huh,' she said after a second. 'She's a bit poorly, though.'

'In which case, they'll have to be gentle cuddles,' he advised. 'You'd better finish your ice lolly first, though, or you'll be dripping it all over her.'

'Oops.' The little girl followed his gaze down to her lolly, then hastily licked up the drips.

'She's good at gentle cuddles, aren't you, Ruby?' Kaitlin's mother said, smiling down at her, then scrutinising Adam carefully as he straightened up.

'Yes.' The little girl nodded earnestly. 'I can just lie next to

her and put my arm around her and kiss her cheek. Like this.'
She pursed her lips.

'Definitely sounds like a plan,' Adam said throatily. 'I'd better get back to the station,' he added, looking back at the woman, who was still studying him curiously.

'I didn't catch your name,' she said.

'Adam. Adam Diaz.' He extended his hand.

The woman hesitated briefly and then reached to shake it. 'Jayne,' she said, offering him a small smile. 'Thank you, Adam, for caring enough about my daughter not to barge in and start bombarding her with questions.'

'It wasn't necessary,' Adam assured her with an awkward shrug. It would be at some point, but not today. 'Please pass on my regards to her.'

'I'll make sure to.' Jayne eyed him thoughtfully for a second longer. 'Do you have a card?' she asked him. 'Should Kaitlin feel she needs to talk to you, it might be handy.'

Adam shook his head at his lack of foresight and groped in his pocket. Finding a card, he hesitated before handing it to her, then took out his pen. 'I'll put my personal number on the back,' he said, scribbling it down. 'Tell her she can call any time, night or day.'

'I'll pass it on.' Jayne smiled and glanced down to her grand-daughter, giving her small hand a squeeze. 'We'd better get back, Ruby, and put your cuddle plan into action.'

Ruby smiled happily up at her. 'It's a good plan, isn't it, Nana?'

'An excellent one,' Jayne assured her. 'Say goodbye to the nice policeman,' she added, looking back at Adam. There was still immense pain in her eyes, but her smile was more relaxed.

'Bye.' Ruby gave him a small wave as the two turned to go.

'Bye, Ruby.'

Adam watched as they headed towards A&E, Jayne chatting reassuringly to Ruby. She seemed nice; a little wary maybe, but definitely not hostile, which surprised him, given the unfortunate timing of his arrival at her house. He was pleased that she didn't appear to hate him. He hoped her daughter didn't either, because even more surprisingly, he found he did care, very much.

Heading for the car park, trying to figure out what was going on with his hitherto dormant feelings, he pulled his phone from his pocket, wanting to check in with Sally.

'Anything on Walker yet?' he asked when she picked up, though he wasn't holding out much hope.

'I think we may have a sighting,' Sally answered quickly. 'I'll have to get back to you.'

THIRTY-SIX

GREG

He was being followed. He could sense the woman behind him, though he'd only caught the odd glimpse of her. She was maintaining a safe distance, ducking out of sight whenever he glanced behind him. What he didn't get was *why* she was following him. If it was Diaz's sidekick – and Greg couldn't be sure it was – then why wasn't she calling for backup?

Perhaps she already had and was keeping tabs on him until they arrived. Expecting a patrol car to pull up at any moment, officers spilling out to wrestle him to the ground, he hurried on through the city centre, making sure he was in the thick of the crowd until he reached the indoor shopping mall, where he had more chance of hiding. He couldn't get caught. They were obviously intending to charge him. They would look into his past, dig up the whole ugly can of worms that he had tried so hard to keep buried. He couldn't allow that, for his past to creep back, though it inevitably did, haunting him in the dark, lonely hours.

His worst nightmare was the most enduring, jerking him awake at night, cold sweat pooling in the hollow of his neck and soaking the sheets beneath him. No matter how many times he silently intoned the word 'stop', as the counsellor he'd talked to had advised him, it never did. He still saw her, his mother, the woman who was supposed to care for him, to nurture and protect him, her eyes barely focused as she stumbled through the front door, some random bloke stinking of booze and fags in tow. Her mind had been focused though, focused on the fix fucking the man would afford her. She never even considered Greg, her own kid, cowering behind whatever piece of furniture they had left that might hide him. He'd vomited, often, at the thought of one of those 'customers', as she liked to call them, coming anywhere near him again. She'd never cared for him. She'd hated him. She'd made that plain enough.

Zoe Weller had also clearly hated him on sight. Frankly, he hadn't thought much of her either, the way she'd tried to turn Kaitlin against him. What was it with women that they felt obliged to point-score their friends' boyfriends, and rubbish men in general? As if women were perfect. Greg scoffed cynically at that thought. Kaitlin, though, she was different. At least he'd thought she was. At first he'd thought she wouldn't listen to this know-it-all Zoe, who'd turned up after God knows how long – what kind of friend was that? – to impart her invaluable opinions. She had been influenced though. She couldn't fail to have been when her so-called friend kept forcing the point home that he wasn't what he seemed. *Why doesn't he have any friends here? There's something not right about him*, she'd banged on like some prophet of doom. It had planted seeds of doubt in Kaitlin's mind, which was exactly what Zoe had intended, jealous cow. He had seen a flicker of uncertainty in her eyes right there in the hotel foyer. He hadn't wanted to acknowledge it, but it had been clear to him then where her loyalties would lie if push came to shove. He'd hoped they were strong enough together to get past it. He'd been ready to forgive her, because he truly did love her. He could still forgive her, if only she would listen to him instead of everyone around her, realise how much he cared for her.

The counsellor had suggested he try to forgive his parents. Not the kind of forgiveness that excused the trauma they'd caused him, she was quick to clarify, but the kind that accepted they were doing the best they could with what they had. They weren't. They didn't even try. Ironically, it had been his attempts to talk to them, when his delightful mother had told him he'd ruined *her* life, that had finally made him realise that there was only one way to exorcise his ghosts. He'd figured they couldn't haunt him if they didn't exist.

He'd been wrong. The dead just wouldn't stay buried.

He'd tried desperately to put it behind him, move on with Kaitlin. And then along had come Zoe bloody Weller, someone too selfish to see what all of this would do to her friend, to spoil things for him.

Glancing over his shoulder, his heartbeat ratcheted up as he caught another glimpse of the woman behind him. Imagining for a horrific fleeting second that it was actually her, he skirted around a mother crouching to placate a wailing toddler, apologised for almost knocking her over, and took the escalator that would lead him to the upper floor.

He tried to steady his breathing, taking long breaths in, exhaling slowly, attempting to oust the images his mind constantly conjured up – out of a sense of grief or misplaced guilt, the counsellor had told him. He shouldn't be carrying guilt for abuse he'd suffered, she'd tried to reinforce that in him. Greg was never sure, though, whether he should be carrying guilt over the positive action he'd taken to end the suffering. He'd felt powerful the last time he'd had any dialogue with his mother, in control for the first time ever. He'd made up his mind as he'd sifted through the embers of his childhood, the charred remnants of his former life, that he would never be a victim again, never allow anything to impact on his welfare or that of the people he loved and wanted to spend the rest of his life with. Kaitlin was his life, his future. He needed to explain all this to her. She knew him. She loved him. Yes, he'd seen doubt in her eyes, but he couldn't blame her for that. It was her friend who was to blame. He'd seen fear there too when he'd told her why he'd had to lie to her. The same fear he felt, that fate was conspiring to destroy them. If the police hadn't turned up when they had, forcing him to run again, she would have come with him.

He had to find a way to talk to her, make her understand why he'd had to run. Finally seeming to have lost the mad bitch who was following him, he focused his mind on how he could achieve that. Readying himself to step off the escalator on the top floor, he barely had time to blink before someone slammed violently into him, sending him sprawling.

THIRTY-SEVEN

SALLY

'Where the bloody hell is it?' Adam muttered, searching again for the Kyle Roberts case. Fruitlessly, Sally gathered. 'There's nothing here.' He stared at his computer in disbelief. 'Not a trace.'

'Maybe it got accidentally deleted?' Sally knitted her brow as she peered over his shoulder. 'Or else someone applied to have it deleted?'

'Fuck it!' Adam banged a hand against his keyboard and then grabbed up his phone. 'Dave,' he spoke to one of the officers out front, 'could you check something out for me? Kyle Roberts, a case going back a while, a murder charge. Could you find out what happened to his records? There appears to be sod all on the DNA database, the national fingerprint database or the Police National Computer.'

'So what do we do now?' Sally asked as Adam threw down his phone and blew out a considerable sigh of frustration.

'Christ knows.' He yanked himself to his feet. Sally guessed why he would be pissed off. Without even a fingerprint or a DNA match between Roberts and Walker, they hadn't got a fat lot. 'Chase forensics, I guess. At least find out whether the blood on the bag belongs to Zoe Weller.'

'I'll do it,' Sally offered. 'Why don't you grab yourself a coffee? You look as if you could use one.'

'Cheers.' Shaking his head, Adam headed for the door, sighing heavily again as he went.

A minute later, Sally had the forensic expert on the phone. 'Hey, Carmen. How's it going?'

'Slowly,' Carmen answered, as Sally had guessed she might. There was never a time when forensics didn't have their work cut out. 'I have news, though,' she added brightly. 'We have a DNA match on the bag from the sample provided by the toothbrush. The results still have to be quality-tested, but it looks like it's Zoe Weller's.'

'Brilliant. Thanks, Carmen,' Sally said, pleased on at least one front. This established that harm had come to Zoe. What they really needed, though, was something to tie Walker in. She was hoping the footwear would at least be a start.

'It's Zoe's,' she said as Adam came back with coffee, a strong black one for her. She needed it. She hadn't slept a wink since the night Zoe had gone missing.

'Anything on the footwear marks?' she asked him, accepting the cup gratefully.

'Nothing helpful.' Adam dragged a hand tiredly over his neck. 'They're a similar pattern to Walker's, could well be his, but there's no way to substantiate that without identifiers, which according to the footwear analyst we don't have. None that match his, anyway.'

Which definitely meant they had nothing. That was a blow. A positive result on the footwear would at least have established he was definitely there.

She was about to suggest surveillance of Kaitlin's parents' house, in case he turned up there again, when PC Michelle Simons tapped on the door. 'Sorry to interrupt.

We found the phone,' she announced, looking a bit breathless.

It took Sally a second to catch up. 'Zoe Weller's phone?' she asked, her heart missing a beat.

'One and the same,' Michelle confirmed. 'Found by a boater letting his dog off to pee. It had been caught up in rubbish washed up on the bank.'

'Christ.' Adam shot Sally an incredulous glance. They'd been searching the river, inch by painstaking inch, but clearly he'd never imagined that the phone would be found intact. Nor had Sally. 'Get it over to digital forensics. It might give us the story leading up to her disappearance.'

'Done,' Michelle said with a competent nod. 'They put a rush on it. No fingerprints, unfortunately. It was locked, so they ran it through the software. Apparently it does give us a story, but possibly not the one we were thinking it might.'

'Go on,' Adam said, a wary look in his eyes.

'There are texts back and forth indicating some friction between her and a male friend. A boyfriend, it looks like. The software didn't pull up the sender's name, so they can't map it, unfortunately, but it appears they'd split up. He'd been bombarding her with texts and calls and she was basically telling him to piss off. They're still working on the data, but it looks like he was playing away from home.'

'He's married?' Adam asked.

Michelle nodded. 'With kids.'

'Shit,' Adam muttered, moving towards his desk. 'We should have been on this.'

'You reckon this Daniel bloke's in the frame then?' Sally asked, vacating his seat.

'Definitely.' Adam parked his coffee and grabbed his phone.

'Oh, right.' Sally nodded.

Adam glanced curiously up at her. 'You look disappointed.'

'No,' Sally said quickly. 'It's not that. We need to find the bastard who attacked Zoe, whoever it is. It's just this Walker bloke isn't someone Kaitlin needs in her life, is he?'

A frown crossed Adam's face. 'Did you chase up the flight information?' he asked her.

'Crap, no.' Feeling hot suddenly in the confines of the office, Sally twirled around to the door. 'On it now.'

THIRTY-EIGHT

KAITLIN

'Come on, cupcake. How about I give you a ride to the exit and we can keep an eye out for the taxi?' Richard tried to entice Ruby down from the bed, where she'd insisted on giving Kaitlin cuddles, persuaded to by Detective Diaz, according to her mum, who'd told Ruby that that was the best medicine for her.

He'd been right. With nothing but cold hollowness in her heart, and in her tummy where her boisterous little baby should be, Ruby's cuddles had lifted Kaitlin from the depths of despair. Depression had been threatening to weigh her down like a cloying grey blanket when her precious little girl had reminded her of all she had to keep fighting for. The love in Ruby's eyes, the fear where once they were crystal clear with the innocence of childhood, forced her to concentrate on those she loved dearly and who loved her unquestioningly back. She needed to get well, get strong, protect her little girl.

She should have protected her baby. Paid more attention to him. She'd thought he was strong, her little boxer. He had been. It had been her body that had let him down, that had failed to keep him safe, ignoring the signs that should have alerted her to him struggling. He'd been tiny – she could have cradled him easily in the palm of one hand – but perfect. How many months pregnant was Zoe? The heartbreaking thought went through her mind again. How tiny was her baby?

'But I want to stay here with Mummy,' Ruby protested petulantly. She was clingy, quite obviously with good reason, but still she was trying to be gentle, her small arm resting lightly across Kaitlin's body in case she hurt her.

Kaitlin stroked her hair. She would tell her. In good time, she would explain that her baby brother had gone to heaven and was nestled safe in an angel's wing. She silently prayed that that was true. But she wouldn't tell her yet; not now, when she couldn't trust her own emotions, when Ruby might be too young and too confused to process all that had happened. Too bruised, as Kaitlin was herself.

'Well, if you insist.' Richard sighed melodramatically. 'I'll just have to ring and cancel the cupcakes I ordered.'

Ruby raised her head, her interest definitely piqued. 'Heavenly Melting Chocolate?' she asked, her expression hopeful.

'Is there any other kind?' Richard said with a conspiratorial wink. 'I thought we could scoff them while we get to grips with those pesky snakes on the snakes and ladders board. But whatever you do,' he lowered his voice and cupped a hand to the side of his mouth, 'don't tell Nana or Mummy, or everyone will want some.'

Ruby eased herself up. 'Silly,' she said with a roll of her eyes. 'They can hear you, can't you, Mummy?'

'I certainly can.' Kaitlin played along. 'Make sure you save one for me.'

Ruby nodded, her expression uncertain. 'Are you coming home soon?' she asked, clearly needing to have some sort of order back in her life.

'I am,' Kaitlin assured her, reaching to brush a copper curl from her cheek. 'I'm just waiting for the doctor to say it's okay, and then Nana and I will be on our way. Promise.'

'Good.' Ruby's eyes flooded with relief. 'Because Cocklepoo missed you last night. I think he was crying, but only a little bit,' she went on innocently.

'Then I'll make sure to give him an extra big cuddle when I get back,' Kaitlin promised, her voice strained as she hugged Ruby firmly to her so she wouldn't see the tear that squeezed from her eye. 'Go on, off you go.' She made sure to smile as she eased away from her. 'You don't want to find the shop shut when you get there, do you?'

'No.' Ruby shook her head. 'But I'm worried, Mummy.'

Kaitlin's breath caught in her chest. 'What about, sweetheart?' she gently urged her. But she knew. How could she not be worrying when her world had been turned upside down?

'I'm worried you'll be lonely.' Ruby searched her eyes, her own full of anxiety, and Kaitlin's heart swelled with love for her. She was a beautiful child, inside and out. This morning she hadn't thought she had any blessings to count, but she knew that she did. She had her little girl, her parents – perhaps more than most people.

'Nana will be here with me, sweetheart,' she assured her, glancing in her mum's direction. 'I'll miss you. I miss you every second I'm not with you, but I won't be lonely. Cross my heart.'

'Okay.' Ruby accepted that with a small nod, but still she looked troubled.

'Come on, angel,' Jayne said, lifting her from the bed and into Richard's arms, ready for her chariot ride along the corridor. 'The taxi will be here soon.'

'Say goodbye to Mummy. And hold on tight,' Richard instructed, smiling reassuringly. Kaitlin could see the pain in his eyes, though. The palpable grief, shot through with anger. The latter an emotion she'd rarely seen in her father.

'Bye, Mummy.' Ruby waved sadly.

'Bye, precious girl.' Kaitlin had to force her smile. 'Make

sure Grandpa doesn't scoff all the cupcakes,' she called after them, as her dad wheeled them through the door.

'And if he sneaks up those snakes, you tell him he'll have me to answer to,' her mum added.

The tears came seconds after they'd gone, pent-up tears of hurt, grief and confusion, plopping fatly down Kaitlin's cheeks. Her mum was there in an instant, circling her arms around her and pulling her close.

Kaitlin stayed there for a second, relishing the comfort of her warm embrace, feeling grateful that she had her there to offer the comfort only a mother could. Zoe had had no one. No one but the person she'd thought was her best friend, and she'd turned her back on her, said some unutterably cruel things. All in defence of a man who'd cared nothing for her. She cried harder.

'It wasn't meant to be, was it?' she murmured, as her weeping slowed to hiccuping sobs.

'I don't know, sweetheart,' her mum answered, stroking her hair as if she were Ruby's age. Kaitlin almost wished that she was, that she could turn back the clock, do things differently. Most of all, listen to those who had always had her best interests at heart. 'I do know you will recover from this, though,' her mum went on softly. 'You won't get over it, as we women are often expected to, or forget, and nor should you have to, but you will recover.'

Kaitlin nodded and eased away from her. 'The bad shit just makes us stronger.' She quoted Zoe with a tremulous smile. *You're a survivor*, Zoe added, a soft whisper somewhere in the shadows of her mind. Dear Zoe, where was she?

'On which subject ...' Her mum wiped a tear from her own eyes and reached for her bag from the chair. 'I ran into DI Diaz in the corridor. I asked him for this,' she said, taking a card from the bag and handing it to her. 'He's put his personal number on the back.'

Kaitlin looked at the card curiously and then turned it over. 'That was nice of him,' she said, surprised.

'I thought so too. He's concerned about you, Kaitlin. He said to call him any time, night or day.'

'What, with any information that might come to mind that might lead him to Greg?' Kaitlin couldn't help her cynicism.

Her mum hesitated. 'That wasn't the impression I got. I don't doubt that he would welcome any information about the man, but I think his concern was more for you should Greg get in touch. I trust him, Kaitlin. I just get a feeling he's genuine, and believe me, I'm as wary as you are. Please promise me you will call him if you need to.'

Kaitlin knew that her mum was concerned, too. That she would be every minute Kaitlin was out of her sight. 'I will,' she promised.

A moment later, she wondered if she would need to keep that promise. A part of her knew it was Greg, even as she'd snatched her phone up, hoping for a miracle, that Zoe was finally calling and answering her prayers. 'What do you want?' she asked without even giving him a chance to speak.

'Just to know that you're okay,' he said after a pause. 'I love you, Kaitlin,' he added. 'I said I would always be there, even if things fell apart between us. I intend to be. Whatever happens, I will always be there, for you and for Ruby.'

Kaitlin's mouth ran dry. Once she would have called that caring. She would have believed that he truly did care. Now, it felt more like a threat.

THIRTY-NINE

GREG

Shit. His foot narrowly missing going through a rotten floorboard, Greg moved back from the grimy window of the property opposite Kaitlin's parents' house. Having recced the place before Richard had arrived again with Ruby and established that Kaitlin wasn't there, he was surprised to see Diaz turn up. Also perturbed. The detective inspector was a bit hands-on, wasn't he? A bit too keen, considering that, as far as Greg could see, they had nothing but circumstantial evidence against him – being in the wrong place at the wrong time. The warrant, what had that been all about? He couldn't be sure they hadn't come up with something that might incriminate him, but he hadn't been about to stick around long enough to find out.

Why was Diaz hell-bent on bringing him in? Did he enjoy breaking up people's relationships? Or was it just Greg's relationship he wanted to fuck up? What did he want with Richard – who, Greg guessed, was majorly annoyed with him for not being straight with his daughter, but who could provide no information about the whereabouts of her missing friend, or him? And where was Kaitlin, come to think of it? He'd assumed she'd gone shopping or something with her mother, but was she really likely to have done that with all this going on? He got that she might have wanted to stay with her parents for a while, but he *had* to find a way to get her on her own for more than five minutes, talk to her and convince her he would die rather than let anything happen to her. That to lose her, the only woman who'd looked at him with affection, with genuine love in her eyes, would mean his life was over anyway.

His gut clenched as his mother's hate-filled glare emblazoned itself on his mind, her mouth curled in revulsion and her nostrils flared as she hissed at him to piss off while she got high or got laid. He swallowed back the enduring shame that always accompanied his flashbacks, flashbacks that had come more frequently since he'd felt his life slipping away from him. No matter how much he tried to push them away, her contemptuous gaze just kept right on boring into him, until he couldn't breathe. *Stop*, he commanded himself as his mind conjured up the last image he had of her, her eyes opaque and blistered, her vile mouth silenced. He smiled with sick irony. She might actually have finally been proud of him. Here he was, out of sight, hiding in shadows, which he'd done half his life. It was what he was good at, best at. He'd thought he would make a good husband and father, but Diaz seemed intent on taking all that away from him. Call him paranoid, but Greg would quite like to know why.

He would also like to know why he'd been unofficially tailed. It had to have been unofficial surveillance given that the person following him had decided to try to kill him rather than arrest him. Had it been Diaz's sidekick? More than likely. Another woman who no doubt thought the female race would be better off without men.

Moving carefully forward again, he watched with growing agitation as the detective climbed out of his car and walked up to the front door – on his own, he noted, his sidekick's company obviously not required on this occasion, which pointed to this also not being official business. Obviously Diaz didn't realise that Kaitlin wasn't home.

Greg narrowed his eyes, watching as the front door opened and Richard wheeled his chair back to allow the detective access with barely a word exchanged. He'd been expecting him, clearly. The knot in Greg's chest tightened as Ruby appeared, smiling up at Diaz. The bastard had obviously met her then, won her confidence. Ruby didn't take easily to strangers. He would have to have met her in Kaitlin's company. Where? When?

Anger rose like acid inside him as Diaz crouched down in front of Ruby, saying something that made the little girl chuckle. Then he laughed in shocked disbelief as the detective actually lifted her into his arms. This was *his* daughter, and this copper had the nerve to be overfamiliar with her? Carrying her into *his* fiancée's parents' house as if the welcome mat had been laid out. Now it was becoming clear, abundantly clear. Diaz was trying to move in on Kaitlin. To do that, he would need Greg out of the way. If he didn't have all the evidence necessary to accomplish that, he was probably fabricating it. He might be trying to coerce her father right now into giving a bad witness statement against him. And Ruby? Was he putting words into her innocent little mouth?

He needed to have a quiet chat with Diaz, preferably in some secluded place, and ask him what the fuck he thought he was up to.

Quelling an urge to put his fist through the window, to go over there and have it out with him now, whatever the consequences, he waited patiently instead for Diaz to come out. He needed to stay in the shadows. He needed to bide his time until he could get Kaitlin on her own. She loved him. *Him.* It had been right there in those forest-green eyes whenever she'd looked at him. She was having his baby. She would stand by him until this shit was sorted out.

FORTY

KAITLIN

Pushing the few things her mum had brought in for her into her bag, Kaitlin jumped as a male voice said her name softly behind her.

'Sorry, I didn't mean to startle you,' Detective Diaz apologised as she whirled around. 'I was passing and I ...' He hesitated. 'Actually, that's not quite true. I wanted to check on you, make sure you were ... well, not all right exactly, I know it will be a while before you feel that, but ...'

'I'm okay, DI Diaz. Thanks for asking,' Kaitlin said, a lump of emotion rising in her throat. 'I'd feel better knowing that Ruby and my dad are okay, though.'

'Adam,' he reminded her. 'I've just left them. They were at the crucial point in some computer game when I called, so I didn't stay too long, but they're fine, I promise you. Ruby said to tell you she's hidden your cupcake from her grandpa. I'm not sure where, but since she hinted that you might have to pluck a bit of fluff off it, I'd treat it with due suspicion before eating it if I were you. I'm thinking she might have secreted it under her bed.' He smiled, a warm smile that reached his eyes.

'Brilliant detective work.' She gave him a small smile back, although even allowing herself to do that felt wrong.

'Okay?' he asked as she dropped her gaze.

Kaitlin's throat constricted. He meant well, but right now his kindness only seemed to prompt the tears that were too close to the surface. 'I feel I've let everyone down – my baby, Zoe, my parents, Ruby,' she found herself saying. She wasn't sure why she was confiding in him. Because he was a stranger, possibly. Someone who, if he did judge her to be as naive and self-centred as she felt she'd been, she might never meet again once this nightmare was over.

It would never be over, though. She wrapped her arms tightly about herself as another bout of the chills she'd had since coming around from the anaesthetic shook through her, making her feel cold inside and out. She would never sleep soundly again, never feel able to laugh with her whole heart again. How could she with part of it still missing?

If she'd been surprised to see Adam Diaz here, she was doubly surprised when she felt his arm go tentatively around her shoulders. 'Don't reproach yourself,' he urged her. 'Falling in love and trusting someone isn't a crime. We'd all be guilty if it was.' He squeezed her shoulders gently before removing his arm.

Kaitlin searched his soulful brown eyes. 'Not trusting your instincts is, though,' she said. 'Or it should be.' She'd known. The exotic wedding plans, the lack of friends and family. Deny it as she might to herself, she had known deep down. She hadn't needed Zoe to point it out.

'In which case, I'm definitely guilty,' he said kindly. 'It took me a while to learn to trust mine.'

Kaitlin could see he was trying to make her feel better, and she was touched. Would that he could.

'Is your mother still here?' Adam asked as she turned back to her bag, zipping it up.

'She left just before you arrived. I've been discharged, so I called a taxi rather than drag her back ... Oh, this might be it.' Her gaze flicked to the door beyond him, where a man in a hoodie appeared to linger for a second before moving on.

Adam glanced that way and then back to her. 'I can drive you,' he offered.

Kaitlin hesitated. She sensed he was trying to make up in some small way for the fact that they hadn't found Zoe, hadn't apprehended Greg, but he did seem genuinely concerned. 'Don't you have work to do?' she asked him.

'I do, most definitely,' Adam assured her. 'I have to pick my daughter up from sixth-form college, though, and you're almost on the way.'

Kaitlin didn't think her parents' house was almost on the way, but ... 'That's really kind of you,' she said. 'I'm desperate to see Ruby. Thanks, Adam.'

'My pleasure,' he assured her, and reached to pick up her bag.

Kaitlin could have carried it herself, but she didn't protest. She'd thought Greg would be the person carrying her bag for her, that it would be him who would escort her to and from the hospital when the time came – the right time. She'd thought he would protect her. She'd told Zoe as much. How wrong had she been? She didn't know much about Adam Diaz, but she did feel protected in his company – and she badly needed his company right now. The thought of leaving the hospital empty-handed and on her own was almost too much to bear.

FORTY-ONE

ADAM DIAZ

Back at the office, Adam checked his emails for one from Sally. He'd reminded Kaitlin again that it would be helpful to have a photograph of this Daniel character in order to pursue investigations; also the name of the hotel Zoe had worked at. That had been the only thing he'd asked her about. He'd made up his mind he wasn't going to go into police mode as he'd driven her to her parents' house. She didn't need questions right now. She'd just lost her child. Her emotions would be raw. He doubted there was much else she could tell him anyway. She was obviously feeling responsible enough without him making her go over it all again. From what she'd told him, it was clear she was questioning herself, worrying that she'd chosen to ignore every nagging doubt she might have had about Gregory Walker.

Pulling up the photograph Kaitlin had sent directly to Sally, he scanned it and then stared hard at it. His blood ran cold in his veins. It was grainy, taken at some beach barbecue late at night. The lighting was poor, but it was clear the man was tall, dark-haired. From a distance, he and Walker could both fit the description given by the eyewitness.

Christ almighty. Clenching his jaw hard, he read Kaitlin's text; then, swallowing back the sick taste in his throat, he called the number of the hotel she'd supplied.

It took them an eternity to answer, another eternity to put him through to the Poolside Café, where Zoe had worked. Finally, after explaining with forced patience to the Portuguese bartender what his call was about, he got the café manager on the phone. The woman remembered Zoe and was furious and clearly upset in turn, describing in too much detail how Daniel Shaw had totally humiliated her, and then asking if there was any news.

Adam supposed she must know about Zoe's disappearance and the fact that they had absolutely nothing regarding her whereabouts. 'We're working on some leads,' he said, his voice sounding hollow even to his own ears. 'Do you have an address for Daniel Shaw?'

'Not to hand, but I can soon find it,' she said. 'He's married to Michael O'Sullivan's daughter. O'Sullivan lives at one of the most expensive addresses in Quinta do Lago, worth at least three million euros. I think Daniel and Jessica live in a house on the same road, probably a wedding gift from her father. O'Sullivan's loaded, owns loads of property. Do you want me to find the address? It shouldn't take long.'

'No need. Thanks. You've been really helpful.' Adam was already googling Shaw and O'Sullivan. 'Oh, one more thing,' he said before she hung up. 'Do you know if Daniel Shaw is in Portugal right now?'

'No idea, I'm afraid,' she answered with an apologetic sigh. 'He hasn't shown his face much around here since he did what he did to poor Zoe, the bastard.'

Seconds later, with several images of Daniel Shaw at a charity event on screen, in some of which he was clearly enjoying the company of his father-in-law, Adam's gut turned over. *Jesus Christ.* He looked from Shaw, who appeared tanned and relaxed, to his blonde wife, who was gazing adoringly at him. Was she still smiling as lovingly now she knew what kind of a despicable bastard he was? Did she know about his history?

Adam yanked himself to his feet. It took every ounce of his willpower to stop himself hitting something to vent his frustration. Why hadn't he worked to get this information sooner? This shifted everything. Daniel Shaw would be aware of the friendship between Zoe and Kaitlin; he would have known that Zoe would was bound to share information about her boyfriend with Kaitlin – which placed Kaitlin squarely in danger. That was down to him. How could he have been so *utterly* fucking incompetent?

FORTY-TWO

DANIEL

Daniel nodded when Jessica's father offered him a drink. He needed one. Sweat beading his forehead, he eyed Michael O'Sullivan's personal trainer, who was standing ominously over him, with sick apprehension. The man was built like a brick shithouse.

'Thanks.' He took the drink Michael passed him, his hand shaking so badly he was sure he would drop it. What were they doing here? If Michael was trying to scare him, it was working.

'My pleasure.' Michael smiled pleasantly. His eyes were as cold as the ice he'd dropped into the glass. 'Don't want you feeling uncomfortable, do we?' Turning away, he walked across the courtyard of his vast mock-Georgian property, back to the purpose-built bar, where he poured himself a drink while Daniel continued to sweat. 'Nice weather,' he commented, glancing idly up at the night sky. 'Portugal has a lot to offer, but there's nothing quite like the British climate when the weather is mild, is there?'

Daniel stared at his back, incredulous. He was sitting here contemplating his fate and they were discussing the *weather*?

Michael took his time, adding fresh ginger to his whisky.

Satisfied that it was just as he liked it, he took a sip, then placed his tumbler back on the bar, twirling it around and studying the amber liquor inside it for a petrifyingly long moment. What was he going to do? Have the personal trainer teach Daniel a lesson for disrespecting his daughter?

Another minute ticked by, the longest in Daniel's life. He reached to wipe away the sweat now trickling stickily down his face.

Michael turned around at last, picking up the glass and ambling towards him. His expression was inscrutable for a second, and then his flinty blue eyes grew dangerously darker. 'Got yourself into a bit of a mess again.' He eyeballed him meaningfully. 'Haven't you, *Kyle*?'

Kyle swallowed against the shard of glass that seemed to be wedged in his windpipe as he considered how to answer. There was no point telling the man he'd had nothing to do with what had happened to Zoe. His gut constricted as he thought about her. Michael would never believe him. Neither would the police. Christ, what the hell was he going to do?

'I got you off the hook, Kyle. Paid good money to make evidence disappear. Got you set up in a nice new life, married into a respectable family,' Michael reminded him, his voice deceptively amiable. 'All you had to do was treat my daughter with the respect she deserves. Not a lot to ask in exchange for your freedom, is it?'

'No, I—'

'A luxurious lifestyle, all your needs catered for.'

'Look, Mike, I—'

'Zip it,' Michael seethed, dragging his now contemptuous gaze away from Kyle and walking back towards the edge of the pool. 'Here's the thing …' He paused to take another leisurely swig of his drink. 'I have no idea what she sees in you, but my daughter loves you.'

Kyle eyed the water with some trepidation.

'What I'm suggesting you do henceforth is behave yourself. Do you think you can do that?' Michael glanced at him over his shoulder and then away again. 'I'm waiting for an answer, Kyle.'

'Yes,' Kyle said quickly. Whatever point Michael was trying to make here, he'd made it. He'd had his balls in a vice for years, and now he was turning the screw.

'Good.' Michael faced him, smiling charitably. 'So I'm assuming you won't be hurting my daughter again,' he went on, his tone casual, chatty almost. 'The woman who gave birth to your fucking children!'

'*No*,' Kyle blurted. 'I didn't mean for it to happen. I just—'

'Couldn't keep your dick in your pants?' Michael suggested. 'I understand. It happens,' he added generously as Kyle dropped his gaze. 'You know, you should take up a hobby,' he suggested, 'other than the one you've been indulging in, obviously. I know you're not much into golf, but I thought some other kind of sport – working out, possibly. We have a fully equipped gym, after all. I'm sure Aaron here wouldn't mind giving you a few ... Ah, here she is.'

He paused as Jessica came through the leafy archway from the lawn to the courtyard.

'We were just discussing Daniel taking up a hobby to keep him occupied,' he said, leaning to kiss her cheek. 'Aaron's about to acquaint him with some of our gym equipment, aren't you, Aaron?'

Kyle looked disbelievingly from Michael to the personal trainer, who folded his arms across his bulging chest and nodded. Jesus Christ, he had to be joking. He really did aim to teach him a lesson, didn't he? Was he insane? He looked back at Jessica, who was sharing an expectant smile with her father. Why was she going along with this?

It was only then that he noticed the mud on the hems of her jeans, splashed up the sides and soaked into the suede of her designer trainers. From where? Jessica didn't do strolls in the countryside. Tramping through muddy fields just wasn't her style. Where else might she have ... Zoe had been on the canal bank. Recalling what Jessica had said about the 'tacky little dress' Zoe was wearing, his heart slammed against his chest.

He had to get out of here. Play for time. 'Look, Jess, I'm sorry. Please don't let him do this,' he appealed to her. 'It's not that I don't love you. It's just ... I don't like *me* very much. I don't think I'm worth loving, and I ... Please, don't let him do this.'

Jessica eyed him stonily for a second, and then looked away.

FORTY-THREE

KAITLIN

'We're playing a new game,' Ruby announced when Kaitlin went to check on her in the lounge.

'I'm incompetent at snakes and ladders, apparently.' Glancing back at her from where they were mooching through the cupboard the board games were kept in, her dad smiled in amusement.

'What's incompetent?' Ruby asked.

'Rubbish,' Richard provided. 'As in, rubbish at playing it.'

Ruby widened her eyes in surprise. 'You're not rubbish, Grandpa,' she said kindly. 'You just get a bit muddled up sometimes.'

Richard chuckled at that. 'Thank you, Ruby. I feel so much better now,' he said with a wry roll of his eyes.

'That's okay.' Ruby beamed him a benevolent smile and went back to delving in the cupboard.

'From the mouths of babes.' Richard sighed and gave Kaitlin a wink.

Kaitlin left them to it and went upstairs in search of her mum, to find her emptying things from the drawers in the room she and Ruby were using.

'Having a tidy-up?' Kaitlin asked, aware of her mum's need to keep busy when she was worried. Her heart caught as she was reminded of Zoe's endless striving to organise her life through the things around her. Simple things. She might have enjoyed her exotic lifestyle in Portugal – until this Daniel, who didn't deserve her, had treated her so abysmally – but the fairy tale for Zoe had always been to have a home with a heart, a family. Kaitlin felt a fresh wave of raw grief crash through her. Zoe would have done everything in her power to be the best mother she could be. The world was a greyer place without her. It was as if the light had gone from her life.

'Just making room,' her mum answered, turning towards her with an armful of clothes. 'All right, lovely?' she asked, clearly realising that Kaitlin felt far from it.

Kaitlin nodded quickly and blinked hard.

Her mum's eyes were glassy with tears too. She knew where Kaitlin's thoughts were. 'I can't accept it,' she said, for once allowing her stoicism in the face of adversity to slip a little. 'I won't.' She pulled herself up, visibly bracing her shoulders. 'Not unless I have absolute proof.'

Dumping the clothes on the bed, she pulled Kaitlin into a firm hug. They stayed like that for a minute, holding back the tears, no words necessary to communicate the immeasurable pain they were both feeling.

'You need to stay here,' her mum said, easing away. 'Detective Diaz says he would prefer it if you stayed with us for a while.'

'He rang?' Kaitlin eyed her quizzically.

'While you were in the garden with Ruby. He's organised a patrol car to drive by at regular intervals. He's obviously worried for your safety. I couldn't help thinking that, as a widower with a teenage daughter, he might be a bit over cautious, but I honestly don't believe that he is.'

Kaitlin was shocked. He'd never mentioned his personal

circumstances. He'd talked about his daughter when he'd driven her home from the hospital, but she hadn't realised ... She felt her heart wrench for him. Had he confided that to her dad, she wondered, when he'd come here to check on him and Ruby?

'Your father and I are worried, too, Kait.' Her mum scanned her face, obvious concern in her eyes. 'We would both feel better if you and Ruby were here with us. Just until ...'

Until the police caught up with Greg. Until they had him in custody. Kaitlin guessed what her mum meant. She was trying to spare her feelings. Looking out for her. Always looking out for her. She should refuse to be intimidated by Greg. Be able to stand on her own two feet. Just now, though, she didn't feel strong enough. Did that make her weak?

'Sometimes being grown-up means admitting you need a little help,' her mum said, wearing her best stern look. 'And before you tell me you're not a child, you're *my* child, which gives me a perfect right to be as bossy as I like.'

Kaitlin laughed in wonderment. She'd plucked the thoughts from her head.

'Right, that's settled then.' Her mum's face softened into a relieved smile. 'We'll go to your house together and collect anything you need.' She reached to give Kaitlin's shoulders another comforting squeeze. 'You can stay as long as you like. Just know I'm always here for you, Kait. Your dad, too.'

As they had been for Zoe. As Kaitlin should have been. She couldn't undo it. She would give her soul if she could. She had no idea how she would go on with the pain inside her where her heart should be, but she had to. For Ruby, for her mum and dad, she had to stay strong; never give up hope. She would take a leaf out of her mother's book and take one day at a time. *Baby steps*, she thought involuntarily, and swallowed hard.

FORTY-FOUR

ADAM DIAZ

'We have an address for O'Sullivan,' Sally said, slapping a piece of paper on his desk.

Adam held up a hand while he finished the call he was on. 'Can you alert me to anything that might be out of the ordinary: anyone loitering in the vicinity, cars parked at the property or thereabouts, anything at all?'

'No problem, sir,' the officer assured him efficiently.

'Cheers, Scott.' Ending the call, Adam drew in a frustrated breath. He couldn't be in two places at once, but he wished to God he could have paid Kaitlin a personal call. He wouldn't have been able to give out any information, other than to tell her there'd been a new development, but the fact that he'd called in person might have made sure she was on her guard. He was confident her mother would keep a close eye on her. That eased his concern somewhat, but still the worry that someone might gain access to the house niggled away at him. He needed to concentrate on what he was doing here. He *had* to find this Daniel character, and fast.

Pocketing his phone, he squinted at the address Sally had placed in front of him and then back to her. 'Solihull?'

'Nice cosy little country property on the outskirts,' she confirmed. 'Around one point five million quid's worth. I thought better of asking the local nick to send a car to see if anyone was home.'

'You thought right.' Adam grabbed his jacket from the back of his chair and headed fast for the door. 'Do you mind driving?' he asked. 'I need to return a call regarding Walker.'

'Just make sure to buckle up,' Sally advised. 'If Shaw is there and gets wind of this, I have a feeling he won't be waiting around for us to pay him a visit.' Following him through the back exit to the car park, she was in the car and gunning the engine almost before Adam had closed the passenger door.

Adam fastened his belt as she skidded out of the car park with blue lights flashing, then pulled out his phone to call the guy who'd gone out on a limb and dug up what he could about historical undercover operations. 'Hi, Paul. Did you manage to find anything?' he asked when the call picked up.

'I did. It makes interesting reading,' Paul replied, a cautious edge to his voice.

Adam braced himself. 'And?'

'It seems his story checks out.'

'Jesus Christ.' Adam felt as if he'd been hit by a freight train. 'You're joking.'

Paul sighed. 'Afraid not. It's not currently authorised, but apparently a local force did use the identities of deceased children to provide passports for officers undercover.'

'So you're saying Walker is kosher?'

'Looks that way,' Paul confirmed.

The man was actually a *copper*? But ... *how*? Adam tried to get his head around it. It was incomprehensible. Why the bloody hell would he run if that was the case? Even if he couldn't reveal his status to Adam, surely he could have got someone to give him the nod. 'Is he in the field now?'

'It appears not. Like I say, his story checks out, but only so far. From what I've managed to find out, it looks like he was given the name Gregory Walker as his alias about ten years or so ago. His real name is Steven Rawlings. He did a long stint undercover infiltrating drugs rings. It seems he cracked at some point. There's a police psych report, but it was bloody difficult to get hold of. Only a few people were privy to the fact that Rawlings even existed, which I guess means he was pretty isolated. He couldn't hack leading a double life and had to get out, I gather. Hold on, there's a note here.'

Adam waited, his gut churning.

'Says there was a probability of PTSD due to being so long undercover,' Paul went on after a frustratingly long pause. 'Witnessed some pretty gruesome things, apparently. Under pressure to take drugs and partake in various nefarious activities in order to maintain his cover. He had a follow-up appointment but disappeared off the radar.'

'When?' Adam asked, feeling sick to the pit of his stomach. He'd messed up monumentally. Christ, Kaitlin. What the hell was he going to tell her? *Sorry for blowing your life apart but it seems I made a mistake?* Had he, though? Being a copper didn't make Walker ... Rawlings clean. There was something. There *had* to be. The man was still using his fake ID.

'It was around about the time his parents died. Both of them burnt to death in a house fire. There's something about Rawlings believing it to be an act of retaliation, or some kind of warning to him to keep his mouth shut. He wasn't close to his parents – there's a note about an unhappy childhood, querying abuse. Whatever, he went rogue after that. I guess it was enough to tip him over the edge.'

Adam sucked in a sharp breath. 'Right. Thanks, Paul. I owe you one.'

'Make that several,' Paul said.

Ending the call, Adam kneaded his forehead and tried to

process what he'd learnt. Rawlings' parents had died in a fire and then he'd told his fiancée he worked as a fire investigation officer. What was that all about? Did he have some kind of fire fixation? Whatever, over the edge was about right. The man was clearly delusional, making up fairy stories whichever way you looked at it. Definitely dangerous – but how far would he have gone to maintain his fantasy? Was it possible he had no involvement in Zoe Weller's disappearance? In which case, Adam had wasted considerable time and police resources barking up the wrong bloody tree.

He'd also put Kaitlin Chalmers, a pregnant woman, under intolerable stress. He didn't think he would easily forgive himself that. He was sure Kaitlin wouldn't. She'd been about to marry the man. All this might have opened her eyes to the fact that he was a consummate liar, but for her to have been under the impression that the father of the child she was carrying was responsible for the possible murder of her friend ... She'd been traumatised, and that was down to him.

'Okay?' Sally glanced worriedly at him.

Adam shook his head. 'Very much not okay,' he answered, his throat tight. 'I may have ballsed up, spectacularly.'

Sally said nothing for a second, then, 'In which case, we'd better unballs it,' she suggested. 'Whatever's happening with the prick Kaitlin Chalmers is involved with, she needs answers about what happened to her friend. Let's see if we can provide them, yes?'

She stepped on the accelerator, causing Adam to brace himself as they navigated the lane approaching the address almost on two wheels. He reached a hand to the dashboard, his pulse racing as he pictured what would happen if they hit something coming in the opposite direction. He'd witnessed the devastating consequences of that scenario first-hand. At this speed, the impact would undoubtedly be fatal.

'Do you want to ease up a bit, Sal?' he asked, his voice strained. 'It might be a good idea to arrive in one piece.'

'Shit, sorry.' She glanced sideways. 'I forgot you had a problem.'

'I don't have a problem. It's just ...' He *did* have a problem. He didn't openly admit it, but Sally obviously knew it. 'Do you think you could keep your eyes on the road?' Sweat wetting his forehead, he nodded towards the windscreen.

'Sorry.' She turned her gaze forward and Adam's pounding heart settled clunkily back into its moorings, only to jerk violently as something emerged from the dense woodland alongside the lane, travelling at speed directly across their path. 'For Christ's *sake*, slow—'

Too late. As he felt the impact, the sickening thud as the car hit, rolling over whatever had come at them, his stomach lurched nauseatingly.

He swallowed back the bile rising in his throat as Sally slammed on the brakes, screeching the car to a haphazard stop several yards further on. His breath stalling, he reached for his door handle. 'Get some help,' he barked. Sally sat immobile, her hands still clutching the wheel. 'Sally! Get some fucking help here now!'

Shoving the door open, he threw himself out, wiping the back of his hand across his mouth. Why hadn't she slowed down? He would swear she'd bloody well sped up.

'Sweet fucking Jesus.' Reaching the body that lay in the road, a pool of rich crimson flowering thickly beneath it, Adam dropped to his knees. 'Daniel?' he said, seeing his eyelids flicker open.

The man winced, clearly in unbearable pain. 'Kyle,' he whispered, his voice emerging as a dry croak.

Adam's heart stalled. 'Kyle,' he repeated. Relief and adrenaline surged through him, tempered with something else:

sympathy. Whoever he was, it was possible he might be about to breathe his last breath. 'Don't try to move,' he urged him and placed a hand gently on his shoulder. 'Help's on its way.' At least he hoped it was. For some unfathomable reason, Sally seemed to still be sitting in the car.

FORTY-FIVE

KAITLIN

'All right, sweetheart?' Kaitlin asked Ruby, poking her head around the lounge door to double-check she and her dad were okay before she left.

'Uh huh.' Ruby looked up from the new game they'd found. Draughts, Kaitlin noticed. A beautiful wooden set her dad had bought for her as a child. She felt a pang of guilt. She'd never really shown any interest in it. Ruby was clearly enjoying it, however.

'Are you moving the white pieces or the black?' she asked, going across to her.

'White. Grandpa says it gives me an advantage, but I don't think that's true,' Ruby answered, her little brow furrowed as she glanced at the board, picked up a piece and moved it. 'Do you, Mummy?'

'You don't need an advantage if that move is anything to go by,' Richard said, picking up the counters she'd just jumped over and placing them on Ruby's side of the table. 'She's a child genius, has to be.' He shook his head in pretend bemusement.

Ruby folded her arms and cocked her head to one side. 'Are

you letting me win, Grandpa?' she asked, her eyes narrowed suspiciously.

'I wish I was,' Richard said with a theatrical sigh. 'I'm going to have to rethink my strategy.'

'What's a strategy?' Ruby asked.

'My game plan. Ways to cunningly outwit you,' he explained.

Ruby nodded, understanding. 'Greg outwits me,' she said. Kaitlin tried not to meet her dad's gaze; she could feel his eyes on her. He and her mum had been watching her carefully since she came home, worrying about her, as she'd known they would. 'He outwits me at Race to Base *and* the Yes! No! game, doesn't he, Mummy?'

Her throat tight with emotion, Kaitlin couldn't speak for a second. 'Uh huh,' she managed eventually, mimicking her daughter.

'He says he watches people so he knows what their next move will be,' Ruby chatted on, and Kaitlin felt a chill run through her. 'Is he coming home soon, Mummy?' The little girl looked up at her expectantly.

Kaitlin's heart squeezed painfully. 'He's working away, sweetheart,' she said softly. 'Remember?'

Ruby nodded, but the small furrow in her brow deepened. 'Will we be going home soon?' she asked. 'Nana and Grandpa could come with us and we could play some more games.'

'We certainly could.' Richard glanced in Kaitlin's direction, his eyes full of sympathy, which only made the ache in her heart all the more unbearable, if that were possible. 'There's a little bit more room here for our chariot, though, isn't there?' he pointed out to Ruby.

'Ah well, we can always bring the games next time.' Ruby sighed good-naturedly.

Kaitlin looked at her in wonder. When had her little girl become so grown-up? She sounded so caring, with a precocious emotional maturity and sense of responsibility Kaitlin hadn't realised she possessed. Blinking hard, she glanced at the ceiling. She couldn't cry any more. After coming home from the hospital, she'd slipped upstairs, wanting to compose herself before seeing Ruby. Catching a glimpse of herself in the wardrobe mirror, she'd placed her hand over the flat of her belly, and she'd cried, though she'd promised herself not to. Shutting herself in the bathroom, she'd sobbed quietly, praying no one would hear her. She'd cried for her sweet, precious baby, for her dear, feisty, beautiful friend. But she had to stop now. She had to be strong for her daughter. She loved Ruby more than she'd thought it possible to love another human being. She had to be there for her, her mind focused on her. She didn't want to miss a single precious second. She had to pull herself together, leave the past behind and keep moving forward, as she'd once promised Zoe she would. Her daughter needed her to. It was as simple as that.

'I tell you what,' she said, making herself smile as she crouched down in front of her. 'Nana and I are going to our house now to pick up some clean clothes. How about you write a list of the games you want and we'll bring them back with us?'

Ruby studied her for a second, her huge green eyes seeming to see right down to her soul. Then she did something extraordinary. Reaching to brush Kaitlin's hair from her face, as if *she* were the child in need of comfort, she whispered, 'Don't worry, Mummy. I'll look after you.'

FORTY-SIX

GREG

Greg's blood pumped as he saw Kaitlin emerge from the house with her mother. He'd tried to convince himself he'd been mistaken. Despite the intimacy he'd seen between her and the *fucking* caring detective at the hospital, he'd tried to tell himself it meant nothing, that the man was just putting a comforting arm around her. Even if Diaz had his sights set on her, Kaitlin would soon put him right, he'd reassured himself, tell him she was engaged to be married ... to him, the father of her child. She wasn't like the other women he'd known, who expected men to be their heroes, to live up to their fantasies of dark, moody and broody, and then threw a wobbly if they weren't in touch with their feminine side. She wasn't his mother, a woman who would drop her knickers for the price of a fix, abuse her own kids. Kaitlin was different.

Seeing her walk to the car, Jayne a step behind her, his mind raced, jerking from one incomprehensible scenario to another as he tried to assimilate, to digest the evidence right in front of him. He hadn't been mistaken. He'd wondered why she was there. Wondered why she would be at the hospital with *him*. He'd given her the benefit of the doubt, been sick with worry as he'd imagined some kind of an emergency that had required urgent medical attention, assuming that to be the only plausible reason Diaz would be on the scene.

Continuing to watch from his vantage point opposite, he ran his gaze over her, disgust and confusion tugging at him. His mother's voice in his head booming echoes from his past. *You're not wanted. You were never wanted. Piss off out of my sight.*

Kaitlin didn't want him either. The woman he would give his life for was treating him with the same utter contempt, right in front of his eyes. A toxic mixture of humiliation and festering rage burned deep inside him. She was seeing the copper, shagging the copper. Why else would the *kind* detective have been picking her up, bringing her home, popping in to see her father, winning him over with his impressive CV? Greg had run because he'd had to – and reliable DI Diaz had stepped right into his shoes. He'd even organised a police car to drive by, pulling strings no doubt, making sure that he, her *fiancé*, couldn't get anywhere near her.

Why would Kaitlin do this to him? Why would she lie to him, so coldly, so cruelly?

Picking up a shard of broken glass lying on the debris-strewn windowsill, he watched as she smiled and chatted to her mum as if everything were normal. As if she hadn't a care in the world. Plainly, she hadn't. Her conscience was clear. She'd aborted his baby and she hadn't shed a single tear. Brainwashed by the copper or not, she didn't have to do that. Greg would have taken him. He would have brought him up. Brought him up properly, not dragged him up like a dog never shown a scrap of affection.

She shouldn't have done it. Inhaling deeply, he squeezed down hard on the glass, hoping the physical pain might detract from the pain in his heart. It was fracturing inside him, he could feel it, each jagged piece piercing his chest like a knife.

Watching her climb into the car, glancing in his direction

almost as if to taunt him, he squeezed tighter. It only served to sharpen his insurmountable loss.

Suppressed fury swirling inside him like acid, he dropped his gaze as the car pulled off, watched in morbid fascination as rich droplets of blood plopped onto the shelf, stark against the peeling white paint.

He'd sworn he would protect her, look after her and little Ruby, his baby. He'd thought she was good, wholesome, honest. She was none of those things. She was just like his mother. Worse. At least *she'd* never pretended to be anything she wasn't. Did Kaitlin think Diaz would protect her now, the copper who got his kicks from moving in on women who were vulnerable? She was obviously far from that. It was all some great big bloody act, wasn't it, the helpless female mercilessly manipulated by men. A ploy to bag herself another man. She looked far from helpless, in fact, with people all around her, her mother and her father, who'd never really warmed to him, clucking over her. Diaz, her white knight in blue, come to protect her from the monster she'd been deluded enough to get involved with.

And what about Ruby in all of this, the little girl Greg had come to love as his own, a genuinely innocent, sweet little girl? Was this any way to protect her from the evils of the world? The people who would play on *her* vulnerabilities? Vulnerabilities she would inevitably have after witnessing her mother's fucked-up relationships. They were messing with her head. Just as his head had been messed with as a child. She would grow up without the skills she needed to interact with people. Her confidence lacking, she would form bad relationships, fall prey to men like Diaz, who would use her and hurt her. Greg couldn't have that. Kaitlin had clearly made her choices, but little Ruby should be allowed to make her own. Kaitlin needed all of this pointing out to her.

FORTY-SEVEN

KYLE ROBERTS

Undiluted fear gripped him as he lay on the road, a puddle of his own blood like warm, sticky treacle beneath him. For a while, he'd been out of it, dissociated, blissfully pain-free and unaware. Now, pain like he'd never felt before seared through his body, red-hot pokers burning his muscles and nerve endings right down to his bones. Apart from his legs. He couldn't feel those. He knew from the look on the copper's face that things weren't good. He hadn't tried to speak again, had no idea whether he could form the words he was screaming in his head. *Help me.* He was petrified, literally unable to move.

'What the *hell* were you doing?' He heard Michael O'Sullivan from somewhere behind the copper, his tone a mixture of fury and fear. A second later, Michael's face hovered above him. Kyle gained some small satisfaction from realising that he was petrified too. No doubt he'd realised that once he was taken away from here, assuming it wasn't in a body bag, he would no longer have control over him.

No doubt Michael was thinking he might be deep in the shit if Kyle talked, imagining he would spill everything. Kyle intended to. He was tired of hiding, tired of running. He was concerned about his kids, the effect on them, but he had no qualms about what the consequences would be for Jessica. She loved him, he didn't doubt that. She'd wanted him. They'd split a few times in the early days; he had found her too possessive, too demanding, always wanting to know where he was, following him around whenever he was evasive, desperate to be on his own, to breathe. She'd enticed him back, reminding him where he would be without her. Kyle had gone along with it, allowed himself to be bought by her father, whose golfing buddies included a high-ranking officer on the police force who had a little gambling problem. Evidence against Kyle Roberts had suddenly disappeared, a new passport had appeared, and Daniel Shaw was born. Jessica had got what she wanted. Michael O'Sullivan owned him.

The irony was, Kyle doubted very much that Jessica, who demanded nothing less than perfection, would want him now. She was scared. He could see the fear in her eyes. On the outside, she looked like butter wouldn't melt. She cultivated her social media image. Seeing herself as a fashion influencer, she made sure to post regularly about her donations to charitable causes, thus promoting her caring persona. Kyle, though, could have posted pictures of a far different woman to the one she portrayed. A woman who, consumed with jealousy, lost control monumentally on occasion. No matter how driven by jealousy she was by his relationship with Zoe, though, would she really have given into her temper knowing what the consequences would be – for herself, her father?

Kyle might never have all the answers. The ambulance was taking its sweet time. He was getting weaker. He could feel his heartbeat slowing to a dull thrum in his chest. He wondered whether he should just give in. Not fight it, but rather go with the flow. At least the dark sleep that was calling him would free him of the living nightmare his life had become. He should have walked away a long time ago. He'd had threats he could have held over O'Sullivan, knowledge that would have made sure he was arrested and investigated. Would the man have been charged with anything, though? Did bribery and police corruption carry a sentence? Kyle didn't know. O'Sullivan, being a solicitor, would know, though, and still undoubtedly had friends in high places. Money might not buy happiness but it could certainly buy people.

His own father's violence had toughened Kyle up. He'd survived the young offenders institute as a teenager because he'd known how to roll with the punches, when to keep his head down. The prospect of going to prison, though, accused of kicking a woman to death, he hadn't been so sure he would survive that. He'd willingly taken the lifeline that was offered by O'Sullivan. Grabbed it with both hands. He'd figured living a luxurious life, even if it was with a woman he didn't love, was better than having no life at all. O'Sullivan had been on the other end of that line ever since, holding the threat of cutting him loose over him. He had known what Kyle now knew. *Hell hath no fury like a woman scorned* – he'd said that to him once, when he'd had one too many drinks on the patio. Kyle had heard it as some sort of warning not to mess with Jessica. In fact, it had been as close as Michael had ever come to admitting he knew what his daughter was capable of. Michael would never have cut him loose, but Kyle could have walked away. He'd had one chance of happiness – with Zoe. He'd been too cowardly to take it.

Life really was full of ironies, wasn't it? He would have laughed but for the gurgle he could feel rising in his throat. He felt sick to his gut. The only other time he'd felt so violently nauseous was when he'd realised what had happened to Melanie Ryan. He never had been able to put all the pieces together. Never imagined that in saving his son-in-law's 'worthless skin', Michael O'Sullivan had in fact been protecting his daughter. Finally the full ugly picture had emerged. And now here he was, unable to walk away. A fitting punishment for the life he'd led, he supposed.

He'd read somewhere that people who were close to death relived moments of sublime happiness and extreme pain, feeling also the pain they'd caused others around them. Kyle couldn't remember having had much sublime happiness, except with Zoe. He'd caused her pain. He shouldn't have.

'Where's the bloody ambulance, for Christ's sake?' The copper glanced urgently up at the woman police officer next to him. 'Did you call it in?'

'Yes,' she answered shakily. 'It should be—'

'Put another call in,' the copper instructed. 'Do it!' he barked as she stayed where she was, appearing to be frozen to the spot. She was sheet-white, visibly perspiring. She'd been at the wheel. Kyle couldn't help wondering whether she'd failed to find the brake. Shock, probably, or else she'd fancied meting out some punishment of her own. Whichever way he looked at it, from where he was lying, he was stuffed.

The copper was willing him to hang in there, but Kyle wondered what the point was. He would probably get fitted up. Much easier to let go, sink into oblivion. His eyes were heavy, his heart too. He would never see his kids again, O'Sullivan would make sure of that. He'd lost anything that was worth living for.

'*Shit*,' the copper cursed as Kyle twisted his head, trying to cough the sour metallic taste from his throat. 'Try not to move,' he urged him, a desperate edge to his voice. 'Help will be here soon.'

The kind of help Kyle needed was a miracle. He didn't think that was going to happen. His eyes were almost closed, everything fading comfortingly, strangely, when he saw her. At least he thought he did: an angel, waiting for him a way down the lane. Beckoning him to follow her. He watched as she slipped silently into the shadows.

He blinked hard, felt his heartbeat flicker inside him. He was hallucinating, had to be. If Zoe were ever to see him again, in this or another life, there was no way she would whisper that she loved him.

FORTY-EIGHT

KAITLIN

Kaitlin knew she should hate him, for the lies he'd told, the things he'd done, one of which she could hardly bear to contemplate. Still, though, she felt the memories of their time together tug painfully at her heartstrings as they pulled up in front of her house.

Her mum switched off the engine and turned to look at her. 'Ready?'

Kaitlin nodded. Her mum knew how she was feeling. Just as Ruby had known. Was she the only person who was so hopeless at reading people she couldn't see the danger signs?

Her mum reached for her hand. 'We'll grab what you need and get back to Ruby. I thought we might go out for a meal tomorrow, as long as you're up to it. What do you think?'

Kaitlin answered with another small nod and tried for some degree of enthusiasm. Her mum was trying to cheer her up, but she wasn't sure how she would ever feel cheerful again. She had to try, though. She would never understand it, why Greg had done what he'd done. She wasn't sure about anything apart from her own naivety, which made her complicit in what had happened to Zoe. She *was* sure, though, that in whatever distorted way he perceived love, he did love her. But now, far from thrilling her, making her feel safe and protected as she had up until her life had started to crumble, that thought terrified her.

What would she do now? She couldn't burden her parents forever, but she wasn't ready yet to bring Ruby back here. She looked towards the house, which had once been so full of hope and now seemed as desolate and empty as she felt.

'We'll be in and out in no time.' Her mum gave her hand a comforting squeeze. 'One day at a time, Kaitlin,' she said softly. 'It's the only way forward.'

Recalling again the promise she'd made to Zoe to do just that, to keep going forward, Kaitlin's heart, already stuffed full of guilt and grief, weighed heavy in her chest. She hadn't moved forward. She'd gone backward. It was her own fault. She'd made bad choices. Adam had tried to reassure her that falling in love wasn't a crime, that trusting people wasn't. She'd been grateful to him for his kindness, but she knew she'd trusted too easily, because she'd needed to feel good about herself. What she actually needed was to believe in herself, believe that she was worth loving. Somehow she had to find the strength to pick up the pieces all over again and turn it around. She didn't need protecting. She didn't need someone else to make her feel safe. She needed to do this for herself. For her little girl. It was *her* job to do that. No one else's. She didn't know how she would ever forgive herself for what had happened to Zoe, whether the image of her lying broken and bruised, lonely and hurting would ever not haunt her. She very much doubted it, but she had to force herself on. She owed it to her friend to do that.

I'll keep going forward, Zoe, she promised her silently, then she gave her mum's hand a hard squeeze back and reached determinedly for her door handle. She was sure she heard Zoe whisper, *I have faith in you* as she climbed out.

Walking down the path, she paused for a moment, taking in

the neat front garden, which Greg had toiled over. It had been a mess when he'd come to live here – Kaitlin had had little time on her hands to tend to the outside of the house as well as the inside. He'd dug it over, returfed the lawn and planted flowers that would bring colour to the garden all year round: daffodils and tulips, amaryllis, narcissus, hyacinth and iris. Kaitlin knew the names, because he kept the plants religiously labelled, religiously watered. Her eyes strayed to the white picket fence. She'd laughed when she'd first seen it, ribbed him about him wanting the perfect life. 'Nothing wrong with that.' He'd smiled, threading his arm around her.

But it *was* wrong. If she was honest with herself, she'd felt a tinge of uneasiness then. It was too perfect. By the very nature of the fact that they were human, there would always be imperfections. When he'd told her those awful things about his parents – which might have been the truth, or yet another unfathomable lie – she'd thought that explained why he'd tried so hard to make her happy. But now, the way things had snowballed so fast, it seemed ... obsessive almost. What might have happened if she hadn't lived up to his idea of perfection? Why had he chosen her? And she felt that he had. He'd known Sean. He must have come to know of her through Sean. And in her and Ruby, hadn't he found the ready-made family he'd clearly craved? How long had he had his sights on her?

A shudder running through her, she wrapped her arms around herself and headed quickly for the front door. Her mum was right. She needed to be in and out. She wasn't sure yet whether she would sell up, but one thing she was certain of was that the white picket fence would come down.

Steeling herself, she pushed through the door, then faltered as she noticed the message light flashing on her answerphone. Hesitantly, she pressed play. Sean's voice filled the hall, as if in thinking about him she'd summoned him up to add another layer to her nightmare. 'Kaitlin, you should know I intend to see

Ruby,' he said flatly. 'She's *my* daughter, so you and your boyfriend can just do one. Call me back, yeah? If you don't, I'll come round there and talk to her. See how she feels about you not letting her have any contact with her own father. Don't piss me about, Kait, I'm warning you. I know my rights.'

'Ignore it.' Her mum had followed her in. 'I'll get your father to call him. And before you say you can fight your own battles, sometimes it's better to let cowards like him know you have people behind you.'

She was right. Kaitlin had no time for his threats and his mind games right now. God, he really was a contemptible bastard. She must have been out of her mind. Still was, if evidence of her recent choices was anything to go by.

Shoving thoughts of Sean and what she would like to say to him to the back of her mind, she hurried up the stairs, while her mum went to the kitchen to collect a few things for Ruby, including her Scooby-Doo cereal bowl, without which she would sulk over breakfast. In Ruby's room, she pulled clothes from the drawers and gathered up the games her daughter wanted, including the two she'd mentioned to her grandpa that Greg had outwitted her at. Kaitlin felt now that that was what he'd been doing with *her* – if not outwitting her, then manoeuvring her to get what he wanted. He hadn't wanted the perfect white wedding, though, had he? Because of his terrible childhood trauma? Because he was undercover? How many lies *had* he told her? How many had she been too ready to swallow?

Another shiver running through her, she went to the airing cupboard to pull out pillowcases. Stuffing Ruby's things into them, she headed towards her own room. As she passed the bathroom, though, she faltered, her eye snagging on the towel rack, where the towels were neatly lined up. Goosebumps prickled her skin. She hadn't done that. She'd left in too much of a hurry to worry about lining up towels. *Ruby*, she reassured herself. The little girl always looked pleased with herself when

Greg praised her for leaving the bathroom as she'd found it. *A tidy house is a tidy mind, Ruby.* She heard him gently reminding her, recalled how she'd once overheard him telling her how keeping things clean and tidy would help with her mental health. She remembered a ripple of apprehension running through her even then. She'd dismissed it. Had she been *blind*?

Hurrying on to the main bedroom, an inescapable feeling that Greg was watching her caused the hairs to rise over her skin. As she pushed the bedroom door open, she stopped dead. The bed was made, the duvet smoothed, the pillows fluffed up. Icy fingers ran the length of her spine. She most *definitely* hadn't done that. In fact, she'd almost laughed at the absurdity of it when she'd found herself about to tackle the task with her fiancé having fled the house to escape the police.

There was something on her pillow. A note? Her stomach twisting in confusion, she walked tentatively towards it. *I LOVE YOU* – the words written in block capitals leapt out at her. There was something else written underneath it. With trembling fingers, Kaitlin picked up the scrap of paper. *I know where she is.*

It was the short lock of copper hair Sellotaped to the corner of it that caused her heart to stop beating. It could be her own. Ruby's. Or it could be Zoe's.

FORTY-NINE

ADAM DIAZ

Where was the damn ambulance? Adam's gut clenched as he looked down at Kyle Roberts, who was growing weaker by the second. The man's face was pale to the point of grey. He was cold and clammy, his pulse slow. The blood oozing from the injury to his legs was congealing around him. Adam had done his best to make sure his airways were clear, but he was coughing up so much blood, it was a wonder he hadn't drowned.

Moving slightly aside to allow Kyle's wife to drape the blanket she'd fetched from her car over his torso, Adam kept pressure on the wound and willed him not to close his eyes. He was bleeding so heavily, probably also internally, there surely couldn't be enough blood circulating to keep his heart pumping. His organs would be starting to shut down. He would go into shock, lose consciousness; he might be dead in minutes. Adam had seen that happen before, right in front of his eyes.

'Stay with me, Kyle,' he urged him, knowing that the man would be craving sleep, ready to give in to his body's natural response. 'The ambulance will be here soon.' He tried to reassure him, all the while cursing inwardly. There was no sign of it. Had Sally chased it up, he wondered, as he'd asked her to?

'Kyle?' he said more urgently, noting his breathing becoming more laboured. The man's eyes flickered open, seemed to focus briefly and then closed.

Adam felt a stab of pure panic. *They* were responsible for this. Why the *hell* hadn't Sally slowed down? 'I'm here, Kyle,' he said, for whatever comfort that might offer him. 'Your wife's here too.' Somewhere. She'd put the blanket over him and backed off, presumably in a state of shock. If this man was going to die here, though, Adam had made up his mind he wasn't going to let him die alone.

Kyle's eyes fluttered open again, and he attempted to speak.

'Don't try to talk, Kyle. Just lie still and—'

'I have to,' he whispered hoarsely. His eyes were shot through with pain, but he was holding Adam's gaze, seeming to want to tell him something.

Adam nodded. 'Okay, Kyle. I'm listening. I'm not going anywhere until the paramedics arrive. Try to keep calm.' Christ, he wished there was something he could do other than offer useless words.

Kyle's features flooded with relief. 'Melanie,' he said, his voice so faint, Adam had to crouch nearer to hear him. 'I didn't do it. I ...' He stopped, a wet gurgle rising in his throat.

Adam's jaw tensed. How long had he got? he wondered. Kyle would be scared. He would want to confess. Adam had seen it before, the hope that a deathbed confession might somehow bring absolution. But was he capable? Coherent?

'Melanie ...' Kyle was struggling.

'Melanie Ryan?' Adam supplied. He probably shouldn't put words into his mouth, but he knew that must be who he was referring to.

Kyle blinked slowly.

'Did you kill her, Kyle?' Adam asked, his pulse thrumming. Would he lie now? He didn't think so.

With an effort, Kyle blinked again, twice.

'Melanie Ryan,' Adam reiterated, 'you're saying you didn't kill her? Blink once, Kyle, if that's what you're trying to tell me.'

Another slow blink. He was coherent enough to understand what Adam was saying, at least.

'Who did kill her, Kyle?' he pressed.

He saw Kyle's eyes shift, guessed he was trying to indicate something or someone behind him. Quickly he glanced over his shoulder, and his heart jolted as he saw the man's wife standing there, her expression one of pure terror.

He snapped his gaze back to Kyle's. Was he saying ...? 'Jessica?' he asked, breathing in hard.

Another slow blink. Just one, then, 'Zoe,' Kyle murmured, desperation now in his eyes. 'I never ...'

FIFTY

ZOE

After the party

Drifting in and out of consciousness, Zoe tried to push away the image that kept creeping back: Daniel's face as his eyes had lighted on his wife standing in the doorway spitting fury. His expression hadn't been one of embarrassment or guilt. He'd looked terrified. Because his wife had found out about them, she'd initially thought – every cheating husband's worst nightmare. The woman would either demand a divorce, meaning there would be financial repercussions, a settlement that might cost him dearly; or else his life would be miserable, deservedly.

She hadn't known then that Daniel's lifestyle was funded by his wife, that it was she who controlled the finances, controlled him. She would never have demanded a divorce. Daniel was hers. She wanted him. She needed him. 'He belongs to *me*,' she whispered, pressing the cup to Zoe's lips. There was no malice in her eyes, as Zoe had expected. Instead, there was fear and uncertainty, the same fear Zoe felt. An almost quiet pleading as she stroked the back of her hand gently over Zoe's cheek and across her forehead. 'I'm not sure what to do,' she said softly, as Zoe fought the desire to sleep, wispy fingers enticing her, curling themselves around her mind like a soft blanket. 'I need time to think, do you see?'

She waited as Zoe stared at her through the haze that was fast descending. Zoe sensed she wanted her to answer, to say she understood.

'He wouldn't be with me if not for my father. That's the dilemma I have, Zoe,' she went on, sighing heavily. 'He doesn't love me. I'm not sure he ever did. He loves you, though. The way he talks to you, laughs with you, walks with you hand in hand on the beach ... Anyone could see it's you he wants to be with, not me, living in a prison without bars, like a trapped animal. That's what he reminds me of sometimes, when he paces around, or stands and stares over the balcony, as if he would rather swim the ocean for his freedom than be with me. I can't let him go, though. I love him.'

She paused, and Zoe jerked as her mind shifted, feeling again the blow that had prevented her escaping, the dirt and the grit biting spitefully into her cheek before she'd let unconsciousness claim her.

'Even if I could let him go, which I suppose you think I should if I truly loved him, my father never would. He's not one to let a debt slide. He thinks Daniel owes me, that he's ruined my life. He might agree, if I begged him, but I know he would want to ruin Daniel's life too, and he could do that easily. All the money in the world can't buy you happiness, can it? It can't buy love either, I realise that now. It does buy people, though, corrupt people.'

Zoe slipped deeper as the woman fell silent. She was with Daniel, floating on her back, the waves rippling gently beneath her, the warm sun caressing her skin. Briefly, sublimely happy.

'I need to think.' The woman stood abruptly, yanking her

from what could only ever have been a fantasy back to reality. This stark reality. 'Decide what to do with you.'

Zoe knew then, as she heard the woman's heels click agitatedly across the wooden floor, the door close behind her, inevitably to be locked, that she might never feel the sun on her face again. Jessica Shaw wouldn't let her go. She wouldn't let Daniel go. She aimed to keep him at any cost.

FIFTY-ONE
ADAM DIAZ

'What the hell kept you?' Adam asked one of the paramedics as they loaded Kyle into the ambulance.

The guy's expression was unimpressed as he jumped down from the back and went around to the driver's side. Adam expected him to say they'd been delayed by traffic, backed up at the hospital on a previous shout. Instead, he said, 'Seven minutes' response time through country lanes? I'd like to see you get here any faster, mate.'

Confused, Adam watched as the guy heaved himself up and set off with sirens and lights going. *Seven minutes?* It had to have been at least half an hour from when he'd first yelled to Sally to call 999. What was going on with her? He glanced over to where she was climbing into another police vehicle, their own being cordoned off for evidence to be gathered. She was normally on the ball. Didn't give in to her emotions easily. She would undoubtedly be in shock, but calling the emergency services should have been her first priority even without him prompting her.

'Is he alive?' asked one of the backup officers Adam had sent for.

'Barely.' Adam kneaded his neck in frustration. He had no idea whether Kyle Roberts would regain consciousness and be able to clarify any of what he'd just told him. His wife's expression had been a mixture of disbelief and confusion as she'd been helped into a car. She hadn't protested, unlike her father, who'd almost blown a gasket, and was now revving his engine aiming to get to the station to defend her. Adam wasn't aware of any law that prohibited a solicitor from acting for a family member, but he suspected that what this woman might need more right now was for him to be there for her as her father.

He sighed, feeling jaded suddenly to his very bones. He'd been sure Walker was Roberts, as sure as he could be. Sally certainly had. He glanced at her again as the car drove off. Looking dazed, she had her gaze fixed forward.

He needed to get to the station. Try to sort out where to start tidying up this mess. He could only pray that Kyle would regain consciousness. He might not have given him the story in so many words, but Adam didn't doubt he was telling the truth. By and large people tended to when they thought they were about to meet their maker. What had he been trying to tell him about Zoe? Seeing the quiet pleading in his eyes, Adam had sensed he'd been struggling to say that he wasn't responsible for what had happened to her either. Had he been implying that Jessica was her assailant? It was possible. The woman was tall. She was toned. Kyle Roberts had cheated on her. If she'd found him with Melanie Ryan, and again with Zoe Weller ... Jealousy was a dangerous emotion. It could consume a person, ruin relationships, destroy families. It was definitely one of the key motives for murder.

Adam guessed that Michael O'Sullivan loved his daughter. His only child, he probably doted on her. There was nothing Adam wouldn't do for his own daughter to keep her safe and ensure her happiness. Was that what O'Sullivan had tried to do, protect Jessica? Had he convinced Kyle it was him he was protecting, buying his freedom with a fake passport just to keep him close? It was all guesswork. They had nothing to back it up unless Jessica Shaw confessed, which was highly unlikely. None of it brought Adam any closer to finding Zoe, whose fate they still had no clue about. Further dredging of the river would be fruitless, he'd been informed. The tides were strong. She could be anywhere. The likelihood was that she would be washed up one day and found by someone out walking their dog. That thought made him sick to his soul.

He needed to ring Kaitlin, he realised, his heart sinking. Tell her they'd been wrong. That Steven Rawlings had been working under the cover name Gregory Walker and that there was now some doubt as to whether he'd had anything to do with Zoe's disappearance. The inescapable fact, though, was that the man was on the run, which made him guilty of something. Why else would he have gone off the radar, adopted his alias permanently? The circumstances surrounding the house fire his parents had died in, the note on Rawlings' psychiatric report about an unhappy childhood, querying abuse, had been niggling away at him, but he had nothing there either. He would look into it, dig up what he could. Meanwhile, knowing as much as he did, he was scared for Kaitlin. This was going to be one of the hardest calls he'd ever had to make, but he had to bring her up to date. He also needed to warn her to stay wary of the man, to call him if he should try to get in contact.

Pulling his phone from his pocket, his heart missed a beat. Kaitlin had texted him, and he reeled on his feet as he realised Rawlings had already made contact. *He's been here at the house*, he read, his stomach tightening. *I've rung the police. There was a note on my pillow. It said 'I know where she is'. There was a lock of hair taped to it. It could be Zoe's. Please could you call me?*

'Jesus.' Sucking in a breath, Adam hit call. 'Where are you?' he asked when Kaitlin picked up.

'Outside the house,' she said, her voice tremulous. 'The police are here. I wasn't sure they would come. It took me ages to explain. What does it mean, Adam? *Is* it Zoe's hair, do you think? She dyed her hair for my party. Oh God, it *was* him, wasn't it?'

Adam heard a sob catch in her throat and cursed himself. If he'd been on top of the Daniel Shaw angle, none of this would have happened. He believed that Rawlings would have been forced to come clean at some stage, that he was manipulating Kaitlin, dangerously so, but it was Adam's investigation that had forced him to run. The note he guessed might be a way of enticing Kaitlin to meet up with him. If so, she might well be in considerable danger. How the hell did he convince her of that on top of what he now had to confess? He took a breath. 'Kaitlin, there's something I need to tell you. What Gregory said about being undercover, it was true.'

'You mean, he really is a policeman?' she asked, her tone a combination of incredulity and confusion.

'Was,' Adam emphasised. 'Gregory Walker was his alias. His real name is Steven Rawlings.'

Kaitlin said nothing. Adam guessed she was trying to process the information, that her emotions would be all over the place. 'Look, Kaitlin, there's no easy way to tell you this,' he pushed on. 'We no longer believe he was involved in Zoe's disappearance. We're focusing our enquiries on Daniel Shaw's family.' He stopped. He'd already disclosed more than he should, but he owed her some kind of explanation.

Kaitlin didn't speak for an agonisingly long second. Then, 'But you did believe he was,' she said finally, angrily. '*You* believed it, Adam. You made *me* believe it.'

FIFTY-TWO

KAITLIN

'I have to go,' Kaitlin said shortly, barely able to comprehend what Adam was telling her. He'd completely dismantled her life, based on what? A whim? Even as she thought it, she knew it wasn't him but Greg who'd done that. She would never have been able to live with his deceit, but that she'd thought him capable of murder ... She'd been appalled by what she might have exposed Ruby to. Devastated that in believing in Greg, being with him, she'd put Zoe in danger.

She'd searched her conscience, her soul, and even knowing all that she had, all that the police had been sure he was guilty of, still she'd wanted the child she carried inside her, an innocent in all of this whose distress she'd ignored, with her mind so preoccupied with the horrors she'd thought to be true.

She'd been furious with herself for being so insecure she'd needed to believe Greg's lies. In the end, she'd doubted everything about him. With her little girl to consider, she'd been right to, but had the police played on her insecurities to achieve their own ends? To secure a conviction? She'd done it again, hadn't she? Would she *ever* stop being so pathetically naive?

'Kaitlin, please, just hear me out,' Adam pleaded. 'I still think you have reason to be wary of him.'

'What?' Kaitlin shook her head, trying hard to keep up. 'Why?' She knew why. Of course she knew she had to be wary of him. The note was clearly another lie to get her to meet up with him, but still she needed to hear Adam's explanation.

'He ran, Kaitlin,' Adam pointed out, a desperate edge to his voice. 'He wouldn't have done that if ...' He faltered. 'Look, I probably shouldn't be telling you this, but he went rogue just after ...' Again he hesitated. 'How much do you know about him, Kaitlin? His past, I mean. Did he talk to you about his childhood? His parents?'

Kaitlin's heart flipped over. 'Yes,' she answered stridently, feeling the need to defend Greg, but with no idea why. Because he was asking about the boy in the man, the child who couldn't defend himself? 'He told me he'd had an awful childhood, that his parents abused him.' She didn't add that he hadn't told her any of that until he'd felt he had no choice but to.

'Right. You were aware that his parents died then?' Adam waited.

Kaitlin swallowed back a sharp stone in her throat. 'How?' she whispered.

'A house fire. An act of revenge, Rawlings believed. Or else someone trying to warn him off. I'm assuming his cover might have been blown and ... Well, it's possible his family was targeted.'

Her blood ran cold. 'And do you believe that?'

Adam sighed. 'I don't know. It's being looked into. Obviously, under the circumstances, it's bound to be. There's not much more I can tell you, I'm sorry.'

Kaitlin had no idea what to think. Believing Greg now to be innocent of the horror she'd imagined him capable of, her mind was so stultified with shock she couldn't think beyond the obvious fact that Adam seemed desperate to want to find him guilty of something. 'I have to go,' she repeated. 'I need to speak to the police and I have to get back to Ruby.'

She glanced at her mum, who she could see was also keen to get home.

'I'll check the incident report. Get back to you,' Adam said.

Kaitlin didn't reply. A confusion of emotion churning inside her, she wasn't sure how to. Was she supposed to thank him for wrongly suspecting the man she was in love with of possible murder? *Had* been in love with. She felt nothing now but betrayed. What was worse, she also felt betrayed by Adam, whom she'd thought was genuine. Perhaps he had been, in his way. Possibly he had cared about her, but he'd obviously had his own agenda.

He drew in a breath. She could feel his tension even over the phone. 'Be careful, Kaitlin,' he warned her. 'I can't give you specifics, I don't have any, but I believe Steven Rawlings might be dangerous.'

'I'm not sure he is,' Kaitlin said after a pause. 'I think he's ill, desperate for a normal family life, which he perceived you were taking away from him, but I can't believe he would ever do anything to harm me.' Did she believe that? She just didn't know.

FIFTY-THREE

ADAM DIAZ

After double-checking with the guy he'd got to look into Rawlings' past, making sure he had his facts right about the timing of the fire and the mention of parental abuse on the psychiatric report, Adam was growing worried. Putting that together with the confirmation Kaitlin had just given him, he was sure that Rawlings was a psychologically damaged individual. Had he closed off his emotions in regard to his childhood? He would have needed to be capable of doing that in order to have worked so long undercover. Adam wasn't sure anyone could ever really close a lid on that sort of trauma. What had he done with all the pent-up anger and frustration? His gut told him Kaitlin had been right in her assumption that the man had been desperate for a normal family life. Her belief that he wouldn't harm her, though, Adam wasn't so convinced about that. He wished he was, but how would a desperate man react if his fiancée were to tell him there was no future for them, that she was taking the family he craved away from him?

He might be wrong, but his instinct was screaming at him that Kaitlin was in danger. She'd sounded flat, deflated and crushed, not surprisingly given what he'd told her. She was probably questioning everything about herself, wondering whether she could ever trust her own judgement again. He doubted she would easily let Rawlings back into her life, but she might agree to talk to the man; to meet up with him, alone more than likely, her natural instinct being to shield her child and her family from further upset.

He tried her number again, and was disappointed to find it went straight to voicemail. She'd clearly decided she couldn't trust him either. He couldn't blame her for that, but he had to make contact with her.

'Are you coming back to the station?' asked the officer who was waiting to give him a lift. He needed to get back. He needed to be in on the interview with Jessica Shaw. To make sure Sally took some gardening leave pending an investigation of the accident. Organise some counselling for her too. She wouldn't be deemed fit for work until the psych passed her as such. Seeing her reactions earlier, Adam was convinced she wouldn't be fit for a while.

'On my way,' he called back, trying Kaitlin again as he walked to the car. Still no answer. Dammit. She probably wouldn't be very receptive, but he would have to try to talk to her face to face. He only hoped she would agree to see him.

Climbing into the car with a nod of thanks to the officer, he placed a call to his daughter, who he guessed wasn't going to be pleased with him. They were due to eat out tonight. Looked like that wasn't going to happen.

'Hey, Dad,' Freya said, picking up straight away. Clearly she'd been expecting him to call, as he had too often before when they'd made arrangements. 'On the basis that you were going to be late, which you already are,' she said pointedly, 'I booked the latest table I could. If you're not about to tell me you're on your way, I may file for divorce.'

Adam's mouth twitched into a smile. She sounded more like a wife than a daughter. 'Sorry, sweetheart. Something's come up. I have an interview to do and then an emergency to attend to. Unavoidable, I'm afraid.'

'Oh *Dad*,' Freya groaned. 'It's your *birthday*. Can't you let up on yourself for one day?'

Adam felt bad. She should be out with her friends, living her life, not weighed down with worry about him. 'Not today, unfortunately,' he said softly. 'There's a woman who might be in trouble. I need to see her asap and alert her to the fact. I can't leave it, Freya. I would if I could.'

Freya sighed wearily. 'Okay,' she said reluctantly. 'I get it. Just ... don't take any risks, okay?'

Adam heard her voice wobble. 'I won't, I promise,' he assured her, his own voice tight. 'I'll be back as soon as I can. We'll do the birthday dinner at the weekend. Okay?'

Freya went quiet for a second. 'Famous last words,' she said.

FIFTY-FOUR

KAITLIN

It was quiet. Too quiet. Something wasn't right. Kaitlin sensed it as soon as she stepped into her parents' hall.

'Richard,' called Jayne, her voice tinged with apprehension as she peered quickly through the open lounge door and then hurried towards the kitchen.

Panic unfurling inside her, Kaitlin flew up the stairs. 'Ruby?' Hearing every creak of the landing above the deathly silence, she pushed open bedroom doors, praying they were playing hide-and-seek, that she would hear a delighted titter from some far corner.

She wasn't here. Her heart thudded. But her dad's car was on the drive. *They'd gone for a walk.* She tried to reassure herself, but couldn't. Her dad wouldn't take Ruby out in the rain. Where were they?

Whirling around, she skidded back to the stairs, then stopped dead, her heart slamming full force into her chest as her mum screamed from somewhere below, 'Richard!'

'*Mum!*' A hard knot of fear climbing her throat, Kaitlin caught hold of the stair newel, swinging around it and scrambling, half stumbling, back down to the hall. 'Mum?' She called, her heart slowing to a dull thud as she went through to the kitchen to find the back door wide open.

'Here!' Jayne shouted. 'Out here! It's your father. He's fallen. Call an ambulance, Kaitlin. Hurry!'

Kaitlin's phone was already in her hand, she realised, because she'd known, in her heart she'd known something dreadful was going to happen even before they'd arrived. Where was her baby? *Sean!* His aggressive tone on the phone sprang to her mind, threatening her, trying to control her, even using his own daughter. What had he done? *Please God, don't let him frighten her*. With trembling fingers, she jabbed 999 into her phone and asked for the police as well as an ambulance as she raced through the back door – and then froze, her stomach lurching as she took in the sight before her.

'Dad?' she said, her voice a parched whisper.

'He's hurt,' her mum cried wretchedly from where she was kneeling beside him. 'Oh Richard.' She reached to brush his hair away from the bloody gash on his forehead.

'I'm all right.' With an effort, Richard lifted his head. His voice was ragged, filled with remorse. He wasn't all right. Kaitlin's gaze flicked from where he lay on the ground to the wheelchair, which was tipped on its side, one of its wheels hopelessly buckled, and rage exploded inside her.

Quickly she swallowed it back, tried to contain the terrifying thoughts rushing pell-mell through her head. She went to him, dropping down next to him to take hold of his hand. 'I'm sorry, Dad,' she cried wretchedly. 'I should have known. Sean rang. He said he would come round if I didn't call him, but I didn't think—'

Richard tugged on her hand. 'Not Sean. Greg. I tried to stop him,' he said, closing his eyes in soul-crushing defeat. 'The back doorstep ... He moved the ramp. I'm so sorry, sweetheart. So, *so* sorry.'

Oh God, no. Kaitlin's heart turned to ice. The note! The

lock of hair. It was Ruby's. But when had he placed it there? When had he cut ...? Her locket. Her hand went to her neck. She'd left it on her dressing table, a lock of Ruby's hair in it. Had he taken that? Been planning this? He was deranged, dangerous. Adam had tried to warn her. She hadn't been listening, too busy being angry with him. And now ... She prayed fervently. Greg wouldn't harm her. He loved Ruby. She truly believed he loved her as his own. Where would he take her? What would he do, a man who was truly desperate not to lose her?

Tears clogging her throat, Kaitlin tried to console her dad, squeezing his hand reassuringly. 'The police will be here soon. The ambulance too. We'll find her. He won't hurt her, Dad,' she assured him with a conviction she wasn't sure she felt. 'Just lie still. Please lie still.'

FIFTY-FIVE

ADAM DIAZ

The interview had been unfruitful. Adam had thought it might be. Michael O'Sullivan had informed him almost before he'd walked through the interview room door that his client was reserving her right to silence. This despite them already having been informed that the interview was voluntary. Without anything other than what Kyle had given him while possibly not thinking coherently, they had no evidence that would justify holding her. The case would be reopened. If Kyle survived and was deemed capable, they might have something, but until then it was all unsubstantiated. O'Sullivan had reiterated that Jessica hadn't left the house on the night Melanie Ryan had died, that there were staff who could bear witness to that. Adam hadn't been surprised when the man had also sworn she was home the night Zoe had disappeared. The rest had been 'no comment' all the way through. Strange response for someone who was guilty of nothing, but there was no way yet to take it further.

Jessica had been quiet, subdued almost, her complexion pallid and her hands trembling as she'd laced her fingers on the table in front of her. All of which could be put down to the trauma she'd witnessed, although, strangely, neither of them had mentioned Kyle or indicated they wanted to be with him. She'd been scared. Again, that could have been because of what had happened to Kyle. The thing that had bothered Adam, though, and was bugging him still as he drove to Kaitlin's parents' house, was the expression on her face when they'd met Sally coming out of the interview room. Sally hadn't stopped – she was obviously on her way home – but the two woman had locked eyes momentarily, and for a fleeting second, Jessica Shaw had looked terrified.

As he was pondering that, he recognised the number coming up on his hands-free. Hurriedly, he picked up. 'Kaitlin?'

'He's taken her!' she blurted tearfully. 'Greg, he's taken Ruby. I don't know what to do, Adam.'

Jesus Christ, no. Adam's blood ran cold. 'When? Where are you?'

'While I was at my house. I'm at my parents' now. My dad ...' She faltered, a sob catching in her throat. 'Why has he done this, Adam?' she asked, her voice now filled with anguish. 'Where has he taken her?'

He hesitated. He had no idea where Greg might have taken her. As for why, at a guess, because he wanted something. He wanted Kaitlin. In his deluded mind, he wanted the family he'd thought he had. In doing this, did he think somehow he could get it back?

'Is your father injured?' he asked her carefully.

'Yes.' She choked the word out.

'And you've called an ambulance?'

'Yes, just now. He's conscious, but bleeding ... It's here,' she said, relief evident in her voice. 'The ambulance, it's just arrived.'

'And the police? You've called them?' Adam asked, then sighed with relief himself as he heard sirens wailing, indicating that uniforms were on the scene.

'I'm on my way,' he assured her, for what it was worth. 'Kaitlin, I need you to do something for me,' he added calmly.

He heard her shaky intake of breath, prayed she was listening and would understand. 'If you're outside the house, can you go back inside?' He didn't want to panic her, but his gut was telling him that Rawlings wouldn't be far away. If any harm came to her because of his thundering ineptitude ... 'Can you make sure you stay inside?'

'Why?' Kaitlin's voice was small, uncertain. She was frightened. Her little girl was missing. She would be fucking well *terrified*. Cursing himself for not seeing this coming, Adam gripped the steering wheel hard.

'I just need to know you're safe,' he answered vaguely.

'But my dad ... The paramedics will be bringing him out. I need to be with him.'

'Your mum will be with him,' he reminded her. 'You need to stay there. Greg might try to contact you.'

Kaitlin took a second. 'Okay, yes. Of course. I ... He tried to stop him. My dad, he tried to ... Greg moved the ramp. He moved the ramp from outside the back door and ... How could he *do* that?'

Adam had no doubt her father would have tried to stop him. He'd struck him as a determined man, one who was obviously blaming himself for not doing more to dissuade his daughter from becoming involved with Gregory Walker. Adam had tried to tell him it would have been attempting the impossible, citing his own daughter's bull-headedness when she'd set her sights on something. Richard had smiled in empathy, but still Adam could see the man's guilt, as if he felt responsible for Kaitlin losing her baby. Guessing that Richard, and Jayne too, would also be grieving the loss of the child, possibly not acknowledging that they were, Adam had shared his own loss with him, telling him how, after losing Joanne, he'd felt weighed down with guilt. How it had taken him a while to realise it was a destructive emotion, one which had prevented him moving forward and being there for his daughter. Richard had got what he was trying to say, though Adam thought he was probably doing it clumsily: that he needed to stop blaming himself; to simply be there for Kaitlin.

He gave her a moment, sensing she was trying very hard now not to break down. Wished he could offer her something other than baseless reassurances.

'Do you think he will make contact?' she asked him eventually.

'I do,' he said, hoping that would give her something to hold on to, guessing it would also increase the agonising apprehension she would be feeling. 'I'm almost at your road. I'll be there shortly.' He prayed his being there might offer her some sort of comfort. He doubted it would. Doubted anything would stop the horrors that would be unfolding in her head.

'Thank you,' she murmured.

'No problem.' He wished there was something she actually had to thank him for.

A minute later, he turned into her road to see the ambulance pulling away. No blue light, he noted, relief on some level sweeping through him.

Parking a way off, behind the two squad cars already out front, he surveyed the surrounding properties. The houses on the opposite side of the road were large Victorian properties mostly, several of them in various states of renovation.

An uneasy feeling creeping through him, he shoved his door open and raced towards Richard and Jayne's house. He was stopped by an officer out front, who asked for his identification. He tried to quash his irritation as he fumbled for it. The man was only doing his job, but he needed to get inside to check out the back, where Richard had fallen trying to stop Rawlings leaving.

Finally locating his ID in his inside pocket, he showed it.

'Sir.' The officer nodded him on.

'We need to get more officers here,' Adam instructed him. 'Uniforms going door-to-door, the surrounding properties searched pronto. Can you get on it?'

'Sir,' the officer replied with an obliging nod, and set about radioing it in.

Adam had almost reached the front door when he felt the impact, like a sledgehammer slamming into his back. His legs failing him, he seemed to fall in slow motion. His first sensation was an odd tingling, surging through his entire body. Seconds later, his left lung began to squeeze, making his breaths short and agonisingly painful. The warm sensation, he supposed, as his vision began to fade, was his blood flowing from the wound in his shoulder. His last thought, as his eyelids grew impossibly heavy, was that he seemed to be extremely competent at letting people down.

FIFTY-SIX

KAITLIN

Hearing the shot, like a thunderclap reverberating through her, Kaitlin froze. For a split second, she was rooted to the spot. And then, her stomach lurching violently as icy realisation crashed through her, she ran.

Flying to the hall, she was through the front door before strong arms were wrapped around her, preventing her leaving.

'You need to get back inside!' someone instructed urgently.

'Get down!' someone else shouted.

'For fuck's sake, call for armed backup. Now!' yelled the officer attempting to force her bodily back into the house.

A mixture of disbelief and primal fear pumping through her, Kaitlin wasn't listening. They couldn't just leave him lying there bleeding. Bleeding so badly. 'Adam!' she screamed. 'You need to help him. You have to *help* him!'

She fought the man. Other sets of arms joined his, and she struggled, though she could feel her own blood draining from her body. She *wouldn't* leave him. She had to go to him.

'Ms Chalmers, you're placing yourself in danger. Endangering other people,' the man who'd first caught hold of her whispered harshly. 'You need to think of your daughter.'

Kaitlin's frenzied gaze snapped to his. *Ruby.*

'He's alive.' He nodded quickly to where Adam lay on the ground, blood staining the road crimson. 'As soon as it's safe to, we'll get help to him. You have my word. Please go back inside.'

Seeing other officers crouching behind cars, a passer-by cradling his dog as he scrambled to join them, Kaitlin felt terror slice through her like a knife.

He had a gun. He had her baby girl and he had a *gun.* Her legs leaden beneath her, she stopped fighting, allowed herself to be guided into the lounge, where she dropped stultified to the sofa. The cacophony of noise outside, sirens wailing, people shouting instructions, had given way to complete silence. It was as if the world had stopped breathing.

Nausea swilled inside her. Dear Adam. He'd tried to help her. She'd thought badly of him, and that was all he'd done. He didn't deserve this. He had a *daughter.* A motherless teenage girl who would need him so much. *Please, please, don't let him die.* A low moan escaped her as she rocked to and fro, as if that could somehow alleviate the excruciating pain in her chest. *Please God, let my baby come home to me.*

'Ruby,' she whispered, wrapping her arms about herself, a shudder shaking through her as she imagined how bewildered her daughter would be, how frightened. Had she seen her grandpa fall? She would have been petrified.

She heard footsteps coming from the kitchen, and a low voice spoke. 'She's safe.'

She snapped her gaze towards him. 'Greg?'

FIFTY-SEVEN

'I wouldn't hurt her. Did you honestly think I would, *Kaitlin?*' He grated out her name, his fingers digging into her flesh as he took hold of her arm and pulled her up from the sofa. 'We need to go.'

'Go where?' Kaitlin swallowed back the fear climbing her chest.

'To join Ruby, where else?' He tightened his hold. 'We need to go now. Please don't try to attract anyone's attention or make a fuss. You won't see her again if you do. They'll never find her.'

'Greg, please ...' With no other choice, Kaitlin stumbled along with him. 'Why are you doing this? Please tell me where she is.'

'Quiet,' he said, his voice now frighteningly calm. 'Please.'

Kaitlin's heart thrashed wildly as he marched through the hall and into the kitchen. Where was he taking her? She glanced sideways at him. His face was taut, his eyes fixed forward. What was he going to do?

'Wait,' he instructed, pausing inside the back door, which was slightly ajar. Pulling it open, he peered around before stepping out – and Kaitlin felt hope fade that someone might see them. There was no one there. Everyone was out in the street, crouching in fear of the bullets that might kill them. That might have killed Adam. It was Greg. He *was* a murderer. *Oh God, Ruby.* Terror twisting her stomach, tears blinding her, she stumbled as he tugged her along with him.

His grip firm on her arm, Greg righted her. He wasn't about to let her go. 'Keep walking,' he ordered, marching her on past the broken wheelchair, the ramp discarded in the middle of the lawn. Ruby would have been with him when he'd done this. She would have trusted him at first, taken his hand happily, and then ... She would have seen all of *this*.

'Greg, please talk to me,' Kaitlin whispered, her voice cracking as he urged her through the gate that led to the garage at the bottom of the garden. The driveway beyond it opened onto a road that was more like a building site, with a new estate being developed. Where was her little girl? *Please don't let her be hurt.*

'It's Steven,' he corrected her. 'But I expect your caring detective has already told you that, hasn't he?'

Kaitlin stared at him as he strode briskly on, clutching her arm so tightly now she wanted to scream out in pain. She bit hard on the inside of her cheek, gulped back the jagged lump in her throat. He was *jealous*. Was that what this was all about? He'd run. After what Adam had told her about Zoe, she still didn't know why he had. He'd lied and he'd run. But he hadn't gone anywhere, had he? He'd been hiding in the derelict house opposite, watching her. Her blood turned to ice in her veins as an image of the man in the hoodie she'd seen hesitating in the hospital corridor flashed through her mind. She recalled Adam's arm around her, and pictured what this man, who she truly didn't know, must have seen. Had he interpreted that small show of comfort as intimacy? He really was unhinged.

'How much further?' she asked him, wanting to lead the

subject away from Adam and whatever ludicrous scenario he was imagining.

'Tired, aren't you, I bet?' She saw his eyes skim sideways. 'Bound to be, I suppose. Did they give you an anaesthetic?' he enquired, something resembling concern in his voice. 'I wasn't sure they did that for routine abortions.'

FIFTY-EIGHT

Kaitlin's heart was thumping so hard, she was sure it would burst through her chest. He thought she'd ... It was inconceivable. If she'd been scared before, now she was petrified. How did she reason with a man who was clearly unbalanced, a man who was so insecure he would imagine she could do such a thing?

'Greg ... Steven, you've got it wrong.' She tried to reach him through the wall of hostility sitting terrifyingly between them. 'I miscarried. I would never have aborted our baby. I *wanted* him. So much. You *know* I did.'

Greg said nothing. Breathing deeply, he stopped abruptly, yanking a car door open and bundling her inside. Dropping the locks – as if he needed to, as if she would try to run; he had her *child* – he went quickly to the driver's side, climbing in and driving off at speed. All of this without uttering a word. She glanced across at him. His grip was tight on the wheel, his jaw tense, his gaze focused on the road ahead, as if he was determined not to hear her.

Please help me. Twisting her fingers in her lap, she prayed with every fibre of her being that he was taking her to Ruby, offering her own life in exchange for that of her innocent child. She would give it in a heartbeat to keep her daughter safe. *Please don't let her be hurting.* She pictured her little face, her beautiful halo of copper hair, her intelligent, trusting eyes. She could see uncertainty in them, she could feel her bewilderment and her fear. It was tearing her apart.

'Greg, please talk to me.' Gulping back her desperation, she tried again to reach him.

He glanced at her then, finally, before returning his gaze to the road. 'So, he was just comforting you then, was he, your big-hearted copper?' he said scathingly.

'*Yes.*' Kaitlin jumped fiercely on that. Aware that he'd witnessed it, there was no point denying the contact between them. 'After all that's happened, that's *exactly* what he was doing. I'd just lost my baby. Zoe's still missing. My world was disintegrating. I was *upset.* Don't you think I was bound to be?'

'Right,' Greg sneered. 'And he just happened to be there?'

'Not by my invitation.' Kaitlin stared at him, incredulous. 'He was at the house. Mum and Dad's house. He was looking for *you.* I passed out, for pity's sake! Have you got no compassion, Greg? No feelings for me at all?'

He clenched his jaw hard. 'Regular little white knight, isn't he?' he said at length, his voice laden with contempt. 'Don't insult my intelligence, Kaitlin. I'm not an idiot. I saw the way he looked at you. I've *seen* him, going above and beyond, looking for any excuse to call on you. Please don't lie to me.'

He was completely irrational. There was no reasoning with him. None. 'I'm not lying.' She couldn't believe the absurd direction the conversation was taking. Biting back her tears, she tried vainly to understand where this was coming from. Had he always been like this? Had she mistaken his insane jealousy for caring? Was it a product of his childhood, the lack of love a child needed to thrive?

'Greg, why are you doing this?' she whispered, her voice cracking. 'I don't understand. I had a miscarriage. I didn't know where you were. I was devastated.'

'Clearly in need of some comfort, then?'

Terror clawed at her chest. There was no way to answer. Nothing more she could say. He truly believed she would welcome the attention of another man having just lost her child.

He glanced at her again, his eyes hard and unforgiving. 'I *saw*, Kait,' he said. 'Even a fucking blind man could see he fancies you.'

'You're *wrong*,' Kaitlin cried, tears of frustration and fear spilling down her face. 'He was being sympathetic. He—'

'And *you* encouraged him.'

'I did *not*!' She choked back a sob. 'Greg, *please* … just stop.'

He shook his head, a wry smile twitching at his mouth. 'Not happening, Kaitlin,' he said, stepping on the brake and yanking the steering wheel hard right, causing her to brace herself against the dashboard. 'You belong to me. If I can't have you, no one will.'

Kaitlin's blood froze. What did he mean?

'We need to walk,' he said, bringing the car to a stop. They were at the dock.

Her mind reeled in confusion and fear. 'Why are we here?'

'To join Ruby,' he answered casually. He climbed out and walked to the passenger side. 'I'm not an unreasonable man, Kaitlin,' he went on, extending a hand to help her climb out. 'We all make mistakes. I can forgive and forget. We can move on together as a family. It's what Ruby wants. She's excited at the prospect of an alternative lifestyle.'

Kaitlin followed his gaze as he nodded towards the river, and hope flickered inside her at the sight of the brightly coloured boats bobbing languidly on the water. *Ruby*. She was inside one of them, she could *feel* her. She looked back at Greg. Saw the nostalgic glint in his eye, the smile curving his mouth as he glanced off into the distance, and realised he was truly mad. After all he'd done, he thought they could just sail off into the sunset together?

'I tried to forgive my parents,' he said reflectively, taking hold of her arm. 'It wasn't something I could easily talk to you about, you gathered that. I would have liked to, though.' He paused. Kaitlin swallowed back the stone in her throat. 'The psychiatrist I saw said it would help me move on if I could learn to forgive them, accept that they were flawed but that they'd done their best with what they had. It was bullshit.' He laughed ironically, then set off at a brisk pace.

'Why?' Kaitlin croaked, playing for time while she sifted through the jumble of thoughts in her head, trying desperately to think what to do. It was growing dark. There was no one about. Even if there were, if she attracted attention, he would run. If *she* ran ... No. She'd made up her mind there was no way she'd do that. No way she'd risk her baby's life.

'They *weren't* doing their best. They didn't give a shit,' he replied, a derisory edge to his tone. 'Their best as far as I was concerned was when they forgot I even existed.'

Kaitlin felt for him. She couldn't help it. Whoever he was now, no child should have to suffer that, to feel so scared and insufferably lonely.

'Do you know what she said when I found the courage to go and see her, the creature who dragged me up?' He laughed scornfully. 'She said I'd ruined her life. Can you believe that? *I* ruined *her* life.' His eyes, full of dark shadows, seemed to be searching hers for understanding.

'No,' she said, attempting to placate him, to relate to him.

'I couldn't believe it either. I reckon the world's better off without people like that.' Heaving in a terse breath, he looked away. 'I thought I might feel some guilt,' he added pensively, after a second, 'but you know what? I didn't. Watching her burn, seeing her beg for mercy, *that* was the best therapy by far. The bastards deserve to rot in hell.'

It took a second for comprehension to dawn. When it did, fear flooded every vein in Kaitlin's body.

FIFTY-NINE

'Where's Ruby?' she asked, attempting some level of calmness through the horror unfurling in her head. Her stomach turned over in revulsion and disbelief. The act of revenge Adam had spoken about had been Greg's. He'd killed his parents. He'd watched them burn and seemed to have not one shred of remorse. Heart thudding, she imagined what might be going through his mind now. In his warped reasoning, hadn't she herself abandoned him too? Thrown away his love as if it meant nothing? He thought she'd aborted his child. A new wave of panic unfurled inside her as she wondered why he had a gun, what he'd intended to do with it before Adam became the focus of his pent-up fury.

He glanced at her, and what she saw in his eyes chilled her to the core. There was nothing. No anger, no hatred, no warmth. Nothing. 'Not far now,' he answered calmly, and fixed his attention forward again.

'Why are we going this way?' Nausea burned in Kaitlin's throat. He was leading her across the footbridge, just a stone's throw from Zoe's apartment. Was it possible he really did have no compassion? No feelings at all, for her, for Ruby, who would surely be distraught? She couldn't believe that. That she wouldn't have been alerted to this cold indifference before. He'd loved her. She was positive he had. She clung to that. Prayed with her whole soul that he would show her some mercy and reunite her with her child. And what then? The thought struck her like a thunderbolt. She and Ruby would be alone with him. She couldn't imagine he would bring them together out in the open, where they might find a chance to escape. Where there was the possibility someone might see them. Assuming Ruby was on one of the boats, they would be trapped.

Her pulse quickened, blood thrumming so fast through her veins, her head spun. She would fight him. She closed her free hand into a fist, squeezed it until her fingernails dug painfully into her palm. With every ounce of strength she possessed, she would fight him. She would claw his eyes from his head before she would let any harm come to her daughter.

'I'm not sure.' His stride faltered. 'Because I need to show you, I suppose. I need you to be able to trust me, Kaitlin.' He slowed a little as he appeared to ponder, and then marched on, leading her over the bridge and down to the bank. 'Just like I trusted you,' he added acerbically. 'I did, you know. Implicitly.'

A few yards along the bank, he paused and turned to her. His eyes had darkened, turning almost to cobalt. 'I know you probably think I'm not capable of forgiveness, but I am. I can forgive you, Kaitlin. I realise you would have been devastated by my leaving like that, of course I do. But I had to. I couldn't have your caring detective digging up my past, looking too closely. My parents got what they deserved, but no jury in the land would come to that conclusion, would they? No one would believe that I didn't go there that day with the intent to kill. When she said what she did, I ... It all came back, the pain, the humiliation, the absolute fucking fear I lived with every single day of my life. I lost it. It was as if I was standing outside myself looking on. I could see what I was doing, but I couldn't make myself stop.'

Clamping a hand over the back of his neck, he looked away. Looked back at her. 'There was no way I was about to let Diaz fit me up for something I didn't do, either. I would have lost you. Then he'd have had free rein, wouldn't he? I know what you did was a mistake, that you were coerced by a man who took advantage of the fact that you felt vulnerable. I can learn to trust you again, though. I still love you.' He shrugged, as if it were something he couldn't help. 'I've tried not to, tried to detach from my feelings, but I can't stop loving you, Kaitlin. I doubt I ever will. I just want what's mine. My family. It's all I've ever wanted. I knew you were the one, the woman I could spend the rest of my life with, the minute I saw you out with that prat you were married to. I watched you with Ruby. I'd been watching you for some time actually, before I dared approach you. I loved how you were with her. It was obvious how much you loved her.'

Kaitlin felt sick to the pit of her stomach. She'd been right. He'd marked her out way before she'd come out of the house one morning to find she had a flat tyre. She'd thought he was a gentleman when he'd stopped while passing by to assist her. He hadn't been passing by. He'd *slashed* it.

'The thing is, I need to know that you still love me.' His expression was hopeful as he studied her, like a needy child. 'Do you?'

Icy goosebumps prickled the entire surface of Kaitlin's skin. He really believed that they had a future together, that it all hinged on him being able to forgive her. Panic rose so fast inside her, it threatened to choke her. She had to get away from him. She had to find a way to get to her daughter. Her mind ticked feverishly. 'I never stopped loving you,' she said, praying her eyes didn't betray her. 'I thought you'd gone for good. I thought I would never see you again, and ... I didn't know what to *do*, who to trust. I ...' She trailed off, swiping tears from her face, willing him to believe her.

His expression softened. 'I'm here now,' he assured her, threading an arm around her. 'I said I always would be, didn't I? I'll take care of everything. You just concentrate on getting your strength back and looking after little Ruby. Once we get away from here, things will be fine, you'll see. Back to normal.'

Kaitlin's blood curdled. He was smiling – kindly, as he would at Ruby. He needed her to need him. To be emotionally dependent on him. And she had been. She'd measured herself through his eyes, by whether *he* thought she was deserving of love, never once stopping to tell herself she was. She'd thought he loved her for who she was, but hadn't she gone along with everything he decided, because she hadn't wanted to disappoint him? She'd *enabled* him.

Nodding tremulously, she forced a smile. 'Can we go to Ruby now?' she asked, her hand trembling as she wiped it under her nose. 'I'm desperate to see her.'

'Shortly,' he promised, relaxing his hold around her to search in his pocket. Kaitlin started breathing again as he produced a tissue and handed it to her. 'I need you to know something before we do.'

Screaming inside, she waited.

'I need you to know I would never harm anyone who didn't deserve it.' He searched her eyes warily. 'Your friend Zoe ... I didn't do what Diaz was determined to prove I did.'

'Prove how?' Kaitlin shook her head in confusion. 'If there wasn't any evidence, then ...'

Greg's smile was now one of indulgence. 'Being a policeman doesn't make him whiter than white, Kaitlin. None of us are that, are we? He would have manufactured any evidence he couldn't find. He wanted me out of the way.' His smile slipped, his eyes, drilling into hers, growing dangerously cold. '*Didn't* he?'

'I ... I don't know,' Kaitlin stammered. Seeing him move closer, she stepped instinctively back.

'Whoops, careful.' He reached out as she almost lost her footing. 'You're very close to the edge,' he said quietly. The look in his eyes, one of amusement, caused Kaitlin's heart to stop beating.

SIXTY

ZOE

She'd waited and she'd watched the woman who had made Daniel's life a living nightmare. She'd tried to resist as the pitiful overindulged creature had spoon-fed her drugs – sleeping pills, she suspected. The fluid she'd crushed them into, along with small sips of water, had been her only sustenance. She'd slept heavily, had moments of clarity, listening as the woman told her life story, as if she were her confessor. How much she loved Daniel. How she would kill for him. Had killed.

She would bet the woman was cursing her incompetence at having forgotten to turn the key in the lock when she'd flown from the bedroom she'd kept her imprisoned in while she decided what to do with her. There'd been a commotion outside, a man yelling that Daniel had taken off, that there'd been an accident outside. It had been enough to give Zoe the strength to fight back. She'd been weak physically, but the will to survive had been strong. That was what she was, what she'd always assured Kaitlin she was: a survivor.

Using walls and furniture for support, she'd found her way down two flights of stairs, out through the open patio doors into the world she thought she would never see again.

She'd watched as Daniel had lain in the lane, his body broken, his blood seeping into the damp, cold earth beneath him. She'd had to leave him there, even though, despite what he'd done to her, she didn't want to. She would make sure Jessica Shaw's story was related to the people it should be, the police. But first she had to bide her time, ensure the person who was parading as a protector of the people was dealt with. Before that, though, her priority was Kaitlin, who as far as she'd known was still at the mercy of a man she had felt in her bones was dangerous. Now, she bloody well knew he was.

She watched as Gregory Walker caught hold of Kaitlin's shoulders, manoeuvring her away from the edge of the bank. 'I left her here,' he said as Kaitlin glanced fearfully from him to the fast-flowing water and back again. 'She was alive. She—'

'I'm still alive, no thanks to you, you bastard!' Zoe snarled, mustering every ounce of strength to spring from the foliage along the bank and plough full force into him. Greg's look was one of surprise as he teetered precariously, giving way to terror as he realised his fate and flailed backward into the river.

'Kaitlin! Run!' Zoe grabbed hold of her arm. 'We have to go. Now!' she yelled as Greg thrashed in the water, trying to stay afloat, attempting to orientate himself. *Shit!* They had to get out of here.

Kaitlin, though, seemed to be rooted to the spot. Clearly shocked, her face deathly pale, she blinked in confusion. 'Zoe ...?'

'We haven't got time for this, Kait. For God's sake, *move!*' Zoe pleaded, tugging on her arm, trying to drag her along the bank.

'Kaitlin!' Greg screamed. 'Don't leave me!'

Kaitlin stopped, her face agonised as she glanced behind her to see him go under again. 'I can't!' she cried. 'I can't just leave him. He'll drown!'

'He won't.' Zoe tugged harder. 'And if he does, tough shit.'

'But Ruby!' Kaitlin struggled to break free of her. 'I have to find her! He—'

'I *have* her.' Facing her, Zoe caught hold of both of her arms, locking her eyes hard on hers. 'She's *safe*. Please trust me. We need to leave.'

'Kaitlin, help me!' Greg shouted, his voice strangled. '*Please*! Don't ...' His words turned to a gurgle as they were swallowed by the water.

'Kait, listen to me. We need to go,' Zoe begged. 'He's dangerous. You know he is.'

Kaitlin scanned her face, her eyes flecked with indecision.

'You owe him *nothing*,' Zoe said vehemently. 'He took your daughter. It's Ruby who needs you, not him.'

SIXTY-ONE

KAITLIN

'Where is she?' Kaitlin asked, as they raced towards Zoe's apartment block.

'With Janice, my neighbour. She'll be safe now. You'll both be safe.' Zoe squeezed her hand tightly in her own.

They'd barely reached Janice's door when it was flung open. The woman immediately pulled Kaitlin into a hug. 'Thank God you're all right,' she murmured. 'I've been beside myself with worry. That *man* ... Who would ever have—'

'Where is she?' Kaitlin repeated, her throat so tight she could hardly get the words out.

'She's here. She's fine,' Janice said softly, stepping back and ushering them in.

Behind her, Ruby appeared from the lounge. 'Mummy!' she cried, her little face a mixture of bewilderment and delight. 'Where *were* you?'

'Here, baby. I'm here.' Kaitlin crouched down, opening her arms for her little girl to fly into.

'Greg said you were coming, but you didn't, and I got lonely,' Ruby said, her voice tiny. 'I didn't know what to do.'

Kaitlin hugged her tight. 'I'm here, sweetheart,' she repeated. 'I promise I'm not going anywhere.'

'Did you have to go to the hospital again?' Ruby asked worriedly.

'No,' Kaitlin assured her, imagining the uncertainty and fear her little girl must have felt. 'I had some errands to run,' she eased away from her to study her face, 'then the car wouldn't start. I would have got here sooner otherwise.'

Ruby nodded, accepting the lie. 'Zoe came for me,' she said. 'I wasn't sure whether to go with her, but she's not strange, is she?'

'No.' Kaitlin emitted a strangled laugh. 'You were right to go with her, darling. She's my best friend.' She extended a hand, and was overwhelmed with relief and gratitude when Zoe caught it, squeezing it gently.

'Are you all right, Ruby? Apart from being a bit worried and lonely, I mean?' she asked, looking her daughter over carefully for any indication that might tell her she wasn't.

Winding a strand of hair around her finger, Ruby studied her silently for an agonising second. Then, 'I'm all right, Mummy,' she said with an assured nod. 'Greg took me on a boat. He said we were going on holiday, but then he didn't come back and I did get a bit scared. I was fine, though, because the boat was cosy, and I'm quite big now, so I didn't cry or anything.'

Her little face was so earnest, so full of concern, Kaitlin felt joy tinged with unbearable pain. She'd put her child at risk. She'd rushed headlong into a relationship because of her own insecurities. The cost to her daughter could have been catastrophic.

'I'm glad Auntie Zoe came,' Ruby added.

'Me too, sweetheart.' Giving her daughter another firm squeeze, Kaitlin got shakily to her feet to finally look at her friend properly. Realising how pale she was, how drained she looked, that the clothes she was wearing, which hung loose on her small frame, weren't her own, she felt her heart wrench. There was blood in her hair, which looked as if it hadn't been washed since she'd last seen her. 'Where were you?' she asked. 'What happened, Zoe?'

'It's a long story.' Zoe's eyes darted towards the front door. 'We need to get out of here,' she said, as Janice diplomatically led Ruby off to the kitchen with the promise of a fizzy drink and a slice of cake. 'I'm not sure where might be best to go.' She walked towards the window, inching the curtain open and peering out.

'We need to call the police.' Kaitlin's head swam with confusion. Greg might be alive, or he might have drowned, she didn't know, but clearly he *was* dangerous. They couldn't just go out there and drive off.

'No!' Zoe whirled around, her face draining of colour, her eyes shot through with shocking fear. 'We can't. Not yet. There's no way we can do that.'

'We *have* to.' Kaitlin stared at her, uncomprehending. 'He might be out there. We—'

'It wasn't him, Kait!' Zoe came quickly towards her, taking hold of her shoulders. 'It wasn't Greg who attacked me. It wasn't Greg who fired that shot.'

'*What?*' Kaitlin felt the strength drain from her body.

Zoe held her gaze, her expression adamant. 'It wasn't him, Kait. I was there. I saw him leaving with Ruby. I've been following him. That's how I knew where Ruby was. I'm positive it wasn't him.'

SIXTY-TWO
ADAM DIAZ

'Are you sure you want to do this?' Amy asked as she helped Adam into the shirt she'd found him in the hospital lost property department.

'Positive.' Gritting his teeth, he suppressed a wince as she eased the shirt over his shoulder. 'The bullet went in and out. I'll survive.'

'You hope. You're as white as those sheets.' She nodded at the trolley he was pulling himself painfully up from. 'You lost a lot of blood, Adam. I really don't think this is a good idea.'

'I'm okay,' he lied. 'I just need to find out what's happening and then I'll go home.'

'That's what modern communications are for.' Amy eyed him, unimpressed. 'I'm sure there's someone at the station who can bring you up to speed.'

Adam had tried that. *The whereabouts of Kaitlin Chalmers are currently unknown. We have everyone available on it* was all the information he'd got. Kaitlin wasn't answering her phone. Her mother was beside herself. He couldn't stay here not knowing what the bloody hell was going on.

'Your daughter's not going to be pleased,' Amy warned him.

Freya wasn't, far from it. Adam had not long spoken to her on the phone. She'd told him the entire force would be out looking for Kaitlin. That him killing himself wouldn't make any difference. She was pissed off with him. 'Sounds like you're determined to make me an orphan,' she'd said, after failing to dissuade him from discharging himself, and then promptly ended the call. She was worried. Upset, with good reason. He would need to make it up to her. Right now, though, putting together what Kyle Roberts had said and what his gut was telling him, he was doubtful that the man had attacked Zoe, which meant someone else had. Jessica Shaw? Someone they hadn't considered who might have followed her from the party? Might it have been Gregory Walker, aka Steven Rawlings, after all? He had no idea. No idea where Kaitlin and her little girl might be. He couldn't stay here. He had to be doing something. Anything.

'Your doctor's *definitely* not pleased. This is against medical advice, you know that?' Amy gave him an admonishing look as he took a second to steady himself.

'I do,' Adam assured her with a weak smile.

She eyed the ceiling. 'Your taxi's out front.' She sighed. 'Go home once you've checked in, Adam. No job's worth risking your health for.'

'Yes, miss,' he joked, leaving her shaking her head in despair.

Twenty minutes later, he was walking through the outer office at the station, earning himself surprised looks from his colleagues, when he spotted Sally through the glass partition. He frowned. He shouldn't be here, but she definitely shouldn't be.

'Can I get you a coffee, sir?' someone asked. 'And a double brandy to go with it?'

Adam's mouth twitched into a smile. 'Yes to the coffee,' he said. 'Probably best to pass on the brandy while taking the painkillers.'

Nodding his thanks, he glanced back to the corridor to see Sally making for the locker room. She'd come to collect her things presumably. She looked distracted; clearly she hadn't seen him. But then it was no surprise she seemed miles away, he supposed, given that she would be facing an investigation into the accident. Deciding to try to offer her some support, he headed after her.

She was searching for something in her locker when he walked in, and didn't see him immediately. When she did, at first she looked startled, and then guilty. Why would that be? Something in her locker that shouldn't be there, maybe? He watched as she reached hastily to retrieve an item crudely wrapped in a carrier bag. Booze? he wondered warily. Might explain her erratic driving.

'Shit, you took me by surprise,' she said, wrapping the bag more tightly around whatever it was, tucking it under her arm and then fumbling to close the locker.

'I gathered,' Adam said, eyeing the parcel. It looked to be the approximate size and weight of a bottle, but he'd never smelled anything on her. Could be vodka, of course, the tipple of choice if you didn't want to reek of alcohol. Then again, maybe he was being overly suspicious, looking for a reason why she'd been driving so recklessly. It was probably no more than that the adrenaline had been pumping. 'You doing okay?'

'Yes,' she answered with a short nod. 'Well, not great, you know, but ...' She shrugged awkwardly. 'You?'

'I'm still breathing. I guess things could have been worse.' He smiled ruefully.

She nodded again and looked away.

'I take it you needed something urgently?' he asked, avoiding pointing out that she shouldn't be on the premises pending investigation.

'Just personal stuff,' she said. She still wasn't looking at him. Adam ran his eyes over her. She seemed edgy, nervous. As she would be, all things considered. He tried not to read too much into it.

'Do you want to go and grab a coffee?' he asked. 'Talk things through. It might help.'

'No.' She shook her head hard. 'I have somewhere else I need to be.' She tucked the parcel further under her arm and moved past him, giving him a wide berth as she did, and all without making eye contact.

Watching her go, Adam felt an uneasiness creep through him. What precisely did she have in that bag? He got that she would be worried, embarrassed because of what she'd done, but the evasive eye contact seemed more than that. She'd been in one hell of a hurry to get away from him.

Running a hand over his neck, he looked from the door back to her locker. Noting that she hadn't closed it properly, he walked across to it, debating for a second. He shouldn't, and if she was secretly drinking she would have removed any evidence, but …

He ignored his conscience and hooked a finger under the door. Nothing much in there. A spare shirt, it looked like, wedged behind a pair of walking shoes. Muddy walking shoes, he noted, frowning curiously. He lifted them out, and cursed silently when something fell onto the floor at his feet.

Glancing down, he braced himself for the pain that would be bound to rip through him, then bent to pick it up. 'Jesus,' he muttered, his throat thick with disbelief as he looked down at the blue gemstone earring shining in the palm of his hand. Realising exactly where it had come from, his heart sank.

SIXTY-THREE

KAITLIN

'Where's the bloody taxi?' Zoe peered agitatedly out of the window again. 'Sorry,' she added, glancing back at Ruby, who, having heard raised voices, had come back from the kitchen. She was sitting on Janice's sofa, nibbling at her cake and watching everyone carefully.

Zoe had stopped talking abruptly when Ruby had appeared, and Kaitlin was none the wiser as to who had attacked her on the riverbank the night she'd gone missing, or where she'd been since. All she did know was that Zoe had stated categorically that Greg wasn't involved. Why then had they needed to flee so desperately? Because he was ill, undoubtedly out of touch with reality, she reminded herself. Because he'd taken Ruby, somehow believing they could have a future together. She recalled what he'd told her about his parents, and an icy shudder ran through her. Closing her eyes against the horrific image the recollection evoked, she went across to sit next to Ruby, wrapping an arm around her shoulders and squeezing her close. Greg loved this little girl. She truly believed that. Would he harm her, though? Kaitlin couldn't make herself believe that, but she didn't know, did she? She'd only ever known a tiny part of him, the better part perhaps, giving her a glimpse of the man he might have been had his life taken a different path.

'That must be it.' Zoe almost wilted with relief as there was a knock on the door.

'Wait.' Kaitlin jumped to her feet. She was about to remind her that whoever it was would have needed the security code for the gate, but Janice was already marching purposefully towards the door. 'I've got it,' she said. 'It will be that nice lady police officer. She left me her number, so I rang her. Best to be safe, I—'

'Janice, don't!' Zoe yelled – too late. The colour draining from her face, she stumbled back as Sally stepped through the open door. 'What do you want?' she asked, her voice a frightened croak.

'Just a chat,' Sally answered, smiling pleasantly.

What on earth ... Catching hold of Ruby's hand, Kaitlin glanced between the two women. Zoe was shaking visibly. She was petrified. Of Sally?

Sally's gaze swivelled briefly towards Kaitlin, and what she saw in her eyes caused goosebumps to rise over the entire surface of her skin. Hostility, bordering on hatred.

'I've called the police,' Zoe said, a defiant look crossing her face as she made a determined effort to stand taller.

Arching an eyebrow amusedly, Sally stepped towards her. 'Oh yes?' she said. 'Not exactly beating a path to the door, are they?'

Kaitlin heard the sarcasm in her voice, saw the contempt in her eyes harden, and her heart lurched in disbelief. She *knew*. She knew that Zoe hadn't called them. Kaitlin hadn't understood her reluctance, but now it was blindingly, terrifyingly clear. She hadn't called them because it might have been Sally who responded to her call.

Her gaze shot back to Zoe, who nodded almost imperceptibly towards the open front door. Torn, her pulse racing, her head screaming the impossible truth, Kaitlin hesitated; then, instinct urging her to protect her child, she inched towards it.

'*Stay*.' Sally's eyes pivoted to her, freezing her to the spot. 'There's no need to leave,' she said, her tone filled with menace. 'You don't think I would harm you and little Ruby, do you?' she asked, surprise crossing her face. 'I'm a police officer, Kait. I'm here to protect you, not—'

'Liar!' Zoe stepped forward. 'She's a *liar*. Go, Kait. It's me she wants, for whatever sad, sick reason, not you.'

'You're distressed, Zoe,' Sally said tightly. 'You've clearly been through a traumatic experience. Why don't you come with me and we'll—'

'It was her!' Zoe looked desperately at Kaitlin. 'I thought it was Daniel following me. He said he was close by and I thought it was him, but it wasn't. It was her!'

'You're not making sense, Zoe.' Sally shook her head. 'Let me take you to the hospital.' She took a brisk step towards her. 'We'll get you some help and—'

'It was *her*!' Zoe screamed. 'She kicked me, she punched me. She tried to fucking *kill* me.'

Sally rolled her eyes. 'Are you serious, Zoe?' She laughed scornfully. 'After all these years, you're still playing the little victim to get Kait's attention.'

Zoe held her gaze. 'It was her, Kait,' she said again. 'Not Greg. She's jealous – of me, of him; anyone who gets close to you. She's—'

'Enough!' Sally growled.

Kaitlin saw her fumble in her jacket and knew before it appeared what she was searching for. 'Why?' she cried, angry tears clogging her throat. 'Why are you *doing* this?' But she knew. It was all some frantic attempt to stop people finding out what she'd done.

'Let Kait go,' Zoe said, standing her ground even in the face of the gun that Sally was pointing right at her. 'She's done nothing to you.'

'No. Apart from not see me.' Sally glanced reflectively down.

Kaitlin couldn't believe what she was hearing. 'But *why* would you attack her, Sally? Why would you want to hurt her?'

'I don't know!' Sally yelled. 'I don't know,' she repeated, her tone quieter, confused. 'I didn't intend to. I knew Greg had gone after her. I thought I could help. I saw him talking to her and ... I just wanted to have a chat with her, that was all.' She looked at Kaitlin beseechingly. 'To ask her what was going on, why she'd suddenly appeared out of the blue, why she seemed dead set on not liking the man you were about to marry. I knew he was a control freak – anyone but you could have seen it – but Zoe didn't know that. She didn't know *anything*. How could she when she'd been off living her exotic life in Portugal? And then she just waltzed back and expected to pick right up where she'd left off.'

'The chat got out of hand,' Kaitlin concluded, her throat dry.

'She was always so appealing, with her fucking sob story of a life,' Sally spat, her expression a mixture of hurt and fury. 'You practically adopted her. You didn't seem to realise you were pushing your friends out. People who cared about you. *Me*. You couldn't see that poor little Zoe was manipulating you just as surely as that prick of a fiancé was, trying to keep you all to herself. You're too trusting, Kait. You've always been too bloody *trusting*.'

She'd done it out of jealousy? Carried out an inconceivable act of violence because she'd been *jealous*. And now she was desperate. That was the overriding emotion now in her eyes – and it was truly terrifying.

Humiliation flooding her face as Kaitlin continued to stare at her, Sally dropped her gaze – and then looked sharply back up as Janice took Ruby's hand in hopes of leading her to safety.

'*Stay*,' she repeated, clenching her jaw hard.

Kaitlin willed herself to be strong, even half as strong as Zoe was. 'She's just a baby, Sally. Please let Janice look after her. Please do that for me.'

Sally wavered. Then, after an excruciatingly long second, she nodded. 'I don't suppose it makes much difference now anyway.' She shrugged.

Kaitlin had no idea what she meant, didn't dare imagine what scenario might play out once Ruby had left, but she was grateful for this one small mercy.

'Go with Janice, sweetheart,' she said, bending to kiss the top of her daughter's head.

Janice pressed a finger to her lips, indicating to Ruby that she should be quiet, then her eyes slid meaningfully sideways to the front door. Kaitlin felt a flutter of apprehension. There was someone out on the landing. She was certain that was what Janice was trying to communicate. Someone who knew the security code to the gate. The new code that Janice had given her.

'What happens now?' she asked once Janice had led Ruby out, her voice calm despite the fear surging through her.

'I'm not sure.' Sally glanced down, as if she couldn't quite hold her gaze. Kaitlin's eyes flicked quickly to Zoe, and she braced herself for what might unfold. It was their only hope, they both knew it. 'I only ever wanted to be your friend, Kait. To be involved in your life. That was all.'

'You can be,' Kaitlin tried.

Sally smiled sadly. 'I don't think so. Not now. Unless you come to visit me in prison, of course.' There was a flicker of hope in her eyes. 'But you won't do that, will you, not with *her* back, monopolising you just like she always has.'

Her attention back on Zoe, her intent clear as her face hardened, she didn't see Greg, had no idea he was there until his arm slid around her neck, his other hand striving to reach the gun.

Zoe dropped in an instant, the shot missing her to shatter the window.

The struggle was brief, violent, two more shots ringing deafeningly out against a backdrop of police sirens.

The last words on Greg's lips as Kaitlin scrambled across to where he lay were 'I love you.'

EPILOGUE

As the crowd dispersed, Kaitlin walked towards the graveside. She'd only ever met her once, but she recognised the slim figure still standing there, staring down at the casket that held the mortal remains of the woman she'd once loved.

'Emelie,' she said softly as she approached her.

Emelie turned her gaze towards her, unseeing for a second, it seemed, and then, 'Kaitlin, you came,' she said, a heartwrechingly sad smile curving her beautiful features. 'I didn't think you...' Overcome, clearly, she trailed off and dropped her gaze to the simple spray of white roses and freesias she held in her hand.

'She was my friend,' Kaitlin said, her throat closing as she saw the tears slide down the woman's cheeks.

'She thought a lot of you. She would be glad you came,' Emelie whispered.

'She would be glad you're here too.' Kaitlin moved to thread an arm around her. Under the circumstances, it must have been a difficult decision for her to make. To have travelled from Paris, she must clearly have thought a lot of her. Had Sally known how much? Kaitlin wondered. She wondered about so much.

Why, most of all, since the terrible night that had ended her and Greg's lives.

Emelie nodded. 'Love, it has a lot to answer for, does it not?' she asked, as if reading her mind. 'It can inspire people to climb mountains, to make great works of art,' she went on, her pretty French accent lending eloquence to her words. 'Unrequited love, or jealousy, I think can also drive people to great acts of despair.'

She fell silent for a moment and Kaitlin felt Emelie's despair as she crouched to place her flowers on the ground rather than throw them onto the coffin. 'Find peace, my love,' she murmured.

After another contemplative moment, she straightened up. 'I have something for you,' she said, reaching into her bag. 'Sally carried it with her.' Drawing out a photograph, she handed it to her. 'I thought you might like to have it.'

Kaitlin was taken aback as she looked at it, and then a turmoil of emotion ran through her. It was a photograph of herself and Sally, arms wrapped around each other, cheeks pressed together, and lips pursed for the camera. It had been taken many years ago. At her hen night, Kaitlin recalled, before her marriage had consumed her life.

'Be happy, Kaitlin.' Emelie reached to squeeze her arm as she studied it. 'We owe it to ourselves to try to be that.' Leaning to press a kiss to each of her cheeks, Emelie gave her another small smile, then turned to walk towards the path.

Kaitlin stayed where she was for a second, and then turned her eyes to the heavens. 'Oh Sally,' she whispered, tears rising for the woman who obviously had been driven to an act of deepest despair.

She sensed someone approach her, but still she let the tears fall. There were so many stuffed inside her, she didn't know how to stop them.

'Okay?' Adam asked quietly, sliding his arm around her.

Kaitlin nodded. It was an instinctive response.

Adam squeezed her closer. 'Tears are good,' he said. 'Therapeutic, so I'm told.'

Kaitlin smiled tremulously. Was he a man who'd allowed himself to cry? She hoped he was. That he had.

'Do you want to walk?' he asked.

Again, Kaitlin nodded. Two visits to gravesides in two days were two visits too many.

After giving her shoulders another comforting squeeze, Adam reclaimed his arm and they walked in silence back to the church, each with their own thoughts. He would be trying to come to terms with things, too, Kaitlin guessed.

'I thought you'd like to know that the case against Kyle Roberts regarding the murder of Melanie Ryan is being re-investigated, with a view to Jessica Shaw being charged,' he said after a while. 'She's admitted to kidnapping Zoe, so she'll be facing charges there too.'

Kaitlin closed her eyes. 'Why did she do it?' she asked. What the woman had done was incomprehensible, inexplicable, but she couldn't help feeling for her, for her children whose lives would be blighted by all of this.

Adam paused before answering. 'Jealousy is often a driving force for murder,' he answered eventually. 'Betrayal and unrequited love can lead people to all sorts of madness,' he echoed what Emelie had just said.

Greg had felt she'd betrayed him. He'd truly believed it. Kaitlin's heart squeezed as she imagined him lying in the cold, damp earth. There'd been no one who cared for him at his funeral to say their last goodbyes, apart from her. Zoe had been right when she'd said Greg would fight for her. He had. There *had* been good in him, the man who'd had no identity he could truly call his own, no family. Kaitlin had loved that part of him. She would grieve for him, be the friend and the family who would visit to put flowers on his grave. She would have a garden full of them, thanks to the tiny plants and seeds he'd nurtured. It would comfort her to see them blooming. She would lay some on Sally's grave, too, whenever she came.

'What happened?' she asked him. 'How did Jessica become involved after Sally ...' She faltered, still not able to comprehend how Sally could have left Zoe for dead.

As they arrived at the church, Adam stopped and turned to face her. 'According to Jessica, she witnessed the attack. She found Zoe unconscious. She claimed she had been going to take her to the hospital. Whether or not she had been ...' He shrugged. 'She took her to her father's house instead. I'm guessing Zoe has filled you in on the rest.'

She had. Kyle was making progress, she'd told her, telling her also that she was determined to be there for him, that he would need a friend. Whether or not there was any future for them, Kaitlin didn't know. She did know, though, that in Zoe the man had the best friend he could ever have. 'Kyle's divorcing her,' she said. Understanding a little more what had driven him, she felt for him too. Jessica had lost him. Despite all her desperate efforts to hold on to him, she would never have him.

Adam nodded and drew in a breath. 'It seems he'll finally have his freedom. It's a cruel irony that in making that bid for freedom, he ran into the path of the car Sally was driving.'

'Do you think she hit him on purpose?' Kaitlin asked.

'Dead men can't talk,' Adam replied cryptically.

Kaitlin frowned in confusion. It wasn't really an answer. 'Meaning?'

'I'm assuming she recognised Kyle from the photograph you'd already shown her, or at least considered the possibility it might be him,' Adam explained. 'It seems she'd accessed files regarding the cold case, possibly to do some background research. The detective in charge of the original case was my wife. I'm guessing that was why she did.'

Still Kaitlin was confused.

'Knowing that Greg had gone out looking for Zoe, that his footmarks were on the towpath, Sally decided to try to frame him,' Adam went on. 'When she thought the case against him might not stick, she went back to her original plan. She knew Melanie Ryan's assailant's MO. She knew Kyle appeared to have been stalking Zoe, that Zoe was pregnant, which gave Sally her motive: him not wanting his wife to find out. It all fitted perfectly, as long as Kyle couldn't tell a different story.'

'So she planned it all from outset?' Kaitlin looked at him, horrified.

Adam hesitated. 'Where Kyle was concerned, I think she saw an opportunity. She clearly had issues with Zoe being in your life. Also with Greg.' He stopped and looked her over in concern. 'Are you sure you're going to be okay?'

Kaitlin's stomach twisted with a mixture of sorrow and disbelief. 'As much as I can be,' she answered honestly. She had to be. For Ruby, for her family, she had to try to process this and put it behind her. Somehow, she had to get on with her life. Thanks to Greg, she had a life to get on with.

Adam hesitated. Then, 'Do you mind if I call you?' he asked. Kaitlin noticed the self-consciousness in his eyes as he glanced down and back. 'Just to check how you're doing.'

'I'd appreciate that,' she answered carefully.

'Great.' Relief flooding his face, Adam smiled and glanced away again. 'I think my lift's here.' He nodded towards an approaching car. 'My daughter. I'd better not keep her waiting. I think I'm probably in her bad books.'

Freya was a lovely girl, Kaitlin soon discovered, friendly and open-faced, and clearly caring of her dad. Also a little bit in despair of him, she gathered.

'Can you believe him?' she asked as Adam headed to the car. 'He's not recovered from his wound, but still he insists on going to work to keep on top of things.'

'Possibly to keep his mind occupied?' Kaitlin suggested.

Freya considered. 'I suppose,' she conceded. 'He's promised me he'll avoid getting shot again. I think that's supposed to be reassuring.'

Rolling her eyes, she followed him to the car. Then paused and turned back. 'We're having a belated birthday celebration for him later,' she said, glancing over her shoulder to make sure he wasn't listening. 'You should come. I mean, no pressure,' she added quickly. 'But after he resorted to such drastic measures to avoid eating out with just me ...'

Kaitlin had no idea what to say. 'I, um ... I'm not sure,' she answered, thinking Adam might not be so keen on the idea of someone just turning up. 'I would need more notice to make arrangements for my daughter. Maybe ...'

'She could come too,' Freya suggested, and then dropped her gaze. 'He cares about you,' she said, her cheeks flushing as she glanced back up. 'I know he'd never say anything, so ... Please come. If you'd like to, obviously.'

After ringing to check with Adam, who'd sounded delighted, telling her he could use a friend, since Freya was now toying with the idea of bringing her boyfriend, Kaitlin had agreed to go. She wasn't sure she was ready for another relationship yet, or indeed whether Adam would even want that. She needed to stand on her own two feet first, to get to know herself. She needed to take things slowly for Ruby's sake and her own. She had an idea that he would respect that.

A LETTER FROM SHERYL

Thank you so much for choosing to read *The Invite*. I really hope you enjoyed reading it as much as I enjoyed writing it. If you would like to keep up to date with my new releases, please do sign up at the link below:

www.bookouture.com/sheryl-browne

I can't believe this is my tenth book published with the fabulous Bookouture. I've loved writing every single one of them and I'm thrilled to bits to be sharing my latest with you, my lovely readers who inspire me to keep writing. Whenever I've been asked what drives me to write psychological thrillers, my answer is always the same: people. I'm fascinated by what shapes people, the internal and external influences that make them who they are. Often we can be affected by our formative years, sometimes negatively, which can impact on our lives into adulthood, resulting in a negative view of ourselves. Low self-esteem can be so emotionally crippling, a persistent little voice in our heads that tells us we are not worthy – of love, of respect. Sometimes, when emotionally damaged, we can view ourselves through others' eyes, our instinct to accept that a critical view is a valid one. We try to fix things, to change and reshape ourselves. In *The Invite*, Kaitlin has survived a controlling relationship. She has grown. She's determined to replace the little voice in her head with a stronger, positive voice that tells her she is worthy of love and respect. She is fiercely protective of her child. She's made the wrong choices in the past. She knows the danger signs. But does she? Is she at risk of pushing away those who truly care for her? Will perceived feelings of jealousy, breeding doubt and mistrust impact gravely on all of their lives?

As I pen this last little section of the book, I would like to thank those people around me who are always there to offer support, those people who believed in me even when I didn't quite believe in myself. To all of you, thank you. Ten books! Now that really is a dream come true.

If you have enjoyed the book, I would love it if you could share your thoughts and write a brief review. Reviews mean the world to an author and will help a book find its wings. I would also love to hear from you via Facebook or Twitter or my website.

Stay safe everyone, and happy reading.

Sheryl x

facebook.com/SherylBrowne.Author

twitter.com/SherylBrowne

ACKNOWLEDGEMENTS

As always, massive thanks to the fabulous team at Bookouture, whose support of their authors is amazing. Special thanks to Helen Jenner and the wonderful editorial team, who make my stories shine. Huge thanks also to the fantastic publicity team, Kim Nash, Noelle Holten and Sarah Hardy. I think it's safe to say I could not do this without you. To all the other authors at Bookouture, I love you. Thank you for being such a super-supportive group of people.

I owe a huge debt of gratitude to all the fantastically hard-working bloggers and reviewers who have taken the time to read and review my books and shout them out to the world. It's truly appreciated.

A special mention to Stuart Gibbon, former UK detective and author of *The Crime Writer's Casebook* and *Being a Detective*, for his excellent advice. Thanks so much for answering my questions at short notice, Stuart.

Final thanks to every single reader out there for buying and reading my books. Knowing you have enjoyed my stories and care enough about my characters to want to share them with other readers is the best incentive ever for me to keep writing.